Advance praise for Jeff Gunhus and *Silent Threat*

"Daddy issues? *Silent Threat* is the book for you. When CIA assassin Mara Roberts is tasked with taking out her hit man father, a passionate, powerful story unfolds—part thriller, part family saga—and all guns blazing. Gunhus's gift of capturing the human spirit leaves you pondering the novel long after you whip past the final page. Unputdownable."
—K. J. Howe, international bestselling author of *Skyjack*

SILENT
THREAT

JEFF GUNHUS

KENSINGTON BOOKS
www.kensingtonbooks.com

KENSINGTON BOOKS are published by

Kensington Publishing Corp.
119 West 40th Street
New York, NY 10018

All Kensington titles, imprints, and distributed lines are available at special quantity discounts for bulk purchases for sales promotion, premiums, fund-raising, educational, or institutional use.

Special book excerpts or customized printings can also be created to fit specific needs. For details, write or phone the office of the Kensington Sales Manager: Kensington Publishing Corp., 119 West 40th Street, New York, NY 10018. Attn. Sales Department. Phone: 1-800-221-2647.

Kensington and the K logo Reg. U.S. Pat. & TM Off.

ISBN-13: 978-1-4967-2622-3 (ebook)
ISBN-10: 1-4967-2622-7 (ebook)
Kensington Electronic Edition: January 2020

ISBN-13: 978-1-4967-2621-6
ISBN-10: 1-4967-2621-9
First Kensington Trade Paperback Printing: January 2020

10 9 8 7 6 5 4 3 2 1

Printed in the United States of America

For Nicole

Always for you

Acknowledgments

Writing a novel is a solitary affair, but the work of bringing it into the world takes a team. When things go well, that team is filled with dedicated, talented people who have a real passion for publishing.

Things went very well for this book.

The first person on the team was my agent, Sarah Hershman. Entrepreneurs are my kind of people and Sarah has showcased all the attributes I love about them. Risk-taker, hard worker, a pro who gets things done without complaint or hesitation. Thanks for believing in my work and taking it out into the world.

Thank you to the entire team at Kensington. Steven Zacharius and Lynn Cully have created a wonderful environment where writers feel valued and respected. I couldn't be happier with my new home. James Abbate was the first read of the book and became its first champion. John Scognamiglio used his experience, wisdom, and insight to help shepherd the project with great finesse. John and James, you have been the dream team and I'm thankful to you both.

Thank you to Kristine Noble for the beautiful cover. You taught me about the joy of thinking outside convention and seeking out originality. Tracy Marx provided the wonderful back cover copy which describes the book much better than I ever have. Carly Sommerstein's powerful guidance of the project throughout production created a beautiful book to hold. Copyediting and proofreading are talents from on high; Sheila Higgins and Emily Epstein White caught details and errors I'd looked at a hundred times and missed. Whatever errors might be left are mine alone. I'm so grateful for the contributions of these talented individuals.

I'm indebted to International Thriller Writers, especially the Thrillerfest held every year in New York. It was through that organization that I took a full-day class with the inimitable Steve Berry. They say it's better not to meet your heroes, but Steve was the exception to that rule. The lessons that day informed my writing greatly and his support since then has meant everything. When I asked for a blurb for this book, he replied the same day saying it would be his honor. Steve is a class act and a hell of a writer.

Kimberly Howe, executive director of Thrillerfest and now bestselling author in her own right, is one of the nicest people I know. She makes Thrillerfest feel personal for each participant and she goes out of her way to make people feel welcome. If you haven't been to Thrillerfest, go just to meet her.

Hank Phillipi Ryan taught me the generosity of writers when she spent the time to do a deep dive with me on the opening chapter of this book. It was made so much better with her insight.

Simon Gervais, a wonderfully talented thriller writer, used his real-world experience to give me feedback on the firepower in the book. It was made better with his help.

I'm indebted to so many other great writers I've met and learned from through ITW: Lee Child, David Morrell, Peter James, Gayle Lynds, Karin Slaughter, Robert Dugoni, to name a few.

James Patterson chose this novel as a finalist for a co-author competition through Masterclass. That early recognition helped spur me on to complete the novel and the insights in that class tightened my writing and taught me to ramp up the tension in my scenes.

My family. Everyone ought to have a cheerleader in their corner, it just makes life easier. I'm fortunate to have a boatload of them. Parents who encouraged my writing and reading from as early as I can remember. A creative brother who has the keenest creative eye I know. Five rowdy, rule-breaking, shenanigan-doing, feisty kids that provide the sound track to my life. And a singular point of calm and grace amid the whirlwind, my wife, Nicole. The best parts of my life have all had you in them.

And my readers. In today's age when things seem to move so quickly and attention spans are measured in seconds on video clips, I'm so thankful to all of you who have committed so many hours to reading my novels. Time is a precious resource and I understand the level of trust you give me (or any author) when you pick up a book and dive in. I do my best to be worthy of your trust. I hope you end this novel feeling that your time was well spent and ready for the further adventures of Scott and Mara Roberts.

If you're ever in Annapolis, cruise by City Dock Café or Old Fox Books. I'll be the guy in the back with the huge headphones on, mainlining coffee, and banging away on the laptop. Come say hi. Maybe you'll end up in the next book.

CHAPTER 1

Mara Roberts knew the Agency would try to kill her father the day he got out of prison; she just didn't expect they'd ask her to be the one to do it.

Before she received the assignment, she would have bet even money he would survive whatever welcome party the CIA had planned for him. Too bad his odds had migrated down to zero now that the job was hers.

She sat in her rented Range Rover, waves of Oklahoma heat shimmering off the parking lot blacktop, bending the prison chain-link fence into wavering lines. Coils of concertina wire topped the walls, razor blade edges glistening in the sun, each loop perfectly spaced. Just like inside the walls of the Cimarron Correctional Facility—orderly but lethal.

Behind the security gate was a low-slung building with a copper overhang at the entrance—more like a school administration office than a prison. The schematics she'd studied revealed the facility extended back into eight separate cell blocks. Each one housed more dangerous criminals than the previous one. She hoped they'd put her dad in the worst of the lot.

The car idled, both for the AC and in case she needed to adjust her plans and leave in a hurry. The few guards she saw moved slow and had dark sweat pits spreading under their arms and on their backs. She pegged them as complacent. Washed up. Bored. Just like she wanted. As she analyzed the prison's weaknesses, she couldn't help but wonder whether her dad had changed much since she'd seen him last.

Sure, he was past fifty now and, according to the photos in the briefing, finally starting to show his age. Wrinkles at his eyes. A close scalp shave, the kind favored by men fighting a losing battle with their hairline. He was still in shape, though. Surveillance camera footage showed a recent fistfight he'd had on the yard, started by some con paid off by the Agency. Obviously a new guy. Anyone who'd been there longer knew not to mess with the quiet guy with the broad shoulders.

The video showed her dad could still throw a punch, but the couple of jabs he took to his face also showed he'd lost a step or two. Yet, the old man still had skills. And she wasn't about to underestimate her target. Hell, four years on the run and the last two months in prison might have even toughened the bastard up. If that was even possible. She wasn't sure it was.

A routine face recognition search through the U.S. prison system by a junior analyst had turned him up. As she read the report, it made her laugh that assets all over the world were searching for him, and there he was serving time under an alias for manslaughter. Seems he took exception to a group of five young men roughing up a prostitute. Four of them ended up with broken bones and long hospital stays. The fifth wasn't going to harass anyone ever again. It was just like her dad to risk blowing his cover to save someone. Typical Boy Scout bullshit.

She'd been raised on stories about him. Even in her macho world of counterintelligence they seemed outlandish. Insanely risky missions. Many of them unsanctioned. Succeeding against insurmountable odds. Like stuff out of bad action movies, and yet people swore to her the stories were true, that they'd seen him do these things with their own eyes. But they always whispered about him, as if just talking about the man and his exploits might suck them into the same darkness into which he disappeared. Still, even with what had happened, she always heard a grudging admiration as they told her about the exploits of the great Scott Francis Roberts, the father she barely knew. The man she was about to kill.

She looked at her watch. Fifteen minutes to go. When she was younger she might have pulled out the 9mm Glock automatic hidden under the seat and rechecked the magazine, or felt for the bulge of the knife strapped under her loose-fitting pant leg. Or pulled out the micro-Taser in her front pocket to make sure it still held a charge. But she wasn't a newbie and this wasn't her first rodeo, so instead she scanned the parking lot, looking for her shadow.

She knew there would be one; there always was on a job like this. A second operative ostensibly there for backup but really just an insurance policy for the higher-ups at Langley to make sure the job was done and done right. This operation was, after all, illegal. She was certain there were a lot of nervous suits back at Langley, waiting for confirmation that Roberts was dead. She just hoped that when the report came through it was the right Roberts.

It was protocol, sure, but having a shadow was demeaning. She tried not to think of it as an insult, but she couldn't help feel a twinge of being babysat. As a game, and also to keep sharp, she always tried to spot the agent watching her. She was usually able to, not because they weren't very good at their jobs, but because she was great at hers.

So far she hadn't found him. And it probably was a him. While women had made strides in the Agency, field operatives with her particular skill set and job description tended to have a pair of balls swinging between their legs. Of course, most of her comrades thought she had a pair of huge ones herself. As much as she hated the association, based on her risk tolerance and her ability to piss off her bosses, she knew the word on her was that there was no doubt she was the daughter of field operative and world-class traitor Scott Roberts.

Ten minutes.

The parking lot was filled with passenger cars and minivans. What if the mission required her to break into the perimeter? She imagined a frontal attack with a full assault team like she'd been trained to do in the Marines. Or a covert entry via the supply chain like she'd been taught at the Farm. Finally, she considered diving from an airplane at 30,000 feet with a squirrel suit on and landing in the middle of the yard. That was what her dad would have done.

No, not her dad. She couldn't think that way. Her target, nothing more.

Seven minutes.

She reached under her seat. Felt the Glock in its hiding place. She took a deep, steadying breath, hating the ice ball churning in her stomach.

"Get your shit together, Mara," she muttered.

She tried to calm herself down by thinking of her little nephew, Joey. His mom, her brave sister, Lucy, had marched through her cancer endgame, from the first shock of the diagnosis, through the treatments, and finally, the closing pain-filled days. Mara had held Joey's tiny hand as they lowered his mother's casket into the ground next to his father's grave. Only this time there was no military salute. No folded flag to commemorate the fallen. There was only a small group of quiet friends to mark bitter truth about the unpredictability of life. The boy had been quiet all day, holding it in. But once the casket started its descent into the ground, he'd lost it. As he wailed, calling out for his mom, Mara had wrapped him in her arms and whispered for the hundredth time that she'd take care of him. She'd told the Agency the next day that she wanted to transfer out of field-work and teach instead. They'd agreed, but then her dad was found. And they asked for one more job.

Five minutes.

She did another scan. *Wait.* That black pickup truck with a camper shell in the far back corner. The driver's cab was empty, which was why she'd dismissed it earlier. This time she saw a round, reflective surface flash on the side of the camper shell, the right size to be a spotting scope. Her shadow. She smiled, pleased that she hadn't lost her touch.

Three minutes.

She took a swig from a water bottle. Her initial request for a long-range shot had been denied. The powers-that-be didn't want a hit in broad daylight in front of a maximum-security prison. There'd be video footage from five different angles, and it'd inevitably leak out to the public. That wasn't good.

Still, it would have been a sure thing. When she'd pressed them on it, they'd come clean. It was the same reason they hadn't killed him inside the prison. They wanted him dead, but they wanted her to question him first. Her instructions were to use their relationship to get him to talk, then incapacitate him and move to a black site to conduct more advanced questioning.

Once done, he was to be terminated. Under no circumstances was he to be killed prior to questioning, nor was he to be allowed to be brought into custody through regular channels. On these two last points, her instructions had been very clear.

The more she thought about it, the more she liked this approach. A head shot was too easy of an out for him. He deserved to suffer first. And suffering was something she was well trained at dispensing.

One minute.

She opened the door and stepped outside, leaving the car running. The heat was dry and oppressive, and it felt like all the moisture on her skin evaporated in seconds. She put on her sunglasses, walked to the front of the car, leaned up against the hood, and crossed her arms. And waited.

Time.

Mara watched her dad scan the parking lot and then settle his eyes on her. He jerked back a little, a discreet movement, but enough that she saw it. At least he seemed surprised to see her. That was a good sign. Part of her had considered that a man like Scott Roberts likely had friends deep in the Agency, friends who didn't believe the charges against him, friends who just might want to tip him off to the planned attempt on his life.

Not that it mattered. She felt confident in her training and her ability, regardless if he knew it was coming or not. She assumed at some point he would realize why she was there, or at least suspect it. All it meant was an adjustment in tactics. No big deal.

He walked toward her, still studying the parking lot. He wore a pair of jeans and a white T-shirt, probably the same outfit he'd been wearing the day he was processed into custody. His build looked good, like he'd taken advantage of the prison weight yard. She had to admit that even with his shaved head, his ice-cold blue eyes and strong jawline made him a hell of a good-looking guy. If grandpas were your thing.

Then again, the guy walking toward her hardly met the criteria to be called a grandpa. Biologically, sure. But he didn't have any kind of relationship with Joey, not since going off the grid four years earlier. She felt a twinge of satisfaction at that. As far as five-year-old Joey knew, his grandpa had died in the same accident that killed his grandma, and Mara intended to keep it that way for as long as possible. There might be a time when she'd have to come clean, but that was a decade or two away as far as she was concerned. And even then she wondered why Joey needed to be burdened with the fact that his grandpa was not only responsible for his own wife's death, but was a goddamn traitor as well.

The thought of what he'd done to both his family and his country made it hard to even look at him. A wave of nausea came over her and she pushed it back. Emotions had no place during an operation. She knew better.

As he came closer, she prepared herself for the first exchange of words. She'd replayed this moment a thousand times in her head over the past four years, practiced a million zingers she could send his way. She expected him to come to a stop in front of her. Maybe apologize. Maybe launch into a defense of his actions. But he didn't do any of that.

As he approached, he put a hand to his mouth, covering his lips as he spoke.

"You've got a shadow, back right corner," he said. "Black pickup."

"That's your hello after four years?" she said, even though she was thinking *oh shit*. "Some paranoid bullshit remark?"

He walked up to her, staying an arm's-length away. His eyes met hers and bore in. They were filled with disappointment and sadness. For a second, she felt like a little girl, the same one who could never live up to her dad's expectations. Fifteen all over again. But the next words out of his mouth shocked her right back into present day.

"They have Joey," he said. "They have Lucy's boy. If you want to see him alive, get in the car."

Her head spun. Joey? It wasn't possible. He was at school. Not just any school, but at Sidwell Friends, a private school where the DC elite sent their kids. Simultaneously one of the most dangerous and one of the safest places to go to school in the country. The fact that high-ranking diplomats, businesspeople, and government officials sent their kids there ostensibly made it a place of interest for the evildoers in the world. But it also meant that the level of security was off the charts. There was actually a special area for the various bodyguards and Secret Service agents who had to wait until their charges were through learning about fractions and adverbs for the day. The idea that someone could have abducted Joey from such a place was ridiculous.

Still, she suddenly found it hard to swallow.

"What are you talking about? Who has him?"

He was already moving. "Who do you think? You're wasting time. Let's go." He opened the passenger door and climbed in.

She stood frozen in place. This wasn't the plan, not even close. Thirty seconds and he'd knocked her completely off balance. The plan had always been to drive him out of there, luring him into a false sense of security with a sob story about her wanting to reconcile. She was supposed to pump him for information; then, once that was done, pump him full of bullets. But that was out the window now.

Joey. It had to be a trick. She ticked through the alternative explanations in her head.

An old friend tipped him off about Joey and told him the name.

He'd either spotted the shadow or guessed there was one there. The term *shadow* was a problem since it meant that he'd already pieced together why she was there. It might have only been a guess on his part, but a damn good one.

Last was his claim that Joey was in danger. Once he knew she was worried about Joey, it was the easiest leverage point he could use to get under her skin, maybe throw her off her game enough to escape once she'd driven them away from the prison.

There, all of it explained. No one had Joey. It wasn't possible. She'd talked to him by phone just earlier in the day, just as the nanny was about to take him to school.

Angry at herself for letting her dad get the upper hand so easily, she pulled the micro-Taser from her pocket and palmed it. The only thing micro about it was its size. It still packed five million volts, and she looked forward to using it.

When she climbed into the car, her dad eyed her cautiously. He paid special attention to her left hand, where she cupped the Taser against her side. She had to admit, he was good.

"Before you do anything stupid," he said, "just listen to me."

She turned in her seat, her finger on the Taser button in case he lunged at her. "Talk fast. Anyone who threatens Joey usually doesn't get a chance to speak for long."

"I don't know what the plan is here," he said. "I expect you're supposed to drive me somewhere nice and quiet so we can talk and then kill me there."

"I don't know what you're—"

"Let's stop with the bullshit, okay? Let's talk like adults."

She hated the weird sense of pride she felt when he called her an adult. It was exactly the kind of reaction that proved she should never have been sent on this assignment.

"Okay, who has Joey?"

He looked disappointed in the question. "The Agency took him earlier today."

"There's no way."

"Sidwell Friends."

A jolt of panic ripped through her.

"How did you—"

"I tried to get word to you when I found out," he said. "But I couldn't. I'm sorry."

She tried to slow her breathing. "You're lying."

"I'm sorry, honey. They took him."

"Don't you dare call me . . ." She stopped herself. There he was again, getting under her skin with a single word. If she was her own trainee, she'd fail her from the program for not being cut out for fieldwork. But this was her nephew they were talking about.

She reached for her phone that was on the coin tray between them. He grabbed her hand to stop her. The second he did, she brought up the Taser and pressed the button. The voltage arc cackled in the air an inch away from his neck.

"Let go of my hand right now."

He relaxed his grip but kept his hand over hers.

"If you call to check on him, they'll know I told you there was a problem," he said.

"So?"

"You're better than this," he said.

The truth snapped into place quick enough. "You have someone inside. You're protecting him."

"The second you call, they'll start tearing through the ranks looking for the mole. That and you'll give up the only tactical advantage we have."

"A little convenient, don't you think," she said. "You give me this information but tell me I can't check it to confirm."

"You have to trust me."

Those words didn't sit well with her. She cocked her head to the side as if thinking of something she'd forgotten. "You know what, Dad? Fuck you." She jammed the Taser into his neck. His body went ramrod straight and then spasmed wildly as five million volts poured into his nervous system.

She grabbed her phone and speed-dialed Sidwell Friends back in Bethesda, Maryland. With the time difference, Joey's kindergarten class would have already eaten lunch and gone back to their class.

A woman answered the phone on the second ring. "Sidwell Friends. How may I help you?"

"This is Barb Newcastle," Mara said, using her alias. It was the name everyone at Sidwell knew her by. Her heart thumped in her chest as she tried to get the words out in a normal voice. "I'm out of town and I'm not able to get in touch with my nanny. I just wanted to make sure Joey made it into school today."

"Yes, Ms. Newcastle," the voice came back. "I saw Joey earlier today."

She gulped for air and felt the sting of tears in her eyes. Until that moment, she hadn't realized how much she'd believed something had happened to him.

"Thank you," she said. "I just wanted to make sure the nanny and I didn't get our signals crossed."

"No problem at all, Ms. Newcastle."

"Ask to talk to him," her dad croaked beside her, still recovering from the Taser blast.

She readied the Taser and nearly zapped him again, but stopped herself.

"Goodbye, Ms. New—"

"Could I speak to him, please?" she blurted out. She saw her dad close his eyes in relief. She didn't like that.

"Of course, let me connect you to his classroom," came the voice.

The line clicked and was replaced by on-hold music.

"What'd they say?" her dad asked.

"They're connecting me to his room."

He shook his head. "They'll say there's no answer. You have to demand to talk to him. Say it's an emergency."

"I thought you said I shouldn't call at all?" she said.

He shrugged. "The damage is done, might as well take it all the way so you believe me. I'm sure they're already going apeshit at Langley to figure out who tipped me off."

"That's kind of your specialty, isn't it? Having someone else take the fall for your mistakes?"

"Hello? Ms. Newcastle?" the voice said on the line.

"Yes, I'm here," she answered.

"I'm sorry, but there was no answer in the classroom."

The pit reopened in her stomach. "It's just after one o'clock. They should be in the room."

"I'm sorry, but sometimes the teachers don't answer. Or they might be visiting the library. You just never—"

"This is an emergency," she said, raising her voice. "I need you to find him and I need you to get him on the phone."

"Ma'am, I assure you he's here," the voice said.

"Then I need you to find him. Do you hear me? I want to talk to Joey."

"Ms. Rober—Newcastle, I assure you that . . ."

The voice trailed away. The woman on the phone knew the mistake was out there. All Mara could hear was her own ragged breathing.

"What did you just call me?" Mara whispered.

Silence on the other end.

"How do you know my real name?"

She tried to swallow and couldn't. Her world had just split in half. The part behind her and the part where her Joey had been taken hostage.

"Hurt him and I'll kill you," she whispered. "I'll kill every last one of you."

A long pause and then finally a man's voice on the line said, "I don't want to hurt him. I hope you believe that. But you know I will if I have to."

"Why are you doing this?"

The man took his time answering. Mara heard her own heavy breathing, her heart pounding in her chest. "You weren't supposed to find out about this," the man said. "It was only an insurance policy if you forgot where your loyalty lies. You haven't forgotten, have you?"

Mara closed her eyes, recentering herself, allowing the fear she felt for Joey to be replaced with something else. Pure rage. "No," she said, her voice ice-cold. "I'm crystal clear about that."

"Good, now do your job, Mara. Evacuate the target from that location and then complete your instructions. We're watching."

Then the line went dead.

And Mara decided that once the mission was done, no matter if Joey was returned unharmed or not, she was going to have to kill Jim Hawthorn.

CHAPTER 2

Four years ago

"Scott Roberts is a true American hero. If you can't see that, then with all due respect, sir, you're a moron," James Hawthorn, Director of Intelligence, told the man in front of him.

A long, uncomfortable silence followed.

Even though Hawthorn had been friends with Preston Townsend's father since their undergrad days at Dartmouth, and he'd known the man since birth, he'd never called him a name like that since he'd gotten his new job. Worse, it was in front of a group of subordinates.

"Can we clear the room, please?" Townsend said softly.

The eight other men and women in the room couldn't get out fast enough, not even pausing to grab their coffees and legal pads on the way out. Once the door closed, a smooth seal forming along the curved wall of the office, Townsend turned to his friend, a wry smile on his face.

"Jim, did you just stand in the middle of the Oval Office and call the president of the United States a moron?" Townsend asked. "Because I'm pretty sure that's exactly what you did."

Hawthorn remained standing with his shoulders squared. "No, sir. What I said was that if you couldn't see that Roberts is a goddamn American hero, then you're a moron. If you come around to seeing things my way, then I technically didn't call you anything."

Townsend blew out a deep breath and crossed over one of the couches in front of the fireplace. He laid down, rubbing his eyes. Hawthorn thought he looked tired. No, more than tired. His friend looked worn down to the nub. He'd noticed the suits fit a little looser now and his skin stretched taut on his cheekbones. Of course his hair had gone gray, but that happened to all of them. Even no-drama Obama had gone the way of the gray after a few years in the world's finest gilded cage. But it was more than that, and seeing how haggard his friend looked took some of the edge off his anger.

"You look like hell, Mr. President," he said, sitting on the couch opposite him. "Are you letting the docs check you out?"

"Funny that you won't call me Preston, even when we're alone," Townsend said.

"Wouldn't be appropriate."

"But you have no problem calling me a moron." Townsend laughed.

"Not when you're acting like one," Hawthorn shot back.

"Your guy shot up the Serbian embassy, killed the ambassador's personal bodyguard, and from what I hear, slept with the ambassador's wife."

"Have you seen pictures of the wife?"

Townsend sat up. "This is a real problem. James Bond is supposed to be working for the British, not us."

Hawthorn gave a *what are you gonna do?* shrug of the shoulders.

Townsend pointed to his desk. "I read the report on this guy. Not the one you sent me, but the full version. By the way, don't do that again. When I ask for something, I expect to see the full, non-redacted version."

"There are some things in there I figured you didn't want to know. Stuff the guys before you did."

"No shit," Townsend said. "I felt like I needed a shower afterward."

"All done in defense of our country."

"Without due process or oversight," Townsend said. He held

up his hand. "I'm not going to debate Civics 101 with you. Look, Jim, I admire your loyalty. Hell, my family has been the beneficiary of it since before I was born. But this guy's a one-man wrecking ball. It's just a matter of time before he goes too far and starts a war."

"Yet, all he's done so far is keep us out of one." Hawthorn stood up. "If it wasn't for Scott Roberts, you and I wouldn't be standing in this room. Washington would be off-limits for the next thousand years while we all waited until the radiation from the nuke he stopped dissipated."

Townsend looked surprised.

"Yeah, that one isn't in your report," Hawthorn said. "The paperwork never tells the whole story."

Townsend stood and looked at his old friend. "Do you trust this guy? I mean, really trust him?"

Hawthorn didn't hesitate. "When there was a terrorist threat against my family, I didn't call the Secret Service. I didn't call my personal protective unit. I called Scott Roberts. And once I did, I knew my family was going to be safe. He's the real deal, Mr. President. Not the right guy to cut loose, especially with everything we have going on right now."

Townsend took a deep breath. "Okay, I'll let you keep him."

"Thank you, sir," Hawthorn said, quickly gathering his things. He'd learned early in life to take the yes and then get the hell out.

"Oh, and, Jim?"

"Yes, Mr. President?"

"Try to look chastised when you walk out of here. I don't want everyone thinking they can walk in here, call me a moron, and get what they want."

Hawthorn grinned. "Chastised and browbeaten. You got it."

He opened the door and strode into the anteroom outside the Oval. Most of the people who'd been ushered from the room after his outburst were still hanging around, most pretending to be typing notes on their devices. He looked down and slumped his shoulders a bit, probably playing it up a little too much.

"Sorry, guys," he mumbled as he left. "He's still pretty pissed off. You might want to give him some time before going back in there."

Worried eyes went to the Oval's open door and no one made a move toward it. Hawthorn thought he might have gotten a few minutes of peace for his old friend. He needed it.

The weight of the office was bearing down on Preston Townsend, and not for the first time, Hawthorn wondered whether he'd made a mistake helping to put the man into office. All occupants of the Oval had the weakness of ego, and Townsend was no exception. Still, Hawthorn worried that he was less capable of dealing with the constant drone of criticism than others. As he left behind the staff cowering outside the Oval, he pushed the thoughts aside. For better or worse, that ship had sailed. He and the country had to live with it.

Hawthorn walked through the White House, out through the east door, and across the road that led to the massive Eisenhower Executive Office Building, the French Second Empire monstrosity that housed most of the staff who claimed to work in the White House. With over half a million square feet of floor space, it hadn't been hard to select a quiet space to meet Scott.

"How'd it go?" Scott asked, standing up from a wooden bench in one of the marble hallways.

Hawthorn frowned. "A cat may have nine lives, but you seem to have eighteen."

Scott looked relieved. "He's letting me stay."

"No, he's letting me keep you on if that's what I decide," Hawthorn said. "I've got to tell you, Scott, maybe it's time you hung up your spurs and rode off into the sunset."

"C'mon, is this some kind of joke?"

"No joke. I fought hard for you today. Maybe a little too hard. I don't think I'll be able to pull your ass out of the fire next time."

"What makes you think there will be a next time?" Scott asked.

"Because with you," Hawthorn said, "there's always going to

be a next time. The country owes you big. *I* owe you big. It's time to collect. Retire. Go relax on a beach. Take Wendy and the girls on some fishing trips."

"Lucy's the fisher. Wendy can't stand it."

"So do two different trips," Hawthorn said. "Take Wendy to New York. See a show. Take a ride through Central Park. You'll have the time for it."

Scott walked over to the ceiling-to-floor window and stared out at the White House next door.

"You've been thinking about this, haven't you? If you were going to try to put me out to pasture, why'd you fight so hard to keep me on?"

"I guess I'm like you," Hawthorn said. "I hate my boss telling me what to do." He put a hand on Roberts's shoulder. "And I want you to leave on your terms. You're owed that much. Think it over, Scott. Take a week. Mara's on leave before she ships out for her second tour, right?"

"Afghanistan," he said, the pride evident in his voice. "My daughter the jarhead. Who would have thunk it?"

"Only anyone who ever met her," Hawthorn said. A long pause stretched out between the two men. "You'll seriously consider this?" he finally asked.

"Out of respect for you, I'll give it some thought."

"I hope you will." He held out his hand and Scott shook it. "It's been one hell of a ride. And no matter what happens, I'll always have your back."

"I know you will," Scott said. "I trust you."

The words gave Hawthorn a sensation he almost never felt. The emotion was so rare, in fact, that he had trouble identifying it at first.

Guilt.

As the two men ended their handshake and parted ways, the feeling hung with him along with Scott's last words.

I trust you.

As Hawthorn walked away from his friend, he knew he didn't deserve that trust. He just hoped Scott never had to discover why.

CHAPTER 3

Mara stared at the phone, trying to process the implications of what she'd just heard.

They had Joey. But why? An insurance policy to make sure she did the job assigned to her? But what reason had she ever given them to think she wouldn't go through with it? Why would they ever involve Joey in something like this? While she didn't know the answers to those questions, there was something she knew for sure. By taking her nephew, someone had wildly miscalculated.

"I'm sorry," her dad said. "This should never have happened."

She startled at the sound of his voice. She was in the car next to one of the world's deadliest field operatives—a man who knew she'd been assigned to kill him. She considered pulling the Glock out right there and then, finishing the job and then getting down to the business of figuring out whose idea it'd been to grab Joey out of his school. When she found out, that guy was going to have a bad day regardless how far up the totem pole his bureaucratic ass was parked.

"Your shadow's on the move," her dad said. "That's not good."

She twisted in her chair. He was right. The pickup had pulled forward slowly so that it was a row closer to them. The shadow didn't move unless the primary operative had failed the mission. But she hadn't failed. Not yet.

"I told you calling the school was a mistake," her dad said.

"Shut up," she said. "I need to think."

The pickup rolled forward one more row. It was still fifty yards away, behind and to the right of their position. There were enough cars in the parking lot that each time it stopped there was just a sliver of the truck visible, but it was enough.

"I see a driver," her dad said. "Guessing one in the back."

"Yeah, there's a cutout in the shell. There was a scope in it earlier." She cringed as she said the words, clearly meant to try to prove she was good at her job. Why she felt she still had to try to impress this man was beyond her.

She shoved the idea aside. None of that mattered. They had Joey. She needed to concentrate and figure out the moving parts. Her stomach turned over as the stakes of the game struck home. She was used to risking her own life, but not Joey's. That changed everything.

"Moving again," her dad said. "C'mon, Mara, he's closing the space. That can only mean one thing."

She looked across her dad and out the window. The pickup rolled slowly between the rows of parked cars, working a parallel line to their position on the passenger side.

"They're not going to do anything here," she said. "Not right in front of the prison. It's why they sent me here to begin with."

He shook his head. "No, they sent you here to get me to talk. Pretty smart, actually. Might have worked if they hadn't screwed up with Joey. But in the end, they were going to get rid of us both. Two Roberts with one stone. Just in case you knew something you shouldn't."

The vehicle came to a stop with a direct line of sight between them.

"I don't think—"

The small, circular cutout in the side of the pickup shell reappeared, but this time there was no scope. Just a rifle barrel extending out of the hole.

"Down," she yelled.

The passenger side window exploded. Mara half expected to find herself coated with blood, but her dad's reflexes were still good. He was low in the seat next to her.

"Time to go," he said.

Still half lying on her side, she reached up and put the car in reverse. The small screen in the dashboard came to life, and the backup video showed her the parking lot behind them.

"You can exit to the southeast corner," her dad said.

"We're not leaving yet."

She hammered the gas and the car surged backward. It swerved wildly as she got used to steering using the rearview camera.

"Hold on," she said.

The pickup appeared in the center of the screen and she punched the gas. Bullets smashed the rear window. Rounds zipped overhead. Whoever was doing the firing wasn't discriminating between targets in the car. And he was about to pay for that.

The car hit the pickup going thirty with a violent crush of metal and broken glass. She guessed the shooter in the back had gone for a ride. Last she checked, sniper stations didn't come with airbags.

But the driver cab did. When the car hit the pickup, it spun to the right so that the passenger window lined with the driver's side of the pickup.

She risked a glance up over the busted-out window. The deployed airbag had pushed the driver back in his seat. He had a gash on the side of his head and looked disoriented as the airbag deflated. Thankfully, she didn't recognize him. That was a small grace. It would have been a hell of a lot worse if it was a friend of hers trying to kill her.

Trying to kill her dad, she reminded herself. She was just in the way.

The man in the pickup seemed to get his wits about him. He turned sharply to his left and saw Mara looking back at him. He immediately reached down for something. She didn't have to guess what it was.

"Oh shit," she said, reaching for the Glock under her seat. But there was empty air where the gun ought to have been. Gone.

Then her dad sat up in his seat, her gun in his hand. He fired two shots into the pickup cab. The sound of the Glock in the enclosed space was deafening.

She saw the man in the pickup jerk backward and disappear inside the cab, a spray of red on the airbag.

Immediately, her dad twisted in his seat and pointed the gun at her head.

"Oops," he said. "Looks like you're not as good as you thought you were."

Mara scowled. She hated looking down the barrel of any gun, but especially when it was her own being used against her.

"About time you showed your true colors," she said.

"Just making sure you don't do anything rash."

"Too late."

He winced as she pressed the tip of her nine-inch blade against his rib cage. She'd grabbed it from where it was strapped to her leg the second she realized he had her weapon. In close quarters a knife was just as lethal as a gun, and they both knew it.

"Give me the gun," she said.

The alarm klaxons inside the prison went off.

"Things are about to get complicated unless we get out of here," he said.

"You think? Now give me the goddamn gun."

He kept the gun leveled at her. "Do you believe me now? They're willing to kill you in order to get to me. That call to the school changed all the math. The fact I'm still breathing has put doubt in their heads about your loyalty."

"You're only still breathing because of Joey. That's where my loyalty is."

"And they're going to kill you for that," he said. "Like it or not, we're in this together."

She pressed the knife harder into his ribs and he grunted. She guessed if she looked down she might see a trickle of blood on his white shirt. But she kept her eyes on his, searching for any sign that he was going to make a move. "The gun," she demanded.

"Joey's in real danger. I'm the way you get him back. I'm the *only* way you get him back."

"Really? And why's that?"

Using her peripheral vision, she saw uniformed guards scrambling inside the prison perimeter. She was running out of time before this scene became a complete shit show.

"Because you don't know the real reason the Agency wants me dead."

"I know what you did. I saw the confession."

"That was all cover," her dad said. "Only a handful of people ever knew the truth, and most of them are dead now."

"That's such bullshit. You can't play me."

"I'm not playing you." He looked out the windshield at the rising activity in the prison yard. "We're running out of time. Get us out of here and I promise we'll save Joey."

Two police cars roared into the far end of the parking lot, sirens wailing.

"These guys don't like loose ends. They're going to kill you as sure as they're going to try to kill me. You think they're going to hesitate to make a five-year-old kid disappear?" He turned the gun around so that he held the handle out to her. "I'm the one chance Joey has. Your call how you want to play it."

Mara grabbed the gun and cocked the hammer.

"I ought to finish this right now," she said.

Her dad didn't flinch. "It wouldn't finish anything. And I think you have enough pieces of the puzzle to know that now." The sirens from the police cars grew louder. "Either way, time to make a move."

Her adrenaline was pumping, but she was trained to think through complex problems under pressure. But with her nephew in danger, she knew her objectivity was shot. Still, the facts were clear. They had Joey. The shadow had tried to kill them both. The Agency wanted Scott Roberts dead, damn the consequences.

And after having two operatives try to mow her down, she didn't feel like giving the Agency anything they wanted.

She lowered the gun, her decision made. For now, her dad was more valuable to her alive. But once that stopped being true, all bets were off. "Okay, but if I find out you had anything to do with Joey being taken . . ."

"After the Agency kills me," he said, "you're more than welcome to kill me again. Now, can we please get the hell out of here?"

She threw the car into drive and hammered the gas as her response. The Range Rover's engine responded with a roar and it accelerated past the row of parked cars. She cranked the steering wheel and the Rover's rear tires slid out on the pavement until she corrected and punched the gas again. Only now they were facing the approaching cop cars.

"You might want to go the other way," her dad said.

"Do you want to drive?" she said.

"Uh, yeah. I do."

"Too bad," she said, gunning it.

The two cop cars raced toward her, side by side, flanked by cars on either side. It was a game of chicken, and the closing speed meant someone had to blink quick or there was going to be a big mess for the prison maintenance crew to clean up.

At the last second, the cop cars veered away, each slamming into the backs of parked cars. Mara's foot never left the accelerator as the Rover split the difference between them, scraping by with a whine of metal-on-metal.

Her dad spun in his chair and looked out the rear window. A few seconds later, he turned back with a grunt. "Lucky."

Mara grinned but didn't say anything.

But once the cops who'd crashed their cruisers got their wits about them, they would find the body of the operative in the truck. After that, there would be roadblocks, helicopter support, and all the makings of a manhunt. It was time to head to the side roads to throw off any search that might be mounted.

"We should turn off and use secondary roads," her dad said.

She noticed strain in his voice, like someone sitting in an uncomfortable chair for too long.

"I know," she said. "Next exit. I know what I'm doing, Scott."

Using his name instead of Dad was petty, but it felt good to see him flinch from it. The satisfaction was short-lived, because the truth was that she didn't know what she was doing. Less than twenty minutes ago, she'd had a well-crafted plan to avenge her mother and punish her dad for the operatives he'd betrayed four years ago. The ones the world had seen executed in Syria on live television. Now she was on the run, aiding and abetting the man she was sent to kill. Worst of all, Joey was being held by God knew who. No, she had no clue what she was doing.

"You better have a good explanation for what's going on," she said.

"It's a long story."

She shot him an incredulous look. "Try me."

He leaned to his right, slumping against the window.

"Are you going to sleep?" she asked. "Hey, listen up. You're going to tell me how . . ." Her voice trailed off as she noticed the blood soaking his shirt and pant leg on the right side. He'd been blocking her view of it until now. "How bad?"

"Had worse," he said. "Been shot in the back before—literally and figuratively. Literally's worse, in case you were wondering."

"There's a med kit in the backseat," she said.

"I'll get it later," he mumbled, closing his eyes and leaning up against the window. "Just going to rest for a second."

"That's the blood loss talking. Hey, c'mon." She swerved the car to the left, which lifted his head off the window, then swerved right, causing him to whack his head against the glass. It woke him up.

"Easy," he said.

"If you're how I'm getting Joey back, then I'll be damned if you're going to bleed out in my car," she said. "Put some more pressure on that wound until I find a place to pull over."

"No time for that," he said, but his voice was getting weaker. Mara knew the signs. The human body did strange things once it leaked enough blood.

She checked her rearview mirror. Empty. Just the way she liked it.

"There's an old barn up here. We're stopping."

"I said no time for that."

"Thing is, you're not in charge," she said. "I am. And this whole escape thing is based on the idea that you know a way to get Joey back. I think it's time you start telling me exactly what the hell's going on here. Hear that, Scott? Hey, wake up."

But it was no use. He was out cold, his head thumping against the window as the Rover bumped down the country road. Even so, she noticed his face contort, eyes darting back and forth behind his lids. His lips curled back and his body trembled.

From what little she knew about her dad's career at the Agency, she figured he had his share of nightmares to haunt him. Clearly, he was locked in one now. She sped toward the barn to take cover and tend to his wound. As she drove, the whimpering sounds coming from the man next to her made her feel sorry for him for the first time in a decade.

She wondered what could have been so terrible to make a man like Scott Roberts cry out that way. Some of her own kills revisited her in the night, plaguing her with nightmares of the dead coming back to life to confront her. She was curious if her dad fought the same battles.

Judging by the way his muscles clenched and by the periodic groans, she guessed that he did. Part of her wished she could see what was going on in his head, but then again she knew it was better that she couldn't. His demons were his own, and as far as she was concerned, he deserved whatever hell they were giving him.

CHAPTER 4

Four years ago

Scott Roberts shot the man in the stomach because he knew he'd die slow that way.

Even though the man sprawled on the carpeted hotel floor was a terrorist, rapist, child-killer and an all-around dirtbag, Scott almost felt bad for the whimpering cur. His psych profile pointed out that his ability to feel empathy for other people's pain is what kept him from tumbling toward sociopathic behavior, but he didn't buy that. When he looked at the man clutching his abdomen, desperately trying to hold his organs in place, he simply knew that there was a good chance he'd be on the receiving end of a bad mission outcome one day. When that happened, he just hoped the son of a bitch who got him did it quick and wasn't a bastard like himself.

He knew if Khalil Al-Saib, the man dying in front of him, had been the one to win this particular game of cat and mouse that the Egyptian would have gladly taken his sweet time killing him. He would have ordered room service and performed any one of his trademark methods. Perhaps flaying the skin from his back, like he did to the Russian agent in Cairo. Or extracting all his teeth with a pair of pliers, like he did to the courier he suspected of spying on him in Limassol. Maybe, like the CIA agent the man had killed in Copenhagen, Al-Saib would have cut off Scott's genitals and shoved them down his throat.

No, Al-Saib would have likely gotten even more creative for him. Their game had been going on for over a year, and each man had come to at least acknowledge the other was a capable operative in a world filled with amateurs.

"Hurts, doesn't it?" he said.

"Ayreh feek. Telhas teeze."

"My Arabic's a little rusty, but I'm pretty sure your mother would be embarrassed to hear you say that. Maybe stick to English. You grew up in Jersey, for Christ's sake."

"Asshole," Al-Saib mumbled. "Give me some water."

Scott walked over to the room service tray. It was still covered with a half-eaten meal on fine China and silverware. Only the best at the Four Seasons. He looked over the remains. "Surf and turf," he said, nodding. "Not a bad call. I would have gone for the crab cakes myself. You are in DC, after all." He picked up a bottle of water, twisted the cap off to break the seal, then put it on loosely. He tossed it in the air. Al-Saib's reflexes weren't quite fast enough, and the bottle hit his stomach where he'd been shot. He cried out in pain.

"Oh shit, sorry," Scott said, not meaning it. "My bad."

Al-Saib pushed with his feet until his head was up against the wall behind him. With some effort, he worked his way up into a half-sitting position. Then he groped the floor next to him until he found the bottle. Clumsily, he managed to get the top off, raise it to his lips, and slurp the water down.

Scott snapped a couple of photos with his phone of the room and meal.

"I wonder what your buddies living back in their desert huts, living on old Russian MREs are going to think about this meal," he said.

"Like I give a shit," Al-Saib said in perfect English. Well, the traces of his New Jersey accent were still there, so it was hardly perfect.

"There you go," Scott said, picking a french fry off the room service plate. "This'll be much easier in English."

"This isn't going to be anything," Al-Saib said. "I want my lawyer."

Scott laughed so hard that bits of the french fry went flying. "Sorry, but damn, that was a good one. What do you think's going to happen here? That you're going to end up in Gitmo or some country club prison in Virginia? You ought to know better than that."

Al-Saib stared at him, the hate burning in his eyes. "A CIA operation right in DC. How many laws are you breaking right now?"

"Just the right number to put you in the ground," Scott said. "But let's just keep that between the two of us. My boss thinks I'm on vacation in the Bahamas."

A fleeting look of fear passed behind the man's eyes, a rare moment of weakness.

"You're unsanctioned." It wasn't a question, just a resigned understanding.

Scott pulled up a chair, a fancy Louis XIV number with carved legs and arms. He sat in it, face-to-face with Al-Saib, his Sig Sauer 226 with the SRD 9 suppressor resting across his lap. "Some guys like to fish or golf on their time off. I enjoy tracking assholes like you and putting them out of commission. It makes me happy. Maybe I could have you mounted and put on the wall in my den."

"I know a guy who can do the work for you."

"I bet you do," Scott said. He leaned forward. "This is more than a social call. There are a few questions I'd like answered."

"Like why I let you track me here?" Scott's face must have registered his surprise because Al-Saib shook his head. "You think the errors I made weren't on purpose? Who's to say who was the hunter and who was the hunted?"

"Where I come from down in Georgia, the animal shot in the gut, bleeding out all over the place, is usually considered the one who got hunted."

Al-Saib laughed, but it turned into a coughing fit, blood spraying from his mouth. Scott figured he might have less time than he originally thought.

"Let's get down to business," he said. "You know what I want."

"You want to know about Omega."

"Yes."

"And if I tell you what you want?" Al-Saib asked. "I get medical attention? I go free? What?"

"ID the leaders. Tell me the names of the men in my government who are part of this," Scott said, "and I'll shoot you square between the eyes."

Al-Saib leaned back and closed his eyes. "You can do better than that."

"I could promise you medical care, asylum, all that, but we're both professionals. We know none of that's going to happen. All I can offer you is a quick death over slowly dying from that gut shot. We both know how that goes. The bullet ruptured the intestine, probably the colon, too, by the smell of it. It could be days until you die, but you will die."

Al-Saib took another drink of water. Scott noticed the man check his watch as he did it. It was a minute movement, probably one most people would have missed. The simple act sent a burst of adrenaline through his system. He regripped the Sig Sauer and looked to the door.

"Expecting someone?"

"I wasn't hunting you to kill you," Al-Saib said. "If I had been, you'd have been dead months ago. I drew you here because I was instructed to make you a proposal," Al-Saib said.

"Oh yeah? How's that working out for you?"

"It could be going better," he said.

Scott stood and walked quickly across the room to the door. It was a large suite, not the Presidential, but the next level down. Still, it was the kind of room used by the rich, famous, and paranoid. For security, there was a video panel by the door with a view of the private foyer outside the door, as well as the hallway. The video feed for the hallway was black. The foyer-cam showed one second of image before it, too, went blank.

But the one second was enough to show a man reaching toward the camera and spraying it with paint. Right before he did, Scott spotted at least two additional men in suits crouched near the ground, both with suppressed MP5s.

"Damn it," Scott said. He hated when a mission went to shit.

"Where I come from," Al-Saib said, "the one caught in the trap at the end of the chase is the hunted."

Scott ignored the comment. The roles had changed and he was in real trouble. He looked around the room for options, finding it funny as he did so.

With all the terrible places he'd been in the world, from equatorial jungles and arid deserts to third world capitals and deep in enemy territory during wartime, he was amazed that he might die only a few blocks from the White House in a luxury five-star hotel.

And if there was one thing he hated to do, it was dying. He'd tried it before and hadn't liked it. As Al-Saib's guards knocked on the door more insistently, he tried to figure out a way to avoid repeating the experience.

Scott pointed the gun at Al-Saib's head. "Call them off or you're dead."

"You said I was dead no matter what," Al-Saib replied. "All you offered me for my cooperation was a fast death. Now you're offering that for free."

There was another knock on the door. That was a good sign. The men in the hall must not have been sure there was a problem inside. Otherwise they would have knocked the door down and come in blazing. Scott already knew the two other ways out of the room; checking for egress was a habit no matter what room he walked into. There was a second door at the other end of the suite. Probably covered by Al-Saib's men, too. Then there was the outdoor terrace. Three stories up. It was an option. Just not a very damn good one.

"I said I sought you out for a reason. Aren't you curious about my proposal?" Al-Saib asked. "Or who's making it?"

Scott crossed to the French door that opened to the terrace. He'd cleared it and the rest of the suite after shooting Al-Saib twenty minutes earlier, but he was happy to see there were not men repelling down from the floor above. That would have been a real problem.

"You want to know where the billions of dollars came from," Al-Saib said. "You want to know what the money is being used for. And you want to know who in your government is part of the project." Another knock from outside. More insistent. A man's voice called out, muffled through the heavy door.

"You want to tell me all that?" Roberts said. "That'd be great."

Al-Saib laughed, wincing from the pain. "A cowboy, even now. No, the men I work for want you to join the project. You're getting older, a little slower, it happens to all of us."

Scott crossed over to the terrace and checked it again. That was looking like the best option. Only he'd have to leave Al-Saib behind.

"You're about to get a lot slower," Scott said. "Like permanently slower."

"Think of your wife and daughters," Al-Saib said. "Don't you want to provide for them? Be able to protect them?" He grinned. "Wendy, Mara, and Lucy, isn't it? They looked beautiful in the photographs, but so much better in person."

Scott froze. Two emotions struck him simultaneously on hearing him say their names. First was cold fear like ice water poured over him. Al-Saib was a pro. If he knew the names, he might just have taken them to get leverage. Scott could endure any threat to himself, any injury, any risk of death. But danger to his family was unacceptable.

This led to the second simultaneous emotion that collided with the first. Pure, unbridled anger. A rage that he always carried with him, usually in check, dormant but just under the surface, masked by his tough-guy, glib demeanor. Al-Saib had found the exact right words to wake it up and make it come alive.

Al-Saib saw the change take place on Scott's face because he held his hands up as he approached. "They're not harmed . . . they're not—"

Scott grabbed one of the man's arms and roughly dragged his

body along the floor. Al-Saib screamed, a trail of blood extending behind him. Scott kicked open the terrace door, pushing aside the refined patio furniture in his way to the low wall on the edge.

In one smooth movement, lifting Al-Saib like he was weightless, Scott hefted him over the edge of the wall, grabbed the cuff of his shirt, and leaned him backward. Twenty-ninth Street below had a few pedestrians on it, unaware of what was going on directly over their heads.

"Has my family been targeted?" Scott demanded.

Al-Saib groaned, looking down at the three-story drop beneath him.

Scott reached with his other hand and dug his fingers into the bullet hole he'd put into the man's stomach earlier. Al-Saib screamed.

"I said, has my family been targeted?"

"You're a fool," Al-Saib spat. "You have no idea what you're up against. How far Omega goes into your own government. Into every government. Men you know and call you friend betray you and you have no idea."

A smashing sound came from behind him. They were breaking down the door to the suite.

"Is my family a target?" Scott snarled.

Al-Saib had a look of peace come over him. He craned his neck to look into Scott's eyes. "The entire world is a target. Your family is no exception." He closed his eyes. "I told Hawthorn you'd never join."

Scott registered the name but refused to believe it. He gripped the man tighter around the collar. "You're full of shit. Disinformation right up to the end."

With a snap of wood, the door frame inside cracked. They were almost through.

Al-Said opened his eyes, a smug satisfaction in them. "It's your end we're about to see. I told them this was how it would go, but they wouldn't listen. And now look at what has to happen. What a waste."

"A waste? Nah, the world's not losing much. Safe travels, Khalil. You piece of shit."

Scott heaved the man over the side, ripping his hands away when Al-Said tried to grab on to him. A couple of seconds later, Scott heard the wet thud of a body hitting concrete. He looked over the edge and saw the man's broken body facedown, a halo of blood spreading around him. For being a botched plan, the result still felt strangely satisfying.

A burst of gunfire exploded behind him and a loud crash told him the men were through the door. He knew they would shoot first and ask questions later. It was time to go.

He leaned over and looked for a path down. At only three stories, he could risk the jump, using the couple of trees nearby to break his fall. But there were already people moving toward Al-Saib's body. And with the new phones, everyone had a camera on them. He'd like to avoid a video of himself on the nightly news if it was possible.

The terrace was the only one in this part of the hotel, so the wall immediately below had windows to regular rooms. Closed with no chance to somehow swing down into one. There was only one other option, and that was to go up.

Once the decision was made, he lost no time executing. He shoved the metal table toward the windows of the suite, then leapt on top of it. There was movement and shouting inside. A bloody smear across the floor probably had something to do with it.

The roof above the suite was flat until it got to the six-story tower in the back of the property. He jumped up, grabbing the roofline. But it was mossy and slick and he slipped backward, crashing onto the table.

He scrambled up to his knees, his breath knocked out of him. When he looked up, he was looking through the wall of windows into the suite's living room. Right in front of him were two men with machine guns staring back at him in shock.

They raised their guns in unison and opened fire.

The window right in front of his face peppered with impacts from the gunfire. Scott flinched, expecting to feel the searing pain of hot metal ripping through his flesh. But nothing came.

The gunfire stopped and he realized what'd happened. The suite's many windows were all bullet-resistant glass, although the designers had likely never imagined the gunfire would come from inside the building. A man shouted orders in Arabic, and one gun reopened fire on the glass. Bullet-resistant didn't mean bulletproof. Scott didn't intend to wait around to see how long the window would last. Not only that, but the movement he could see through the spider-webbed glass told him he wouldn't be alone on the terrace for long.

He made another attempt at the roof, this time knowing what to expect for his handhold. It was hard, but he was able to scramble up before anyone shot him in the ass. It was only a matter of seconds before he heard men's voices below. He took off running across the black tar roof, ducking behind the air-conditioning units bolted to the surface. Anything to take away the line of sight between himself and the guys with the guns.

Speaking of guns, he still had his. He considered doing a doubling-back maneuver, grabbing an ambush spot and letting the new arrivals walk into his field of fire. But as much as he loved his Sig Sauer, he didn't like the idea of going up against an unknown number of opponents equipped with MP5s. All it would take was one misstep and it'd be a showdown with him on the wrong end of the firepower calculation. No thank you.

Instead, he intended to go with the time-honored tradition of just running like hell.

But even that plan had its issues. The roof ended abruptly with a thirty-foot drop into a central courtyard in the middle of the hotel complex. He spotted a door in the side of the attached tower that housed extra floors of the hotel, but that was a hundred feet away across open space with no cover. He was sure the gunmen behind him would be on the roof and after him any second.

As if on cue, bullets zinged off the air-conditioning unit next to him, sparking against the sheet metal.

With only a two-step run, he leapt from the roof, arms and legs frantically moving to get every last inch of horizontal distance. He hit the small branches of the tree first, crushing them like twigs. But these gave way to thicker branches that slowed his fall, then abruptly to a main branch that stopped him with a jolt to the side of his rib cage. There was a loud crack and he wasn't sure if it was the branch or his ribs. From the way it felt, he guessed it was both.

The primitive part of his brain, the instinctual part that somehow sensed danger before it even happened, told him to move. He pushed off the branch and fell the last eight feet to the brick sidewalk just as the tree above him was peppered with machine gunfire.

He rolled on his shoulder and came up running, his ribs screaming in pain. The bricks around him came alive with chips flying up in the air as the gunman tracked his movements. Scott zigzagged his way through the courtyard toward an opening to the street. Just as he made the entrance, white-hot pain exploded in his calf and sent him tumbling forward. Having been shot over a dozen times in his career, he knew exactly what it was. Not that knowing made it any less painful.

He pulled himself up using the brick wall and staggered out of the hotel property. He tasted blood in his mouth, a sign that one of his broken ribs might have punctured a lung. His leg was a bloody mess and pretty much useless. There was a narrow sidewalk in front of him, then a strip of well-tended grass followed by a wall of trees along the C&O Canal. He knew what he had to do. Plans B and C were long gone. He wasn't sure what variation of his mission plan he was on now. Maybe P or Q. But as the old saying went, every plan became worthless after first contact with the enemy. Damn if that wasn't true.

He hopped on his good foot down to the water's edge and waded in. The C&O Canal ran through Georgetown, a relic from a time when barges were pulled up and down the waterway for trade. The water was flat, dark, and stale. Bits of floating trash dotted the surface, and it smelled like a sewer. Scott could only imagine the zoological wonders crawling into the open wound on his leg.

Sirens erupted in the distance. This was the nation's capital, after all. Machine gunfire at an establishment with Pennsylvania Avenue in its address drew an immediate and what would surely be a massive response. He knew they'd be too late to save his sorry ass, though. He was on his own.

He hugged the edge of the waterway and lowered himself until he was completely submerged except for his head. Seconds later, faster than he'd expected, he heard Arabic voices coming his way. He took a deep breath and went underwater.

Grabbing handfuls of the slimy mud on the bottom, he pulled himself downstream, moving methodically so as not to leave a wake on the surface above him. This was a high-risk, high-reward move. If he made it around the bend in the waterway into Rock Creek, then he was in good shape. If they spotted him before that, he was a fish to be shot in a barrel.

God, grant me the serenity to accept the things I cannot change, the courage to change the things I can, and the wisdom to know the difference.

The Serenity Prayer, commonly used in twelve-step meetings like Alcoholics Anonymous, served him well on missions. He recited it again, pulling his way hand over hand through muck, fighting to keep his legs from floating up to the surface behind him. He couldn't change the fact that he was in the water with gunmen on the prowl on the shore looking for him. All he could do was disguise his movements to the best of his ability and keep underwater for as long as possible.

On a normal day, one where he hadn't been shot in the leg or punctured a lung with a broken rib, Scott could hold his breath for four minutes easy. If he had time to prepare with breathing exercises to oxygenate his blood, he could get that up to six. But with the raging pain in his leg and with his right lung slowly filling with blood, the serenity prayer did little to keep him from blowing through his air in less than two minutes. He fought it hard, gulping and swallowing the air in his mouth, before giving in and raising his head as slowly as possible.

No one shot him in the head the second he broke the surface, so that was positive. He drew in a sharp breath and opened his eyes. It was hard to see because he couldn't risk the movement of wiping the muddy water from his face, but he got his bearings. And he liked what he saw. He was almost to the bend in the waterway. He was going to make it.

Then a man shouted in Arabic behind him, and all hell broke loose.

The water sprayed around him with gunfire. A second voice shouted at him. Scott pushed off the grassy bank and swam for the bend. The pain in his side was so intense that it blocked the pain in his calf. Without the adrenaline rushing into his system, he might have passed out. But he wasn't going to let some two-bit protective detail take him out. Especially one that obviously sucked at their jobs since their protectee was a blob on the Twenty-ninth Street sidewalk.

Digging deep, he splashed his way downriver and by some miracle made it around the bend. The river was wider here and had some current because it was joined by Rock Creek. He kept swimming even though his body begged him to stop. But he knew he wasn't out of it yet. The sirens were getting close, but the gunmen seemed to be the motivated type. Scott hated those, much preferring the low-level goons who liked to hide as soon as the bullets started flying.

He pulled out his phone from his pocket, knowing it was water-proofed and would be fine even though it'd been submerged in the C&O cesspool. He was unsanctioned, so there weren't very many people he could call for help. The one person he could was also the one person he most wanted to avoid asking. But he was a re-alist, and things just weren't going his way that day. She picked up the phone on the first ring.

"Mind if I drop by?" he said.

The building he was looking for loomed up ahead, down-stream on his right. It was four stories of beautiful design, clean lines, and glass walls that seamlessly integrated into the river's edge. Even though this was the back of the building, there was a large blue flag with a yellow cross shifted to the hoist side and a sign announcing that it was the Embassy of Sweden.

A small knot of security left the lower level of the building and took positions at the river's edge, guns pointed directly at him. He held his hands in the air the best he could to show he was unarmed. A line was thrown out. He grabbed it and was dragged to shore and half carried into the building. The men, military by the way they moved, put him down in what looked like a maintenance room filled with cleaning supplies. An older man with gray hair and a neatly kept beard was there waiting for him. Scott knew him as Dr. Peter Gurtz, although he wondered if that was his real name. Dr. Gurtz removed his suit jacket and rolled up his shirt sleeves.

"Welcome back to Sweden, Mr. Roberts," he said. "Last time I saw you we were both in tuxedos and drinking champagne."

He tried to smile, but it came out as a grimace. "You were drinking champagne. I was drinking bourbon."

"Yes, I remember now," he said, cutting away Scott's pant leg to expose the gunshot wound as if everything happening was just another typical day at the office. "A pleasant evening." He made a *tut-tut* sound as he looked at the bullet wound. "This will not go over well."

"How about you stitch me up and we don't tell her about it," Scott said. "Say I tore it on a metal post or something."

Without looking up, Dr. Gurtz raised his voice slightly. "Would you accept that explanation, Wendy? That this gunshot wound came from, what did you say, a metal post or something?"

Scott cringed and turned. Maybe it was because he'd just had a near-death experience, or maybe it was because she was dressed in his favorite yellow dress with her blond hair pulled back into a simple ponytail, or maybe it was because she was simply a drop-dead gorgeous, brilliant woman, but Scott had never felt so happy to see his wife.

He couldn't say the same for her. She looked about ready to slap him around.

"No, Dr. Gurtz," she said. "I don't think I would believe that."

She softened when Scott flinched from the doc poking around in his leg, and leaned over him. "But then again, you're hard to believe under the best of circumstances, aren't you?"

"How's your day going?" he asked.

"Good," she said, willing to play the game with him. "Yours?"

"Same ol', same ol'."

She leaned down to his ear. "Did you get what you were after?"

He shook his head. "Not enough. He gave me a name. . . ." His voice trailed off. It was the first minute he'd had to think about what Al-Saib had told him. Jim Hawthorn. The man was like a father to Scott. There was no chance he was involved. He looked at Wendy. "It was nothing. Just misdirection."

"Who was it?"

Scott glanced down at the good doctor. She caught his meaning. She always did.

"How is he, Dr. Gurtz?" she asked.

"The leg will be fine. Bullet passed through the muscle. No damage to the bone. Very fortunate."

"Yeah, that's exactly how it feels," Scott said.

Wendy nudged him on his side and he grunted in pain.

"Oh shush, you big baby."

"I want an X-ray of the ribs," Dr. Gurtz said. "As soon as possible."

"We're arranging transport," she said.

"Good." Dr. Gurtz felt around Scott's rib cage. "Let me take a look. Let me know if this hurts."

He pressed down, not hard, but hard enough so that lightning bolts of pain raced up his side.

Scott cried out and . . .

CHAPTER 5

Mara stepped back as her dad pushed her hand away.

"Damn, that hurts," he said.

"Oh shush, you big baby," Mara said. She was almost done suturing the opening. It'd been a lot easier while he'd been passed out from the blood loss. She noticed an odd look had come across her dad's face. "What?"

"Nothing," he said. "Forget about it."

She took a step back and stood in the middle of the barn. It was old and had a definite lean to one side. An old tractor that was more rust than metal hunkered down in the back corner. The whole place smelled of dust and machine oil. The most interesting find was an old Chevy pickup truck parked next to the tractor. There was only a thin coat of dust on it, so it hadn't been in the barn for long. There weren't any keys in it, but that wasn't going to be a problem. If they could get it going it was their ride out of there. A little less conspicuous than a Range Rover riddled with bullet holes. She held the suturing kit out to him. "Do you want to do it yourself? You're more than welcome."

"No, I'm sorry. Please finish." He peered down at her handiwork. "Looks like you've done this before."

Mara doused the area a second time with antiseptic. "Yeah,

on Marines. Only they didn't whine about it." She went back to stitching.

"I heard about your tour in Iraq," he said quietly. "I'm sorry."

A long silence strung out between them; the only sounds were the rustling of some kind of small animal in the moldering hay piled in the back of the barn. Mara focused on suturing the flesh in front of her, willing the memories from her last mission to stay sleeping in the corner of her mind, where she'd pushed them. Four years later and it was impossible to think about it without hearing the gunfire in her head. Not to mention the screams.

"Who told you about that?" was all she managed. "Same person who told you they were going to take Joey?"

Scott remained silent.

"You need to tell me who your contact is," Mara said.

Scott winced as she pulled the stitch tight, cinching his flesh back together. "We went over this. I'm not telling you that. Not yet anyway."

She poked the needle back through his skin with a little more force than necessary. "If you get killed, then I'm left not knowing who to trust."

"Let me make it easy for you," he said. "Trust no one."

She tied off the last stitch and took out the scissors to snip the ends of the sutures. "Don't worry. I've got that part down. It's one of the side benefits when your larger-than-life hero of a dad kills your mom and betrays his country. You learn that lesson real quick."

She threw the scissors back into the med kit and took out two large area bandages. She put one over the entrance wound and another over the exit, then wrapped tape around his torso to hold it in place. She felt him staring at her, but she purposefully avoided his eyes as she finished the last touches. She cut the tape and pressed the dressing into place. "We're done here."

Scott held on to her arm. It startled her and she had to fight the urge to retaliate, but his grip was soft and nonthreatening.

She turned to him and was surprised to see tears in the big man's eyes.

"I loved your mother. From the first second I saw her until the night she died right in front of me. I loved her more than you could possibly imagine. The idea that I could ever hurt her is . . . is . . ."

"Is what you admitted on your video confession," she said, yanking her arm back. "I saw it. Not the transcript. Not someone telling me what you said. I saw the actual video of you admitting it."

"There's a reason that I said those things."

"I know the words," she said. "I memorized them. Not because I wanted to, but because I watched it so many times."

"I didn't—"

"The questioner asks, 'Are you responsible for the death of Wendy Roberts.' You look down at the table for a second, then back up with these big crocodile tears in your eyes and say, 'Yes, I killed her. It was the hardest thing I ever did, but it had to be done.'" She choked up as she said the words, mad that she was giving Scott the satisfaction of seeing her so vulnerable. "It had to be done?"

"That was just theater," he said. "Your mom's death was the hardest thing I've ever been through. Still is. There's not a day that I—"

"Don't say it," she said, cutting him off. "I don't want to hear you talking about her. You don't deserve to."

"I didn't kill her."

"Then what happened?"

"It's complicated."

"Try me," she said, crossing her arms.

Scott stood and stretched gingerly. "I can't. Not yet."

"That's such bullshit," she said. "I'm just supposed to trust you?"

"You don't have to trust me. You just need to stay out of my way."

Mara let out a short laugh. "Oh really?"

"What's your second option for getting Joey back?"

"Kill you and go in for a full debrief," she said. "Take every lie detector test they can think of to prove you didn't tell me this mysterious information you say they're worried about."

"You mean those lie detector tests you've been trained to fool?" Scott asked, walking over to the pickup and opening the door. "They'd do that just to see if they could get a positive out of you. If they did, then they'd bring in the real heavy hitters. Even if you passed all the tests, and they'll hook you up to more than just lie detector machines, you'd still be a loose end. What they do then is just a measure of how paranoid they are. Maybe they stop there. But maybe they don't."

"That's why you're not giving me any details," she said, suddenly realizing his motive. "I don't just have plausible deniability, I have actual deniability. You're trying to leave this option open in case I need it."

"See?" Scott said as he climbed into the truck. "It's not because I'm just an asshole."

"I wouldn't go that far," Mara said, half to herself. She had to admit, there was a ring of truth to the idea. It didn't make it any less frustrating. Seconds later, the engine slowly turned over, then fired up. The old man could still hot-wire a car. "I'll drive," she said. "It'll be hours before you're not feeling the effects of the blood loss."

He held up his hands. "No complaints here. She's all yours."

Minutes later, they were headed north on a rural gravel road, nothing but hundreds of acres of corn in every direction. There was a helicopter to the west toward the prison, but it never came toward them.

"Where are we going?" she asked.

"Chicago."

"Chicago?" she said, pumping the brakes. "No way. They have to be holding Joey somewhere in DC. I need to—"

"If you want to get him back, we go to Chicago. Trust me."

She laughed. "Trust me? Really? That's where we're at now?"

"There's an old friend in Chicago I need to talk to. He has information that will lead us to who's really behind all this."

"In case you were wondering, the Agency is who sent me here. They're behind this. You're not getting senile on me, are you?"

"Nothing's as simple as it seems. It may have been the Agency, but there's someone else pulling the strings. There has been for a while now." He must have noticed her skeptical look because he turned away. "You'll see. Once we talk to this guy, you'll understand better what's going on here. How far it reaches."

"You sound like one of those conspiracy nutjobs. Who is this guy? This friend of yours? Please don't tell me he's some tinfoil hat–wearing, black helicopter–fearing guy you met online."

"More of an acquaintance. I need to ask him a few questions."

"I'm not driving to Chicago when Joey's in DC unless I know who it is," she said. "If you can't—"

"Preston Townsend," he said.

She took a second to process the name, thinking at first he was playing with her. But his tone was dead serious. "You mean President Preston Townsend?"

"Ex-president, I think. Unless they changed the Fourteenth Amendment while I was locked up."

"We're going to go just chat with the president?" she said, exasperated.

"It might need to be more of an interrogation, but yeah. That's the general idea."

"That should be easy enough. I can write the newspaper headline: RENEGADE CIA OPERATIVE APPROACHES EX-PRESIDENT. SECRET SERVICE SHOOTS HIM ON SIGHT."

"Are you always this much of a Debbie downer?" Scott asked, closing his eyes and leaning his seat back so that he was almost horizontal. "I don't remember that about you."

"You don't know me at all," she said. "Remember that."

"Used to be nice. Smiling all the time. Saying nice things," he mumbled, drifting off to sleep. "Just like your mom. Nice . . . so nice . . . to everyone."

His voice trailed off and his breathing grew deeper. Soon a soft snore filled the cab.

Mara saw a turn up ahead that would take them east. Toward DC. Toward Joey. She felt the battle rage inside of her, trying to make the best decision possible with the limited facts. The turn east came and went. She took a deep breath and settled in for the long drive north.

Mara drove, alone with her thoughts, watching the sun descend in the sky and sink down beyond the sea of green leaves. She worked through everything that'd happened over the past day. Replaying every conversation, considering the implications of her dad's claims. What if he really had been framed? What if he hadn't killed her mom? What kind of daughter did that make her?

But it wasn't possible. She'd watched his video confession. Read through the classified field report. Pored through the notes from the attempts by body recovery teams for even more clues. She'd even had a meeting with the DCI, Director of Central Intelligence, Jim Hawthorn himself to go over the circumstances. He'd been a family friend and even with all of his resources, he hadn't seen a way out as the evidence piled up against his top agent. It was one of the reasons Hawthorn was an ex-director who now ran his sphere of influence out of a small shop inside the Special Activities Division.

She wondered what her dad would think if he knew it'd been Jim Hawthorn who'd personally recruited her for this assignment.

As she drove north into the darkening sky, she considered all of her options. Every fiber of her being still told her to get to DC as fast as she could to look for Joey. But on that count, her dad was right. Joey was a lever to get her to act. But a lever only worked when direct force was applied. When that force came it would be in the form of a deadline to perform a specific action or suffer some consequence to Joey. By not opening the dialogue, whoever was holding him couldn't threaten her or give her a deadline. It was brilliant in its simplicity, but it was driving her crazy.

The idea that Joey was being held by strangers filled her with rage. She was used to taking action, not sitting and waiting for things to develop around her. Her insides twisted around themselves, and she felt for a moment that she might need to pull over and throw up. She clenched her fist and punched the steering wheel. Over and over again. It wasn't like her to lose control; it was a weakness she rarely allowed herself. But they had her baby and he was her responsibility. Nothing in her training prepared her for the way it made her feel.

What her training did give her was complete certainty that if anyone were to actually hurt Joey, she would make every single person involved pay for it. She thought of her dead sister and felt sick all over again at what she would say about how Mara had taken care of her son.

"It's all right," Lucy said, her voice so frail that it hurt Mara to hear it. The hospice was an improvement from the hospital wing, where they'd been for the last two months. Mara had brought in framed photos and paintings from Lucy's house. There had been a flat-screen TV on the wall opposite the bed, but Lucy had told Mara to take it down. "I'll be damned if I'm going to spend a minute of the time I have left watching TV," Lucy had said on move-in day. True to her word, she hadn't.

The spot where the TV had been was where Lucy's favorite photo hung. It was a beautiful image, her and Mike next to a garden filled with sunflowers.

Lucy was pregnant in the photo, Mike's hand on her stomach, grinning like he'd won the lottery. There was so much hope and love in the photo, but such sadness, too. It was the closest Mike ever came to meeting his son. A month later, a uniformed Casualty Assistance Calls Officer knocked on her door, the visit dreaded by every military spouse. Training accident was what she was told. But Mara had arranged a second visit, this one unofficial, from Mike's Force Recon squad leader Lt. Dan Suarez. She'd held Lucy's hand while Suarez told them the real story.

The mission had been a target in Afghanistan, a terrorist the military intelligence analysts had decided was worth the risk to try and grab. Only it'd been a setup. Mike had died a warrior's death, fighting for his country but dying for his men. Suarez left no doubt that without Mike's sacrifice, neither he nor the rest of the team would have made it out alive. Openly weeping, he begged Lucy's forgiveness for leaving her husband's body behind.

Mara found it hard to look at the photo of the two of them without feeling the gut-punch, but it was a source of strength for Lucy. Maybe it was the joy framed in that moment. Or maybe the consolation that she'd be back with her husband soon, able to tell him that his son had been born strong and healthy. Mara didn't ask. She just made certain that the flowers brought into the room from Lucy's friends never blocked the photo from her line of sight.

Lucy spent hours staring at the photo. Sometimes, she told Mara one day, it was her focal point when the pain came, when the agony raged like a storm inside her. Other times, it just soothed her and transported her to the scene in the painting, far away from the machines hooked up to her, far away from the cancer consuming her, far away from the inevitability of leaving her son an orphan. But after Mara's confession at the edge of her sister's bed, she saw in her eyes that not even the painting could ease the pain that day.

"I'm sorry . . . I just can't . . ." Mara said again. She'd cried when she'd practiced the speech, but she didn't now that she was there doing it for real. She almost wished she could, thinking that would somehow make her sister understand that this wasn't a decision she took lightly. "I thought I could when you first asked me, but now . . . now . . ."

"Now it's real," she said. "Now it's really going to happen and you know it."

"Don't say that. You could still . . . there's a chance . . ." They both fell silent. The only sounds in the room were the faint hum of the machines monitoring her sister's gradual descent into Death's open arms.

Lucy reached out and put her hand over Mara's. It was cold and thin, mostly bone. Yellowed skin hung loosely from it. "Don't worry, kid. It'll be all right. Joey will be fine. I've talked to Ted and Marie already. They'll take him."

This caught her off guard. Ted and Marie were Mike's parents. The image of their grief-stricken faces as they lowered their only son into the ground flashed in her mind. They'd seemed so old that day, so worn-out by life. How could they raise a little boy? "You already spoke to them?"

Lucy patted her hand. She closed her eyes, the slight wince telling Mara that the pain was back. "It's all right," she said softly. "Maybe it's for the best. I just wanted him . . . I don't know . . . you can still be part of his life."

"Teach him to be a screwup?"

"I was thinking you could give him that fire you have inside you. But being a screwup works, too." Lucy smiled, but it was a strained action, pushing its way through the wave of pain she was riding. "I wish Dad would come visit again."

Mara looked away, blinking back tears. The hallucinations of seeing their dad had started a few days earlier. Another sign the end was near.

"Should I get the nurse?" Mara asked. "Get you something for the pain?"

Lucy's eyes wandered first to the ceiling and then tracked back down to the photo on the wall. "Joey's off school soon. I want to be awake. I don't want to miss it."

Mara brushed her sister's hair back. "I'll wait with you. Do you want me to sing you a song?"

Lucy's chest bounced as she laughed. "God, you trying to kill me or what?"

Mara laughed with her, but somewhere along the line, it turned into crying. She tried never to do that in front of Lucy, always trying to be strong for her, but she couldn't stop herself this time. She edged herself onto the bed and laid next to her big sister, the way she used to do during thunderstorms when they were kids. They didn't say anything more, but just waited there for Joey to get back from school. It wasn't long until Mara fell asleep.

A nurse woke her up, an older woman Mara didn't recognize. The woman's face was kind, but laced with sadness as she spoke. Mara didn't understand the words at first; then she understood them but didn't believe them. After putting her hand on her sister's still chest, she believed but didn't accept. When the nurse told her that Joey was at the front desk, home from school and eager to see his mom, she accepted and didn't know what to do.

And so she did the only thing she could think of and went out and wrapped Joey in her arms and promised to take care of him for the rest of his life.

She rolled down the window, gulping down the fresh night air, trying to clear her head from the memory of her sister. Only a year and yet it was so raw that the wound ripped open at the slightest pull. She couldn't afford to have her judgment clouded. Whatever path her dad was leading her down, she was going to need to be sharp and ready to take advantage of any opening she had to twist things to her advantage. She'd already made the decision that if she could sacrifice her dad in exchange for Joey's safety, she'd do it in a heartbeat.

Still, being around him had been tougher than she'd imagined. After so many years of hating him for what he'd done, she'd successfully turned him into a cartoon villain in her head. A scheming double agent who'd lost his moral compass and sold out his family and his country for a big pay day. A narcissist who'd skipped out on visiting his daughter's deathbed to avoid capture. Lucy had wanted so desperately to see him that she'd imagined he visited her, even speaking to him in her sleep. One more thing that broke Mara's heart in two.

The psych guys had prepared her pre-mission about the risk of feeling the pull of the father-daughter relationship once she was around him. She'd dismissed the idea. Her hatred of the man who used to be her father was rock solid.

But with his claims of innocence, the way his voice cracked when he talked about her mother, even the familiar sound of his breathing next to her, she did feel the self-doubt creep into her mind. She hadn't forgotten that she was dealing with a professional manipulator, perhaps one of the best in the world. Whatever feelings she had for him were likely only there because he wanted her to feel them.

But there was a chance that he was telling the truth. He might somehow hold the key to getting Joey back. Certainly there was someone high in the Agency who was still his ally. His knowing about Joey being taken before she knew had been proof of that. Perhaps that same person who fed him information would be able to tell her where they were keeping her nephew.

She rifled through her contacts in the Agency, thinking who she might call for help. Who she could trust. The problem was that Jim Hawthorn would have been on that list only a few hours earlier. In her line of work, paranoia was part of the skill set that made her good at her job. Now it kept her from having even a single lifeline back into the Agency for help. With one possible exception. There was one person who might be able to help, but she needed to figure out how to reach out to him. She'd dumped her phone after the prison to avoid being traced, not that she would have used it anyway. The NSA would be sitting on that phone like barn cats waiting for a mouse to poke its head out of a hole in the wall.

No, she needed to find a new phone. She tucked an idea in the back of her mind to revisit later.

She checked her watch. They'd be in Chicago by the morning. She decided to let things play out once they got there, but if there wasn't clear progress by noon, then she was making the call to Hawthorn and risk coming in.

As the moon rose up over the rural landscape and turned the swaying cornstalks into eerie oceans of silver, she thought about where Joey was sleeping that night and whether he was being brave. The sudden mental image of him alone and afraid in a dark room caught her off guard and she choked back a sob. She glanced over to make sure her dad was still asleep. Satisfied he was out, she allowed the carefully constructed walls holding back her emotions to break down. Mara Roberts, hardened CIA operative and decorated ex-Marine, did something she hadn't done since her sister's funeral. She let herself cry.

CHAPTER 6

Jim Hawthorn was pissed.

He sulked in the back of his Lincoln Navigator, the privacy window up between him and his driver, watching the lights of Washington, DC, pass by. Nothing had gone to plan. He was used to some degree of improvisation from his field agents and deviations over a long mission, but this was supposed to be a simple exercise. Then again, nothing involving either Scott or Mara Roberts was ever simple. He'd known that but failed to think through all the variables they introduced into the mix. Was it really possible to predict the path any destructive storm would take?

The cell phone he held in his hand rang. He thought about just not answering it, but he knew that wasn't an option. There weren't many people in the world who could make him nervous, but the woman sure to be on the other end of the line was one of them.

"You didn't call," the voice said, slightly modulated from an electronic distortion device. She wasn't going to let him hear her real voice. And she left no path to discovering her true identity; Hawthorn had put that to the test. "I find that disrespectful," she said.

He felt his body tense at the way she said the word. It came across as an expletive.

"I wanted to bring the situation under control before I contacted you."

A pause. He parted his lips and heard the tackiness of his suddenly dry mouth in the silence.

"Is it under control?" the voice finally asked.

"It will be."

"Which means it's not," she said.

"There was a complication, but nothing we can't recover from."

"You said *we*," the voice said softly.

Hawthorn tried to swallow and found it hard to do so. He leaned forward and grabbed one of the water bottles in the drink holder. "It's nothing I can't recover from," he said. God, he hated this woman. She called herself the Director. He had more descriptive names for her.

"Because if you fail at this, it's you who has a problem. Not we," she said. "Unless the we you're referring to is your family. Your wife left behind quite a legacy. Three children. Six grandchildren. Your first great-grandchild is due, when? Three weeks? Are Megan and Travis planning on having the baby at Bangor Memorial? It's a twenty-minute drive from their home, so it only makes sense."

His stomach tightened. He'd argued against her plan to take the five-year-old Joey as leverage. He'd thought it was an unnecessary complication, but she'd insisted, so he'd complied. Taking the kid was supposed to have been a trump card if things went south with the assignment, not the reason the thing went south. Part of him wanted to tell her he'd been right about leaving the kid out of it, but he didn't dare. It was what it was now. Just one more thing that had to be dealt with. Ultimately, using the kid as leverage was just business. But hearing his own family threatened was a different matter. "You've made your point."

"Have I? If this isn't resolved in the next twenty-four hours, I will need to do something to make certain of it."

Hawthorn gripped the phone so hard that he thought he might crack it. It took every bit of his self-control not to lash out. He held the phone in front of him and flipped it off, mouthing the words he really wanted to say. But fear is a powerful deterrent and he held his tongue. He took a deep breath to steady himself and put the phone back to his ear.

"Don't worry," he said. "The plan will be on track before noon tomorrow."

A long pause. Too long this time.

"Hello?" he said.

"I've been told you have some problems in your house."

She was referring to Mara's call to Sidwell Friends. That call only happened if Roberts told his daughter about the abduction. It followed that Roberts only knew if someone on the inside told him. Goddamn shit show. "I'm on it."

Hawthorn thought he heard another voice in the background, then the stillness of a phone being muted. He waited. It was thirty seconds before the voice returned.

"There's some conversation about activating an additional asset," she said.

"With all due respect, I don't think—"

"This is not an option I want to pursue at this time," she said, cutting him off. "I've told the Council that you can handle this. Am I correct in that calculation?"

"I can handle this."

"Next time I want an immediate situation report, good news or bad. Understood?"

"Yes, ma'am."

"One last thing," she said. "Don't ever flip me off again. It's unseemly."

The line went dead. Hawthorn was left alone in the car, looking back and forth at the interior of the Lincoln Navigator, wondering how the hell they'd gotten a camera past his security team. The answer was simple: They had someone on his security team.

Omega had someone everywhere.

It's what made the group so dangerous. And so powerful.

He lowered the privacy screen and called up to his driver. "Change of plans. We're going to the house in Silver Spring."

"Yes, sir," his driver said.

Hawthorn wondered if the driver was the traitor in his group. The truth was that there was no way to know. And if he switched out his entire protective detail, there would probably just be another infiltrator in the new group. It was better to just assume his employer was always watching and act accordingly. It made his job all that more difficult, like threading the eye of a needle in the middle of a hurricane.

His driver made the turn and headed out of DC into the upscale Maryland suburb of Silver Spring. It was where Mara Roberts's nephew had been taken. He hadn't planned on the kid seeing his face just in case it worked out that he could let the boy go when it was all over. But he realized now that he was on a trajectory that was inevitable. There was no turning back now.

The kid had started out as an insurance policy, but now he was an integral part of piecing this mission back together. No matter what lies Hawthorn was going to tell Mara Roberts along the way while others were listening, there was only one way he was going to let things end for Joey. And that meant it no longer mattered if the kid saw his face.

CHAPTER 7

Mara yawned as she pulled off the freeway. The adrenaline from the escape was long since gone, and even her worry about Joey had settled into a dull ache instead of the throat-constricting panic of the first few hours of the drive. As hard as it was not to call Hawthorn, her dad's logic was solid. A hostage was no good dead. And there was no upside to hurting him except as a punishment for her noncompliance. The second she talked to them, they'd ask her to do something and attach something specific to Joey. Do X or he loses a finger. Do Y or he loses a foot. She knew exactly who she was dealing with. She only hoped they remembered who they were dealing with, too. If there was one hair out of place on the boy's head when she got him back, she intended to open a world of pain on whoever was responsible.

There was a massive truck stop, brightly lit with signs promising great food, showers, and clean facilities to the weary road warriors passing through the Midwest on their great treks across the country. As tempting as it was, she passed by the gleaming palace and drove down the road another two miles until she found a tiny, broken-down gas station; BILLY-RAY'S GAS AND CONVENIENCE, it proclaimed on a sign that was only half lit up in the predawn sky. She knew the big truck stop down the road would have had dozens of cameras around the property, all of them linked and their feeds accessible to the CIA's intercept teams. The supercomputers in Langley's basement would be chewing through terabytes of data, using advance facial recognition software to spot them. She didn't want to take the chance. Billy-Ray's would have to do. She doubted there were any cameras there.

She pulled in and saw that most of the pumps had little signs on them that said NOT WORKING. She rolled the pickup past these until she came to the single pump that had a sticky note on it that said CREDIT CARD BROKE PAY INSIDE. She parked in front of it and turned off the engine, eager to get out and stretch her legs. Scott stirred next to her and looked around.

"Where are we?" he asked.

"Texas," she said.

Scott sat up straighter in his chair. "What are we . . ." His voice trailed off. It didn't take a genius to figure a gas station in Texas wouldn't have a Chicago Cubs banner hanging on one side of the building. "I see your weird sense of humor hasn't really changed."

She opened the door. "Driving for ten hours will do that to a person. Especially sitting next to someone snoring the entire time."

He stretched and opened his door. "I would have driven some if you'd woken me up."

"Don't worry, you're next. I'll pay, you pump, chump." She hesitated before getting out of the truck. That was one of her dad's sayings, said to her a thousand times when she was growing up because her dad always had her pump the gas. *I'll pay, you pump, chump.* She hadn't heard or said that in years. It made her feel weak that she was letting him get inside her head.

"You got it," he replied. If he'd caught the saying, or thought anything of it, he wasn't letting on. He climbed out of the cab and went to look for the gas cap.

She got out and walked toward the concrete building. There were two service bays with rusted doors and weeds growing up in front of them. Looked like it'd been a while since anyone had trusted Billy-Ray to change their oil. Why bother when there was a state-of-the-art facility just down the road?

She tried the door. Locked. Walking around the service window to the thick bulletproof glass, she spotted a teenager asleep in a chair, his face on the counter. She walked back over to the locked door, picked up a metal bar that was leaning against the wall, and slid it through the handles of the double door. Now it was locked from this side, too. Satisfied it was secure, she knocked on the glass. The teenager didn't move.

"Hey, buddy. Look alive."

The teenager raised his head, a string of drool extending from the corner of his mouth to the countertop. He rubbed his eyes, blinking hard to bring things into focus.

"Cash only," he mumbled.

Mara slid two twenties into the rusty metal box and the kid pulled it back into his safe room.

"Pump four," she said.

The kid snorted. "Uh . . . yeah. It's the only one we got." He pressed some buttons, still blinking the sleep from his eyes. "Right, all set."

"Got a bathroom?"

"Side of the building. You ain't gonna like it, 'specially if you got to take a dooger. Better off going in the trees out back. That's what I do."

Mara saw the kid's cell phone on the desk inside. She glanced behind her and saw that Scott's view of her was blocked by the pump.

"I lost my cell phone. Can I use yours? Just for a quick call?"

"No, you can't use my phone," the kid said, protectively grabbing it as if she might come at it through the window. "What if you take off with it?"

"Do I look like I'm going to take off with your phone?" Mara said. "If I do, you can call the cops."

"With what? I wouldn't have a phone."

Mara pulled out a hundred-dollar bill and held it against the glass. "Maybe this will help you be a little more generous."

The teenager licked his lips and scratched at the faint hint of stubble growing on his chin. "Did my mom send you down here?"

"Do you want the hundred dollars or not?"

He thrust the tray forward. "Put the money in."

She did and he jerked it back. He pulled out a counterfeit pen and drew a line across the bill. Then he grinned. "You're so stupid. Why would I give you the phone now? I'll just keep the hundy."

"I wouldn't do that," she said.

"Oh really? What you going to do about it?"

Mara narrowed her eyes. "I'm going to change my plans and sit out here the rest of the night, waiting for your shift to get over. Once you unlock the door, I'm going in there and punch your teeth so far down your throat you'd have to stick a toothbrush up your ass to brush them."

Her tone left no doubt that she was dead serious. The teenager turned pale and put the phone in the tray and pushed it forward. She grabbed the phone.

"Thanks," she said. "I appreciate your generosity."

The teenager looked like he wanted to throw her a snappy comeback, but he held his tongue. Even locked inside with bulletproof glass between them, he appeared to have picked up on the fact that Mara Roberts was not someone he wanted to mess with.

She pocketed the phone and walked back to the car.

"I'm going to use the bathroom," she said. "Be right back."

Scott waved, indicating that he'd heard her. He was gingerly picking at the stitches on his side, barely paying her any attention.

Mara made her way around the outside of the cinderblock building to the bathroom. There was trash all over the ground, mostly empty beer cans, broken bottles, and piles of cigarette butts. The bathroom door was open a few inches, and even from ten feet away the smell of urine and shit filled the air. Even if she really had to go to the bathroom, she wouldn't have gone in there.

She dialed the phone quickly, glancing up to make sure her dad was still at the car.

"Hello?"

"Jordi, it's Mara."

There was a long pause on the other end of the line. She imagined her friend pushing back from his workstation in his basement room at the FBI, his considerable girth making the chair groan as he did. Jordi Pines was one of the most brilliant minds she'd ever encountered, and one of the most bizarre. Although born in New Jersey, he spoke with a fake British accent for reasons he'd never explained.

"Mara, luv. There are all sorts of people talkin' about you today. You've been naughty, it seems."

She listened close for any of their safety words to tip her off that he might be in a room filled with agents tracking the call. And if he were under duress with people who knew what they were doing, even a change in his cadence would have been enough to tell her they weren't alone. She'd called on his cell, but it was a burner phone he had just for this purpose. One thing about being friends with a computer and communications genius was that he was an excellent guide for how to subvert the system.

"Where are you?" Jordi asked. "Everyone in North America with Tier 5 clearance and above is looking for you."

"No lie, I'm in the shit this time, Jordi. I could use your help. Are you in the mood to give the middle finger to the higher-ups?"

"Bureau or Agency assholes?"

"Does it matter?"

"Not really," he said. "But I really like serving up shit sandwiches to those CIA monkeys."

The CIA had turned down Jordi's offer of his services. The powers-that-be worried about his stability and decided he was too much of a security risk. The FBI surveillance program had no such qualms. They just stuck him in a basement office and let him do his work. One thing about Jordi Pines was that the man held a grudge.

"They have Joey," she said. "They took him."

"Who did? How could . . ." Another pause. This time she heard heavy breathing. When Jordi's voice came back on the line, she could tell he'd pieced it together. "What a bunch of fucking rotters."

"Like I said, I'm in it, man. More than ever. So I need you to find him for me, all right? Use all that Jedi, voodoo magic of yours and find him."

"Full rectal exam. I'm on it," Jordi said. "How do I contact you?"

"You don't. I'll reach out to you."

"Mara," Jordi said softly, the accent fading to what she assumed was his actual voice. "I'm really sorry. We'll find him. I promise."

"Thanks, Jordi. I'm counting on you."

"Destroy the phone you called me from. Rotate the phone number like we discussed to reach me next time."

"Be careful."

"You too."

She hung up and smashed it against the wall. She felt a little pang of guilt for destroying the kid's phone, but he'd been a jerk so it didn't last long.

Besides, she had bigger problems.

Like the fact that she was about to join her dad in a plan to interrogate the ex-president of the United States.

What could go wrong with a plan like that?

"How well do you know him?" Mara asked.

"Who?"

"The Pope," she said, lacing the comment with sarcasm. She'd let her dad drive, thinking she'd get some sleep, but that'd proved impossible. Every time she closed her eyes, she saw Joey's frightened face, tears streaming down his cheeks.

"I actually know the Pope," Scott said. "Saved his life once."

"Of course you did."

Scott shifted his weight, checking the rearview mirror for the hundredth time. "Preston Townsend? I know him well enough. He was the chair of the House Intelligence Committee before he made his run for the White House, which was both good and bad. Jim Hawthorn was a lifelong friend of Townsend's dad. They were college roommates, best men in each other's weddings. Tight. Jim's even godfather to Townsend's younger brother. It's why he always had the president's back."

"No love lost between the two of them now," she said.

He slowed down as they passed an Illinois State Trooper posted up on the side of the road with a radar gun. "No, I suppose not after everything that went down."

"I can't think he's going to be very happy to see you either."

Scott grinned and gave her a wink. "I think you're discounting how charming I can be."

She leaned toward him. "I don't know if you're trying to reduce the stress between us with his whole shtick you have going on, but it's getting old in a hurry. I get it, you don't know Joey. He's just another hostage to you. But it's pretty goddamn real to me.

There was a flash of anger, but he restrained himself. "He's my grandson."

"Only by blood," she said. "He doesn't even know you exist. You're nothing to him. Just like you're nothing to me."

She looked out the window at the passing suburban landscape, and a long silence stretched out between them. The faint *thump thump* of the tires on the highway the only sound.

"You're right," he finally said. "About the joking and the bravado. It's always been my way to deal with things. But you're not right about Joey. He's not just another hostage. He's family. And believe it or not, being family still means something to me."

"We stopped being family four years ago."

His face fell. The comment struck a chord. "Not for me. But I guess that's going to have to be enough for now." He let that sit for a beat, but then took up a new thread. "To answer your first question, Preston Townsend owes me a favor, or two, or three.

He's a politician, so he's better at asking for favors than paying them back. So, no. I don't think he's going to be happy to see me."

"So, then what's the plan?"

"You don't go after the target. You go after his protection."

She didn't like the sound of that. "We're not hurting anyone on his detail. That's a nonstarter."

"Of course," he said, the cocky grin coming back. "We're not going to hurt them physically. But I imagine we're going to bruise a few egos along the way."

"How do we even know where to find him? How can you be so sure he's in Chicago? I'm guessing they weren't sending you his schedule with your morning breakfast tray in prison."

"And I'm the one with the snappy one-liners, huh?"

"Just answer the question."

"It's common knowledge he has an office in downtown Chicago. It makes the news, just like Clinton made a splash when he opened an office in Harlem. And yes, they do provide us inmates with access to newspapers."

"That's nice," she said. "I thought they just gave you access to long showers with the other guys."

He ignored the comment. "Tomorrow, ex-president Townsend is delivering a speech at the Chicago Tribune building. They're turning the whole damn thing into condos now. We've been there before, remember?

Mara did remember. She knew exactly where that was. It triggered a memory of a trip to Chicago with her mom and dad when she was ten. Lucy must have been thirteen. It was the four of them living it up, playing a normal family for a few days when both parents had been together and available. They'd eaten deep dish pizza, had ice cream late at night before bed, done the rides out on Navy Pier, the whole nine yards. The Tribune Tower stuck out because the walls of the building were unlike anything she'd ever seen before.

Embedded in the façade at street level were bits of rocks from places and buildings around the world. A brick from Buckingham Palace, a stone from the Parthenon, even a sliver of moon rock. It was the epitome of cool for a ten-year-old girl to be able to touch something from so many exotic places in the world. But what stood out in her memory was when her mom and dad started to point to the stones that were from places they had been.

The Great Wall of China. The White House. St. Sophia in Istanbul. Notre Dame in Paris. Dozens and dozens of locations, the two of them playing a game and laughing as they took turns finding someplace they'd been. The Berlin Wall. The Kremlin. The Pyramids at Giza. The whole thing blew her mind at the time because, of course, she'd had no idea at that age who her parents really were. Looking back later, it made sense. Her parents weren't well-traveled tourists. They were describing a lifetime of covert operations around the world.

"I've been there before, but I don't remember being there with you," she said. "Maybe it was just Lucy."

"No, you were there. All four of us were. You remember."

She played dumb. "If you say so."

The lie was petty, maybe even childish, but she didn't care. She doubted if it hurt him at all, the fact that his daughter had no recollection of their family together, but she hoped it did. She hoped it stung.

"What time is the speech?"

"Noon."

"Where'd you get this intel?" she asked. "Same guy who told you about Joey?"

"Same guy."

If the information was right, it was exactly what they needed. A specific time and place was great intel. Not only that, but the fact that he was going to a nonsecure location was helpful. Something like an embassy or bank would have been trickier. "So that's where we do it?"

"I think so. We'll get into Chicago just before eight. That gives us four hours to check it out and decide."

"Plenty of time to work out how to kidnap the president."

"Ex-president," Scott said. "I've done harder with less time. And so have you from what I hear. Tehran? Hong Kong?"

She was surprised to hear him reference two assignments that were so black they were nearly nonexistent. Whoever his source was, it was high up in the organization. Or someone on the outside who had a way in. But she didn't want him to think she was impressed, so she didn't bother answering.

"I hope you have a good plan. I've dated a few Secret Service guys. They're no joke."

"You dated a few of them?" he asked. "How many is a few?"

"Oh please." She noticed a small facial tic. For some reason it bothered him, so she pushed a bit. Just for fun. "I had a reputation to live up to. My dad was Scott Roberts, the notorious womanizer. I wanted to be just like you."

The muscles in his jaw clenched, but he didn't say anything for a while. When he did speak, it was in a low, steady voice, like he was trying hard to keep in control. "I never cheated on your mom. Not once. Think what you want about me, listen to the stories if you want, but not once. I would never have done that to her."

She laughed. It was an unexpected reaction and it burst out of her without warning, laced with so much anger and bitterness that she hardly recognized the sound. He flinched at it, but kept his eyes on the road.

"Let's not talk about Mom," she said. "If we do, I think it's going to go bad in a hurry, and right now, I need your help."

"We're going to need to talk about it eventually. I want you to—"

"Not now," she snapped.

He drew in a sharp breath, paused as if he was about to say something, but then let it out as if he'd thought better of it. They drove without speaking for a few minutes, both of them needing the time to get their emotions in check. She was the first to break the silence.

"So, let's go over your plan," she said.

"Don't you want to be surprised?"

"The last thing I ever want from you is to be surprised. Walk me through it, step-by-step."

He did, and she had to admit the plan wasn't half bad. It would almost definitely get them both killed, but there was a small chance it might work. They tweaked the details and then ran through it over and over, thinking of different scenarios, one after the other. By the time the sun was up and the Chicago skyline rose up on the horizon, the plan was better.

Instead of almost definitely getting them killed, she considered the newest version was only likely to get them killed. A major improvement and the best they were going to get under the circumstances. She took a deep breath, thought of Joey, and got herself ready for the job ahead.

CHAPTER 8

Asset read the instructions on the phone screen a second time. And then a third. He had an eidetic memory, a trait that he'd further trained so that he could perfectly recall complicated schematics or blueprints after viewing them for only a few seconds. But these instructions, just three sentences long, were unlike anything he'd received before. He wanted to be absolutely sure he understood.

After the third reading, he entered his affirmative response, deleted the text, and then destroyed the phone with a hammer. He checked his watch and felt his muscles tighten in his neck as he considered the time line. Placing two fingers against his throat, he felt his pulse well above where it ought to have been. His training kicked in and he responded to his body's physical stress response with a deep, cleansing breath and cleared his mind of anything superfluous to the immediate task at hand.

Twenty seconds later, his heartbeat was back to normal. The tension in his shoulders eased. He was in control.

He crossed the sparse room of his long-term rental unit, a studio with a sleeping bag in one corner and a bathroom in the other. Asset had spent time in prisons in four different countries. The experience had hardened him in ways helpful for his profession, but had made normal comforts unbearable. He could pretend to fit into high-society and move through a five-star hotel as if he were the scion of the wealthiest of families, but he took no joy in it. The bare essentials were all he needed. All he wanted.

Some of those essentials were on display when he opened the studio's single closet. Hanging on wooden hangers were various uniforms. UPS driver, Chicago Police Department, Chicago Fire Department, Pizzeria Uno delivery, and several others. Alongside these were three tailored dark suits and pressed shirts. He pulled out one of these suits and the Chicago PD uniform, and laid them on the round table, where he both ate his meals and built his bombs. He stared at the two disguises, undecided which would be better for the job. He checked his watch again, then pulled the single chair up and sat in it to think.

This was going to be the most important job of his life. He didn't want to fuck it up.

CHAPTER 9

"You trust this guy?" Mara asked, looking at the run-down pawn-shop across the street.

"He owes me one," he said.

She noticed him scanning the utility poles on the street. "Three cameras," she said. She pointed them out. Two on lights poles and one above them on the roof of a mechanic shop.

"You missed the one over there," he said, pointing to a black-ened husk of a burned-out row house across the street.

She turned in her seat and looked the ruin over, not seeing the camera for a full thirty seconds. He watched her and gave a lit-tle cluck of his tongue when she finally saw it tucked into a shadow on the second floor.

"Details, details."

She was mad at herself for having missed it. Not that it mat-tered since they were already there parked in front of the damn place, on display for whoever was inside watching. But mad be-cause it was sloppy. And like it or not, she wanted to impress the great Scott Roberts. Missing a surveillance camera wasn't the way to do it.

"Why don't you wait here?"

"Yeah, right," she said, opening her door and climbing out. There were a few guys at the end of the block, but they took one look at her and walked away.

"You look like a cop," her dad said.

"I look like I need to look," she said. "Figured the less company we had the better."

He glanced up and down the empty street. "I guess there will be fewer witnesses if Harry tries to kill us. So that's a plus." He walked toward the pawnshop, slowly, his hands open and slightly out to his sides. Mara looked around at the empty windows in the abandoned buildings on the street, every one of them a potential hiding place for a sniper.

"I thought you said this guy was a friend of yours."

"No, I said he owed me one. Not the same thing."

The unmistakable sound of a pump action shotgun being racked filled the air. It echoed on the street, making it impossible to tell where it came from. "You're damn right it's not the same thing," said a rough voice. "And for the record, I don't owe you shit."

The voice was easier to track, or at least Mara thought it was. Her eyes keyed on the spot where her brain told her the voice originated, only to find a small speaker attached to the brick of the pawnshop building. She suspected there were more speakers around just like there were cameras covering every angle on the street. Clearly, Harry was not the typical pawnshop owner.

"Harry, how about we come in there and we talk it over?"

A pause, then the voice came again. "Is that your girl? Mara?"

"How does he know who I am?"

"Yeah, that's Mara. You going to let us in now or what?"

Another pause. Then a buzzer sounded. It was the door to the pawnshop, some kind of electric lock being deactivated. "Come on in. But that's not a promise that I'm not still going to shoot you in the ass at some point."

Scott held his hand toward the door, as if he were offering to let her walk in front of him as they entered a fancy restaurant. "Some friend," she murmured as she walked past him.

"He has his moments."

Mara ignored the comment. She reached the door and pushed it open with her foot. The inside looked like any other pawnshop she'd ever been in. A U-shaped glass case filled most of the floor space, displaying a wide assortment of junk from costume jewelry to baseball cards. There were rows of collectible silver dollars and an entire cabinet filled with porcelain plates. The walls were an even more eclectic assortment. There was a neon Budweiser sign that lit up only halfway. A deer head with a broken antler and wearing sunglasses and a straw hat. To her right, a painting of all the Republican presidents playing poker together.

The place had a feel like it was someone's personal museum. It didn't look like many of the items had been moved in a while. She had a sneaking suspicion that anyone wandering into the place would have discovered many of the items suddenly not for sale if they had the poor taste to actually make an offer.

At the far end of the room, behind the bend in the U, was a cabinet filled with guns. And standing in front of the guns, still brandishing one himself, was the owner of the establishment. And he didn't look happy to see them.

The man was older than her dad, but not by much. It was hard to tell because his dark skin hid any wrinkles that might have been around his eyes, but that same complexion made his shock white hair and beard stand out all the more.

"Jesus, Harry. You look like a black Santa Claus," her dad said.

"Fuck you. And the horse you rode in on." He gave her a short nod. "Sorry 'bout the language, miss."

"I tell him to fuck off all the time," she said. "Why should you deny yourself the pleasure?"

That made Harry break out into a wide smile, his teeth mostly silver fillings, except for the front two, which were gold. "You don't take no shit. I can see that."

"Which is why I'd appreciate you lowering that shotgun," she said. When the man didn't budge, she followed it up with, "Please."

Harry lowered the gun. "See, Scott? That's what I'm talking about. Some goddamn manners."

"Yeah, then she'll punch you in the head when you're not looking," Scott said.

"You wouldn't do that, would you?"

"Depends on if you deserved it or not."

This got a genuine laugh out of Harry. The big man's whole body shook, making Mara think of her dad's comment about Santa Claus. A foulmouthed St. Nick that trafficked in guns and ammo in the middle of the Chicago war zone, but a jolly old elf nonetheless.

"I already like her a lot more than I ever liked you," Harry said. "Your other girl this scrappy?"

Her dad's eyes found the floor. He took a beat to answer. "My other girl's gone. Cancer."

Harry turned serious. "I'm sorry to hear that, Scott. I really am. Lost my wife to cancer. That whole disease is bullshit on top of bullshit."

"Yes, it is," her dad replied softly.

Mara fought the urge to point out that her dad didn't know. That he hadn't been there while Lucy wasted away to no more than a skeleton. He hadn't been there when the smell of food made her dry heave until tears streamed down her sunken cheeks. He hadn't been there when Lucy said goodbye to her son every day not knowing whether it might be her last. Cancer was bullshit on top of bullshit, but her dad didn't have a right to pretend like he knew a damn thing about it.

But she held the words in check. No good would come from them right then, so she chewed the inside of her lip and held on tight, riding the surge of anger she felt until it dissipated enough for her to think straight again.

"I'm guessing you didn't come for a social visit. Especially as how you're supposed to be dead. Or locked up in some CIA black site getting the shit kicked out of you for all eternity."

"You heard about that, huh?"

"I've got friends in the Agency still. I know things."

"And?"

Harry shrugged. "You always were a rotten sumbitch, that

much is a fact." He pointed at Mara. "I want to hear what you say. You think he did all the nasty things they say he did?" The next words came out slow and filled with venom. The Santa Claus image was gone, replaced by a dangerous man whose narrow eyes threatened violence. "You think he gave up those nine agents the Russians executed for all of us to see? You think he betrayed his country? And, here comes the big one now. You think he killed your momma?"

She expected her dad to turn to gauge her reaction to the question, but he didn't. He kept his eyes fixed on Harry. She considered how best to answer. Was he looking for some validation that there was a chance he was innocent of those things? Or just that he could trust her to be honest?

She went with the truth. "Don't know yet, Harry. But if I confirm that he did those things, especially the last one, I'm going to put a bullet through his head. So don't think for a second that the two assholes behind that wall are going to beat me to the punch."

Harry stared her down like she'd just called his mother fat. He walked toward her, hitting his shoulder against Scott's as he passed. She stepped forward slightly with her left foot, putting herself in a better position if she had to fight the big man coming at her.

He stopped right in front of her, towering, standing at least six foot six and wide as an NFL linebacker. She craned her neck and met his stare, looking tough but wondering how she was going to be able to avoid getting crushed if he attacked.

With his eyes narrowed, top lip pulled back in a snarl, he reached back and pointed at the wall behind him. "What I want to know," he growled, stretching it out, trying his best to intimidate her, "is how you knew Drey and Whitey are both assholes?"

He let the question hang in the air for a second and then burst out laughing so hard that she not only heard it, but felt it, too, as specks of spittle pelted her face. He noticed her wipe it off. "Oh shoot, sorry about that."

Her dad turned and was laughing, too. The both of them having a good chuckle at her expense.

Harry wiped tears from his eyes. "'Cause they are assholes. Both of 'em." He noticed that she wasn't smiling. "Aw, c'mon now. I'm sorry, just having a little fun."

The back door opened and two young men stepped out, each holding an M1 rifle. The muzzles were pointed at the ground, and Mara noticed their hands were in the safety position, fingers nowhere near the trigger. These boys may or may not have been assholes, but by the way they handled themselves, they were ex-military.

Her dad slapped Harry on the back. "As much as I'd like to watch Mara here kick your ass for messing with her, we have a shopping list."

Harry directed him toward the open back door. As they walked, he fake-whispered so that Mara could still hear him. "She's a little uptight, huh? Didn't even crack a smile. That was some funny goddamn shit."

"You're an acquired taste, Harry. You know that."

Mara watched the two of them disappear into the back room, hanging out like old school buddies. Drey and Whitey watched her, both of them with smirks on their faces, half amused and half looking like they should apologize for a crazy old uncle.

She sucked up her pride and followed Harry and her dad into the back of the pawnshop.

The real goodies were in a basement storeroom. To get there, Mara passed by the rows of M1s and AK-47s locked in cabinets faced with heavy security bars. She turned a corner around a stack of Kevlar vests and watched as Harry typed in a code on a keypad next to a metal door. The keypad lit up and chirped, but instead of opening the door, Harry stepped back and pulled away the carpet on the floor.

Beneath it was the real door he'd unlocked. She guessed the one in front of her was a dummy, or opened to a room with some contraband in it, but nothing special. It was the perfect decoy. What burglar or cop would think of looking for a second door when there was one staring him in the face?

The cellar door revealed a metal ladder that descended into a brightly lit room. Harry motioned Scott to go first and he obliged. He motioned for Mara next, but she hesitated. She didn't know this man, nor did she know what was waiting for her at the bottom of the ladder. As far as she knew, Harry's plan was to just slam the door behind them, call his buddies at the CIA, and turn them in.

Her concern must have registered on her face because Harry's expression softened. "You don't remember, but I met you a bunch of times when you were just a little thing. I knew your momma. Hell, I loved her like she was my own sister. Cried my eyes out when I heard what happened to her."

"Funny that you're still friends with the man who killed her."

Harry pursed his lips and squinted at her, a flash of anger at what she'd said. He waited a few seconds before he responded. "Listen, you might not know your daddy's innocent, but I do. Most people you meet in life are a hard read on the best day. Not your dad. I know him like I know myself. He didn't kill Wendy, not in a million years."

"Yeah, but she's dead, isn't she?"

"And I have a suspicion you being in my store, in the same town where Preston Townsend likes to make a scene in public all the time, has something to do with sorting all that out."

She felt her stomach tighten at the mention of Townsend's name. She'd thought pawnshop Harry a fool, but she was clearly wrong. She decided it would serve her best never to think of him that way again.

"Do you have the things we need?" she asked.

"I've got pretty much anything a person can think of, even a crazy motherfucker like your daddy."

She smiled. "You do know him."

"We served some time together. Been in some scrapes along the way. Ol' Harry wouldn't be here if it wasn't for your dad saving my sorry ass. You may think you know stories about him, but maybe, if we ever have a chance, I'll tell you some things I guarantee you ain't never heard."

Mara smiled. "I'd like that," she said, realizing that she meant it. She walked up to the ladder, turned, and descended the first two steps. She stopped and looked up.

"Can I trust you, Harry?"

"You can't trust no one in this business," he said. "But I suppose you can trust me more than most."

"I guess that'll have to do," she said, and climbed the rest of the way down the ladder.

They loaded a small duffel bag with their supplies into the space between them on the front bucket seat of the truck. After they'd sorted through all the options Harry had available, the end result was only a few very specialized pieces of equipment. Once Harry heard what her dad asked for, he understood the broad strokes of his plan. He didn't say much about it, but just kept shaking his head like they were both crazy.

"Harry's a character," she said as they drove away.

"Known him for a long time."

"He said you and he served together. Said he knew Mom."

"The last time I was in the field with Harry we were on an op in Afghanistan. We had tracked a target to a remote village in the Hindu Kush. Wild country."

"I know it," she said softly. She'd left blood of her own in the Kush.

"So you know the drill. Tough terrain. Opposition can come from any direction, at any time. Especially when the target has been tipped off."

"How many men?"

"Seven-man team. Lost three. Four injured."

A shudder worked itself through Mara's body. Her own memories of a mission gone wrong flashing back at her. The feeling of one of her men's hot blood spraying across her face, the metallic tang of it her mouth, the cries for help from the rest of her squad as they took fire. She shook away the memory. "Harry told me you saved his life."

"Is that what he said?" He let out a low chuckle. "I caught some shrapnel that he figures was meant for him."

"Was it chance, or did you try to save him?"

Scott stared out the window, maybe lost in his own flash of memory of whatever hell he'd been through with Harry. She respected that he wouldn't say. Real soldiers rarely talked about their own acts of courage. Mostly because they knew that even acts of valor are born in fear and steeped in terror.

"What he never mentions about that day," he continued, "is that he carried me two clicks on his shoulders to get the hell out of there, fighting off Jihadi assholes the entire way back. He was a thing possessed, all rage and death. But he refused to put me down. Wasn't until we were at the base, taking our gear off, that he saw his clothes were drenched in his own blood. Turns out he took some shrapnel after all. He was just a tougher son of a bitch than I was."

"And now he sells guns to gangs in the mean streets of Chicago."

"Don't be so quick to judge."

"Seems pretty clear to me."

"Not everything is what it seems. You think you'd know that better than most by now."

"Like how my dad turned out to be a traitorous scumbag?"

Scott took a deep breath, obviously fighting the impulse to rise to the bait she'd dangled in front of his face. As she watched the emotions play across his face, she realized she wanted the confrontation. She needed to let all the hurt and pain out that she still carried from his betrayal, and she wanted to do it in a fight. She sure as hell didn't want to do it with tears.

But he wasn't going to give her what she wanted. Typical of him.

"He still has ties to our world," he said. "Only caters to a very specific clientele."

"People like us don't use AKs. In this city, those are just cop killers and you know it."

This time his voice took on a sharp edge. It was the tone she remembered from her teenage years when the two of them used to butt heads on the simplest issues. "Before you got on your high horse and decided to cast judgment on all of us low-lifes, did you ever stop to ask if maybe you had it wrong? Maybe the most obvious scenario wasn't the truth?"

Mara was taken back by the comment, but then chastised herself for being manipulated. "In the face of overwhelming evidence, I'd say it's pretty clear that—"

"That what? An African American war veteran set up shop in America's murder capital to sell automatic weapons to help his community destroy itself faster?"

Mara sensed that he wouldn't push that hard unless he was on the right side of the argument. She had a sinking feeling that she was about to get her comeuppance. She rifled through the possible outs her dad had. How he could be right, even with all the evidence she'd just seen with her own eyes.

Then, like an image popping up on a screen, she got it.

"He's not selling the AKs," she said. "Or the other guns."

"Nope."

"He's buying them," she said. "Trying to get the big stuff off the streets."

Her dad didn't say anything. He didn't need to. Just like when she was a teenager, once he'd won an argument, he just let her stew in her own juices. It was far worse than if he'd just come out and say she'd gotten it wrong. Not once, but twice about Harry.

But two could play that game. Even though he'd won, she wasn't about to give him the satisfaction of an apology. Instead, she thought back to the way the big man had pulled her dad into a bear hug when they'd left. "What'd he whisper to you?" she asked.

"Offered to come with us. Didn't figure that would be a good idea." The light ahead turned yellow. He could have made it in time, but he slowed down and came to a stop.

"You're getting cautious in your old age."

"Caution isn't always a bad thing," he said. "In fact, we need to talk about the operation."

"I'm listening."

"This whole thing would be easier if just one of us did it," he said. "Smaller footprint. Easier to slip in and out."

"I agree."

He looked surprised, but pleased. "Good. I thought this was going to be a hard conversation."

"Just let me know the questions you want me to ask Townsend, and I'll let you know what he says."

"Mara."

He growled her name, and for a split second she was a kid again, caught not doing her homework, or sneaking out to meet her boyfriend. She pushed the feeling away. "Do you really think I'm going to bow out? If Townsend has the information we need to get to Joey, then I'm going to be there." He turned the corner and the Tribune Tower loomed up before them on the other side of the bridge, imposing as a medieval fortress. "So this plan had better work because we're both in."

CHAPTER 10

Preston Townsend stared out of the window of the black Suburban, barely registering the Chicago landmarks as they whisked by. The job of ex-president didn't suit him. After a lifetime of laser-like focus on getting the world's top job and eight years leading the Western world, he felt adrift since handing over the keys to 1600 Pennsylvania Avenue to that numbskull Patterson.

They were in the same party, but there was no love lost between them. After the scandals hit Townsend during the Republican primary to see who would run to replace him, he'd expected the others to distance themselves. But Patterson had not only run from Townsend as fast as his stubby little legs would carry him, he'd thrown him under the proverbial bus every chance he had. It wouldn't have bothered him as much if Patterson hadn't been his own goddamn vice-president.

Townsend had plucked the junior senator from Ohio from obscurity. The ungrateful son of a bitch had polled a one percent name recognition when they'd announced. Eight years later, Patterson was leader of the free world. And what thanks did he get? On the campaign trail, the puke had done nothing but kick his old boss in the dick every chance he got.

"Five minutes, Mr. President," said the Secret Service agent from the front seat. He didn't know the man's name. Didn't care to. He didn't care about much, if he was being honest.

He had enough money in the bank, more than he or his wife could ever hope to spend. He'd seen the world and done it in style. After arriving in a foreign country in Air Force One, it was hard to fly any other way. Women still held his interest, and his wife didn't care about his extracurricular activities, not after the entire world was now privy to his infidelity. But women weren't really a challenge. No, he pined for the combat of politics and the national stage. He wanted to be where the action was. He wanted to be relevant again.

Instead, he was posing for photo ops, shilling for investment groups, giving the same, tired speech for a couple hundred grand a pop, half the fee that other ex-presidents commanded.

At least his memoir was keeping him busy. Random House had bought it for a record sum after he'd promised there would be honest revelations about the two scandals at the end of his presidency. He knew they, and the public, wanted the crude details of his affair with the wife of one of the Democratic party's biggest donors. He would give them some of that. Why not? What did he care?

He felt his jacket pocket and the small bulge there of the silver cigarette case. The only copy of his manuscript. It was a risk, because if he lost it he'd have to start over from scratch. The thing was encrypted, completely useless to someone who might find it if it somehow fell out of his jacket, but he guarded it like it held the nuclear launch codes.

Some may have found the precaution extreme, but as president he was all too aware of the abilities the intelligence agencies had at their disposal. It was Hawthorn who had cautioned him while he was still in office to take care of what he typed, even into the computers in the White House. For all his most sensitive work, he used an air-gapped computer. No connection in any way to the Internet. Not even a modem in the machine that could make it possible. The thumb drive he stored his material on was one he'd purchased himself from a small electronics store in a Chicago suburb. He recalled how one of the greatest successes in cyberespionage had come from planting cheap thumb drives for sale in the stores around the NSA. Only those thumb drives had contained malware that infected whatever system they contacted.

He'd been careful. The only thing more hack-proof would have been to handwrite the book on paper, but that could be stolen. And it couldn't be encrypted. No, he thought, feeling the slender case in his pocket, he'd taken all the right precautions. He didn't want any leaks. Nothing to steal his thunder.

When he was ready, they would get more than they bargained for regarding what had really happened at the CIA and the outing of those agents in Russia. He was going to name names, consequences be damned. Not only that, but he was going to make a lot of fringe conspiracy theorists out there very happy. He planned to acknowledge the existence of Omega.

That was going to blow people's minds.

Too bad he didn't know more than he did. He would have loved to take all the bastards down and return the favor they'd done him when they'd ruined his legacy. All he had was the end of the smallest thread, but he knew others would pull on that thread to see where it went. He had an inkling that some of the world leaders who had turned their backs on him would find themselves implicated in Omega's web. It would be his pleasure to watch them scramble.

He predicted that he'd have to fend off accusations that he knew more than he would admit in the book, but that would make for even greater controversy. There would be TV interviews, magazine covers, perhaps even congressional hearings with him as the star witness. The controversy would ensure the world's spotlight would be on him once again.

History would forgive him schtupping some other guy's trophy wife. Clinton had taken advantage of a poor intern and he turned out all right. But he was damned if he was going to let history judge him for the thing at the CIA. That hadn't been his fault, and he was going to make sure blame was properly assigned where it belonged.

Even if doing so meant unleashing the powerful forces of Omega against him.

* * *

"Victorious arrival," said the agent in the front seat into the radio in his sleeve. "Victorious" had been Townsend's own pick for a name. The Secret Service historically picked their own call signs for their protectees, but when he'd heard that they'd chosen "Retriever" as his because he'd used his two Golden Retriever dogs in most of his campaign commercials, he'd put the brakes on it. Retrievers worked for a master, and Preston Townsend acknowledged no master over him. Victorious suited him better.

Or at least it had. As they pulled up to the Tribune Tower, six paparazzi waited for him. Only six. He felt like taking a bullet. As an ex-president, it was a poor choice of words, but on some of his darker days he wondered whether it would be better to have been assassinated. Those guys got all the ink in the history pages. Lincoln may have screwed up Reconstruction if he hadn't been killed. JFK may have gotten caught having his affairs and popping pills, except for Lee Harvey Oswald and a mail-order rifle. Instead, those guys were deities now, all of their imperfections washed away by the gush of national tears.

God, he wished that had happened to him. Maybe revealing the existence of Omega to the world would get him his wish.

Except that wish was self-pitying bullshit and he knew it. He didn't want to die. It was too final. Talk about really being taken out of the action. No, his perfect scenario was to Tom Sawyer the whole thing. He wanted all the outpouring of love and grief, but he wanted to watch it on CNN from a suite at the Four Seasons.

"It's the same speech as the Wells Fargo meet and greet," said Mirren Lefoust, his post-presidency chief of staff. His old chief of staff, Travis Belmont, a college buddy no less, had abandoned ship as the Townsend presidency was taking on water in its last days and looked unsalvageable. The man had tendered his resignation via e-mail. E-mail, for Chrissakes. Preston Townsend remembered every slight, and he intended to get even.

"Did you hear me, Mr. President?" she said, holding out the speech to him.

"You want me to carry that around like some kind of jack-ass?" he said. "Keep it until we're up there, for God's sake."

Mirren was unfazed. They were all used to him now, and that just depressed him even more. He used to make the Chairman of the Joint Chiefs of Staff quake in his boots. And now his staff disregarded him like he was someone's crazy old uncle they'd agreed to watch for a while.

An agent opened the door and he climbed out. His sixty-one-year-old body had no complaints. He'd dropped a needed fifteen pounds since leaving the White House and he was in fighting shape. That was the problem with being a young president. You became a young ex-president.

His protective detail, four men this morning, took positions on either side of him, scanning the area from behind dark sun-glasses. Townsend found himself wondering how effective his little team would fare if a terrorist group pulled up in a rented minivan and opened fire with machine guns. Despite his sporadic fantasies of martyrdom, he hated the idea of dying. He shuddered at the idea of an attack and tried to push it out of his head.

He'd pissed off more than his fair share of people while in office, even before the scandals. That list included every major terrorist organization, every gun nut in the United States who held a grudge over his gun laws, every white supremacist group who thought a Republican president ought to have been on their side; they hated him for his Civil Rights Bill and for appointing two African American judges to the Supreme Court, and the list went on.

He was glad ex-presidents continued to have protection details. But while the Secret Service would never admit it, the level of protection loosened up over time. The world moved on, and the threat to the old men who once held the nation's top job moved on with it. The world's haters turned their attention to the new person in office, and the old politicians were left out to pasture.

Two years removed from office and he already felt like he

was wallowing in a Jimmy Carter type of obscurity. Although even Carter had a presidential library in Atlanta. So far discussions for the Townsend Library were on hold, waiting for "a better fund-raising environment," according to the planners.

"Mr. President, so good of you to come," an elderly gentleman said as Townsend approached a small clutch of people waiting in front of the door to address him.

"Stan Goldman, COA Investments," Mirren whispered under her breath, just a little too loud so that the old man noticed.

Townsend caught it and faked a disappointed shake of the head. "Of course, I know Stan," he said. "How are you?" Truth was he had no idea who Stan was and he didn't care. His brain was on autopilot while he made small talk and cracked jokes. Stan showed off the tiny sliver of moon rock on display in the lobby and showed a model of the luxury condos being built in the building. Then, they went in the elevator for the ride to the thirty-fourth floor. He nudged Mirren and held out his hand for his speech.

He glanced it over on the ride up, made a few marks on applause lines and a joke that'd killed the last time he'd delivered it. There was nothing to it. Just a walk through the glory of the Townsend presidency, nary a mention of the scandals. He just wished that was the version in the history books.

The elevator door opened on an area that would one day be the showcase luxury penthouse apartment. The space was blown out, just white walls, high ceilings, and massive windows showing the Chicago skyline. The room was set up with a dozen round tables, eight seats each, just under a hundred people. Townsend noticed most of the tables were covered with the remains of a luncheon, but the two tables in the back were bare. He hadn't even generated enough interest to fill a hundred-person room. At least they wouldn't be eating during his remarks.

There was a small podium in the front of the tables with an American flag on either side of it. Red, white, and blue bunting on the podium was the only other attempt at decoration for the event. It made Townsend think of a kid's birthday party more than a presidential address.

Still, as he entered the room, people rose from their seats and burst into applause. He still enjoyed that part. As a recorded version of "Hail to the Chief" played from the speakers, he dove in, his protection detail spreading out to the sides and one staying at his right elbow as he shook hands and posed for selfies.

After a minute of this, he turned to Mirren. "Let's get this damn thing going so I can get the hell out of here. Old man Stan gives me the creeps."

When Mirren moved to the side, Townsend saw Stan Goldman standing behind her. The elderly man's smile was gone. He obviously overheard the comment. Townsend's old impulses gave him three different ways to quickly fix it by taking Stan by the arm and turning it into a joke. But he stopped himself. What did he care? That was one of the benefits of being an ex-president, what could they do to him?

"This way to the podium, Mr. President," Mirren said.

Townsend held up his hands and played it up as if he would have preferred to shake hands and visit with each person in the room individually. "Does Stan work all of you this hard, too? Sheesh." Laughter from the crowd.

He walked up to the podium as people began to take their seats.

Then the fire alarm went off.

Everyone froze for a beat, looking at one another for confirmation that it was a drill or a false alarm. Everyone except for the Secret Service detail, which pushed through the crowd to get to their protectee. No one was shoved and no guns were drawn, but they got from their standing posts into a protective stance around the president in a matter of seconds.

"Status report?" the lead agent said into his mic.

Townsend saw each agent nod as the voice in their earpieces told them what to do next.

"What is it?" he demanded. "What's going on?"

"Roger that. Moving Victorious to service elevator."

As a team, the agents moved through the room, each with a hand on Townsend, helping him along.

"There's a fire on one of the lower floors, sir. We're taking you to a secure location until they contain it."

Townsend shook the agents off of him. "Let go. I can walk on my own."

The agents did as ordered, but they didn't slow their forward momentum through the room, banging through a set of swinging doors into a staging area for the caterer. Cooks and waitstaff stepped back against the wall as the ex-president of the United States passed by. There was an agent already standing by the service elevator, holding open the door.

"I thought you weren't supposed to take the elevator in a fire," Townsend said.

"The fire's on the opposite side of the building. This is just a precaution."

"It's ridiculous is what it is," Townsend said, but he climbed on the elevator anyway.

The doors shut with Townsend and three agents inside. As the elevator began its slow descent, the sudden silence felt awkward. Townsend pulled at his cuffs and smoothed out his suit.

"You guys didn't have to . . . What the hell is that?"

He pointed up to the ceiling of the elevator. From openings in two different corners, white smoke was pouring in.

"You said the fire was on the other side of the building."

The smoke continued to pour in. All of them coughed violently. One of the agents pulled his weapon, only to have it fall from his hand and clatter to the floor as he keeled over. The agents sagged to their knees, hacking. Townsend was the longest on his feet, but that didn't last. He fell to the floor, collapsing on top of the agents under him, his face turned up to the ceiling.

As he lay there, he realized he was going to die. And all he felt was anger that his death was to be so much less dignified than what he deserved.

But then part of the ceiling moved. A large square lifted up and slid away. Then a flashlight shone down into the compartment, cutting through the smoke. A man wearing a mask swung into the elevator. The man pressed a button, stopping their descent.

The man was here to rescue him. He was going to live.

"Hi, Preston," the man said, putting his face right in front of Townsend's. "Remember me?"

Townsend blinked hard. He did remember. And he knew that voice.

Scott Roberts.

His last thought as he closed his eyes was that maybe he was right the first time. He was going to die in the elevator after all.

CHAPTER 11

Four years ago

Scott slugged back the last of his Sam Adams and motioned the bartender for two more. Hawthorn waved the order off. "It's all right, Jose," Hawthorn said. "We're good."

Jose the bartender looked back at Scott. "Sorry, Dad said no."

Hawthorn snorted. "Dad, hell. If I were your dad, you could bet your ass you'd have already been out to the woodshed for this last thing."

Scott tipped his mug back again, getting the last drops from it. "Instead I get drinks at Old Ebbitt Grill. I'm sure glad you're not my dad."

Hawthorn turned serious. "What the hell were you thinking? Right here? In DC?"

"Well, technically it was in Georgetown."

"Don't get cute with me. I'm not in the mood."

Scott glanced around the bar. He'd surveyed the place already, but it was habit. He knew Hawthorn had his own people posted around the room, and they were easy to pick out. He wondered again why they were having this conversation here as opposed to Hawthorn's office.

"I saw an opportunity to bring in Al-Saib. I had to take it."

"No, Scott. You saw an opportunity to bring in Al-Saib, and then you went and screwed it all up. You should have come to me. We could have done it right."

Scott crunched an ice cube in his mouth. "You know the problem with that."

"Again with this thing. I've checked my shop out every way possible over the last three months. We don't have a mole. Not one I can find anyway."

"That's not what Al-Saib said."

Hawthorn hadn't been in on his debrief after the incident in Georgetown, but Scott knew he'd watched the recording of it. This was information he hadn't shared with the goon squad and Hawthorn knew it. Scott wanted to do this part in person because he wanted to see the reaction for himself. Hawthorn was an old pro, so if there was anything, it would be no more than a microexpression. A twitch. An eye movement.

"Al-Saib said he had someone inside?" Hawthorn said.

Scott watched his friend carefully. "He implied it."

"Christ, Scott. This is why we needed to bring him in."

"Right after he told me, he lost his balance and fell."

"A lot of folks think he had a little help falling off that building."

"What do you think?"

Hawthorn grinned. "I think the only thing you would have liked better than seeing him splat would have been to see him locked up and interrogated for the next ten years. If he lost his balance, it was for a good reason."

Scott grabbed Hawthorn's beer and took a swig. "Thanks for the vote of confidence."

Hawthorn grabbed his beer back. "Did he give you a name?"

"Yeah, he did."

Hawthorn glanced at the nearest one of his guys in the room, as if measuring whether he was within earshot or not. "Who?"

"You, James. He said it went all the way up to you. And higher."

Hawthorn locked eyes with Scott for a beat, then burst out laughing. "And that's what you want to tell the president? You want to drink these beers and go into the Oval and tell the guy that some terrorist said both he and his director of Intelligence are in cahoots with the bad guys?"

"I know you're not part of it. Hell, if you were, you're responsible for helping me kill half their roster of hitters."

"Wouldn't make me very popular at the bad-guy Christmas party," Hawthorn agreed.

"And I wasn't planning on using the word *cahoots*," Scott said.

"Well, that puts my mind at ease. Thank you very much."

"The point is that there's something big going on. Al-Saib wasn't an ideologue. At the heart of it, he was a professional. But something had him spooked. Enough to make these wild claims. Enough to commit suicide to evade capture and interrogation."

"And you think you're the one to put a team together to go hunt this down?"

"You're damn right I am."

"After you just engaged in a running shootout on the roof of the most expensive hotel in the city, left a dead body in the middle of the street, and leveraged your wife's position to involve the government of Sweden in your exploits. The Swedes are pissed off at her and at us."

Scott winced. He'd already paid that bill, sleeping on the couch for a week even though he'd been recovering from the gunshot. Then the Swedish government had quietly asked her to make other arrangements, no longer comfortable with housing a CIA operative as part of their diplomatic team. That'd earned him a second week on the couch. "Al-Saib planned the coffee-house bombing in Stockholm last year. They wanted him dead."

"Yeah, but they just wanted us to take care of it. You know how they are; they hate getting their hands dirty."

"Why are you bringing all this up?"

"Because the president will." Hawthorn checked his watch, then pulled out a twenty-dollar bill and left it on the bar. "We should be going. Always a negative to keep the president waiting in the Oval."

"Really? We're going right now?" Scott said.

"Why did you think I didn't want to have that second beer? It'd be nice if you called him sir, Mr. President, that sort of thing."

"So, no calling him jackass?"

"Maybe we should have had that second beer."

They walked through the dark wood and brass interior of Old Ebbitt Grill out into the street facing the Treasury Building. Hawthorn's car pulled up, but he ignored it.

"What do you say we stretch our legs. We have time," Hawthorn said, obviously not asking it as a question.

They turned left down Eighteenth Street and walked parallel to Treasury toward the mall, where the Washington Monument loomed up in front of them. They didn't say much, content to walk in silence. Scott processed the idea of meeting the president in the Oval. He'd met Townsend's predecessor, President Simmons, but that had been in a private ceremony out at Langley when the man had hung a medal around Scott's neck. The difference was that Simmons was an honorable man who Scott respected. Townsend was a different matter. It wasn't just the man's policies that rubbed Scott the wrong way, he could live with that. It was the man's character that bothered him. He was a narcissist who made everything about him. He demanded loyalty from the people around him, but showed none in return, publically embarrassing even his allies if it could make him look better.

He didn't understand how Hawthorn had not only tolerated the man, but helped him along the way. Being college buddies with the man's father was good for a few beers and maybe a weekend golf trip to reminisce. Endorsing a run for the president of the United States was another thing altogether. He could only assume that there was a good man buried beneath the hubris, a man Hawthorn had seen there over the years and thought he could find again.

Then again, maybe Hawthorn was human and just liked the access to power that came with backing the winning horse in the most important race on the globe. He liked to think Hawthorn was a better man than that, but Scott understood the draw of power on a man's soul. Still, he held out hope that his friend was a moderating influence on the president's temperament. If Townsend had to be in the White House, Scott was happy Hawthorn was on the inside to help guide him.

They crossed Eighteenth Street at the W Hotel and walked through the park bearing the statue of William Tecumseh Sherman astride his horse. "Funny how we honor a man like Sherman so close to the White House," Scott said.

"He got the job done," Hawthorn said. "His taking Atlanta probably ensured Lincoln won a second term. Without that there might be a border crossing just south of here into the Confederate States of America."

"His scorched earth campaign burned down towns, killed livestock, laid waste to the South. They still spit on the ground down there when you mention his name."

"They were disloyal," Hawthorn said. "The price for that is high."

Scott stopped. Hawthorn took a few more steps, but then he slowed and turned, facing him. "Is that why we came this way?" Scott asked. "Just so you could let out that little line?"

"You're overthinking." It was clear from the expression on his face that Scott had it right.

"You've always shot me straight. This is the first time I can think of where you've tried to handle me. What's going on, Jim? How bad is it?"

The muscles in Hawthorn's jaws twitched and he clenched his teeth. Scott noticed, but he was in work mode now, and he knew Hawthorn could have done that just so he would notice. The trap inside a trap inside a trap.

"I want you to meet the president and then I'll answer that afterward."

Scott closed the space between them until they were toe-to-toe. He had Hawthorn by four inches, but the older man wasn't intimidated. Not in the slightest. "I'd prefer you tell me now. If I'm walking into a buzz saw, I want to know about it ahead of time."

Hawthorn held out a hand to the men in his protective detail striding toward them once Scott had moved into his personal space. They stopped, but clearly didn't like what was going on. "What in God's green earth makes you think I give a shit what you'd prefer?" Hawthorn said. "Now, snap to or I'll break you over my knee and send you crawling back to the Farm to teach raw recruits how to wipe their asses. You got that?"

Hawthorn turned on his heel and walked toward the White House gate. Whatever pleasant buzz Scott had from the beer at Old Ebbitt was long gone. Every once in a while, it was easy to forget the career James Hawthorn had before becoming a political animal foraging in the Washington jungle. A decorated Marine, then CIA field operative before being promoted up the chain of command, Hawthorn wasn't some limp dick political appointee. As evidenced by the way the man had just made him feel like a teenager being scolded by his dad. He followed Hawthorn up to the gate and showed the guards his credentials. After they were waved through, they headed across the South Lawn toward the West Wing. When they reached the Rose Garden, Scott finally broke the silence.

"And I thought you'd gotten too old to be such a giant prick," he said. "Is it the Viagra?"

Hawthorn let out a loud laugh, flashing Scott a grin that put them back on firm ground again. "Just behave yourself in there, all right?"

"I respect the office," Scott said. "No matter who the son of a bitch is who's sitting behind the desk."

"Even this son of a bitch?" came a voice from ahead of them. Both men looked up at the colonnade that marked the walkway from the West Wing to the Main Residence. There stood a man smoking a cigarette. He looked older than he did on TV. Scott swallowed hard.

"Hello, Mr. President," he said.

Townsend took a long drag from his cigarette, then tossed the butt down and ground it out. "Come on, let's get this over with."

The president turned and walked toward a double set of French doors. A Secret Service agent opened the door as he approached.

Scott took notice that the president didn't even acknowledge the agent as he passed.

"We're off to a good start," Hawthorn said before walking up the steps to the colonnade.

Scott followed, but as he ascended the stairs, he bent down and picked up the cigarette butt on the ground. He deposited it in a brass receptacle discreetly hidden behind a bush, a foot away from where Townsend had been standing. Just one more reason not to like the guy.

"Thanks," he said to the agent holding open the door. Then he walked into the Oval Office and the worst meeting of his life.

CHAPTER 12

Mara watched the ex-president of the United States slowly regain consciousness, his eyes fluttering open and then squinting in the lights of the storage room. It was a cramped space, most of it taken up by wire shelving units that stood empty because they were in the new construction area of the building. The covers for the LED bulbs in the ceiling were not installed yet, so everything was bathed in stark, harsh light. As Townsend slowly cleared his head, she wondered what must be going through his mind. Probably not a lot of good thoughts about his Secret Service detail.

Mara still couldn't believe how simple it'd been to pull Townsend from the elevator.

It almost made her feel sorry for the Secret Service agents. A month from now she figured they'd find themselves assigned to the most remote outposts the Service had, probably chasing counterfeiters in border towns in Texas or something. Certainly none of them would protect a president again.

"C'mon, Preston, wake up," Scott said, kneeling in front of the man. He rifled through his pockets, pulling out a thin wallet and a silver cigarette case, handing both over to Mara. Scott slapped his cheeks lightly. "Haven't got all day."

Townsend coughed, hacking up some phlegm and spitting it

on the floor. He blinked hard and then settled in on Scott's face. "Roberts. You're supposed to be dead."

"That's the rumor." Scott put the palm of his hand on Townsend's forehead and stared at him. "Are you all there? Do you know what's happening?"

Townsend swatted his hand away. "Don't touch me. What the hell do you think you're doing?"

Scott looked satisfied. "Something I've waited to do for four years."

Without warning, he delivered a brutal right cross to the man's face. Townsend's head popped backward, his hands covering his nose. Within seconds, blood gushed from between his fingers and he howled like a wounded dog.

Mara pulled her gun and pointed it at Scott.

"This wasn't part of the plan," she said. "You said we're here to ask him questions. We wouldn't hurt him."

"I'm gonna have you killed for this," Townsend said. "Both of you."

Mara turned the gun on Townsend. "You shut up."

"He had it coming," Scott said. "More than you know."

"Ask him your questions," she said. "You know they're tearing the building apart looking for him right now."

Scott edged closer to Townsend. "She's right. We don't have much time. But you can see I don't give a shit about hurting you or not. My government trained me to get answers out of people as efficiently as possible. I hope you don't cooperate, because I'd love to show you what Uncle Sam taught me."

"You don't scare me," Townsend said, his shaking voice telling a different story. "You can go fuck yourself." His eyes lit up as if he'd just figured something out. "My God, this is about the book, isn't it? I knew they might come after me, but this? You know what? You can tell whoever hired you that they can go fuck themselves, too."

Scott clamped his hand over Townsend's mouth. He knelt down so that they were face-to-face. "I don't want to hear another word from you unless it's a direct answer to a question I ask you. Understand?"

Townsend's wide eyes were answer enough. Scott removed his hand.

"First question, who gave the kill order on my wife?"

Townsend looked confused, but then his shoulders relaxed and he let out a snorting laugh. "That's what this is all about? Your wife?"

Mara felt a chill wash over her. She didn't know that what happened to her mom was even on the table. The questions made no sense. Her dad had killed her.

"Answer me," Scott shouted.

Townsend looked away. The fear was gone now. His usual dismissive, smug attitude was back in force. "I don't know anything about that. You need to talk to—"

Scott grabbed the president's pinkie finger and snapped it at the middle joint like it was a pencil. In the same motion, he covered Townsend's mouth with his hand, muffling the man's scream.

Mara flinched at the suddenness of the violence. As much as she wanted an answer to the question, her gun was still at her side. Her dad looked out of control, and she's wasn't sure whether it was an act to scare Townsend into talking. She was starting to suspect it wasn't.

"This is entry-level pain," Scott snarled. "Next time I ask a question and you don't cooperate, I'm skipping the intermediate stuff and going right for the permanent disfigurement. You'll give your next speech without a nose. Got it?"

Townsend nodded.

"Good." Scott removed his hand. "Now, who gave the kill order on my wife?"

"I gave the order to bring her in alive."

Mara looked closer at Scott. All of the play was gone from him. He was deadly serious.

"Why did you want Wendy Roberts brought in?" Mara asked.

Townsend jerked his head toward her as if he'd forgotten she was there. His lips curled in contempt. "He hasn't told you? He brought you all the way here to kill me and he didn't even tell you the truth about why you're here."

"Kill you? No one is talking about . . ." She caught the look in her dad's eye and she knew. Townsend was right. Her dad was there to kill the ex-president.

She raised her gun slowly and pointed it at him. "Are you crazy?"

Scott wouldn't even look at her. His eyes were fixed on Townsend. "He killed Wendy," he said. "Same as if he pulled the trigger himself."

No, you killed her, Mara thought, but that fundamental truth, that fact that had consumed her waking hours for four years, now suddenly seemed shaded gray. Why would her dad be asking these questions unless he really didn't know who'd killed her mom? But why would he have confessed to it? It made no sense.

"Admit it," Scott raged at Townsend. "You gave the order."

"Bullshit, I had nothing to do with that," Townsend said. "I told you, I wanted her alive. You're the one that went off the reservation."

"She told me, before she died, that the U.S. government had a kill on sight order on her. That if I brought her in, she was as good as dead."

Mara studied her dad's face, searching for any sign he was lying. There was none. She leaned against the shelving unit next to her, light-headed. Trying to catch her breath.

"When did she tell you that?" Townsend snapped. "Right before you shot her?"

Scott slammed his fist into Townsend's face, making the man's head snap backward. When he righted himself, he spit out a gob of blood.

"Say I killed my wife again," Scott said. "Say it."

Townsend showed no interest in taking the bait. He rubbed his mouth where he'd been hit. "I'll pass."

Mara crouched down next to him. "Jim Hawthorn took my

nephew. Is Hawthorn CIA only? Or does he work for someone else?"

"What am I? The goddamn missing persons bureau? How would I know anything about some missing kid?"

"You said you thought we were here because of a book. What information do you have that people want silenced?" Mara asked.

Townsend pointed at her. "See, she knows what matters. That's the question that needs answering. And it might just tie into your first question."

Scott pulled his fist back. "Then answer it."

"In exchange for what?"

Mara's fist connected with the other side of Townsend's face. His head snapped back again. This time when he righted himself, he spit out a tooth.

"Jesus, you hit harder than he does."

Mara couldn't deny that she loved hearing that. She snuck in a discreet look at her dad, not bothering to hide the smirk on her lips. He let out a *humph* and turned his body as if to make sure he had a better angle if he needed to hit the president again.

"How about in exchange for keeping that telegenic face of yours pretty? Or I can let my daughter knock the rest of your teeth out," he said.

"Daughter?" he said, surprised. He glanced between her and her dad. "What does she know?"

"She knows how to get answers in a hurry, just like I do," Scott said. "She knows the value of sticking only to the salient facts. Do you?" He pulled a knife from his side, then grabbed one of Townsend's hands. "Which finger are you least fond of?"

"Stop," Townsend said. "Okay, listen. I'll tell you. But not because I'm a coward. But because you knowing the truth might be the only way to stop these people."

"Omega?" Scott said.

Townsend smiled. "That's one of the names for them. I don't know if Jim Hawthorn gave them the name or he uncovered it. The last letter of the Greek alphabet. The end times. These people, they're outside government. Outside any jurisdiction. Old money. Old power. Old ideas about how power ought to be wielded over the masses."

"And they helped you get elected?" Scott said.

"Don't you get it? They've helped every president get elected," Townsend said. "If there was an order to kill your wife, then I'd look at your employer." He noticed the puzzled look on Scott's face. "You *are* working for them, aren't you?" When Scott didn't respond, Townsend began to laugh.

"I'm not working for anyone," Scott growled. "You said they're worried about what you'll say in the book. Give me the names."

Townsend leaned back, suddenly looking very old. "They didn't even need to buy you off. You're working for them and you don't even know it."

"Bullshit."

"They aimed you at me and let you fly." Townsend righted himself, some of his dignity seeming to come back to him. "Think about it. I start work on a memoir where I plan to share what I know about them. It's not much, but a former president, even if it's me, giving credence to all the conspiracy theories out there is more than they could handle. They want me dead to silence me. How better to accomplish that than send you?"

"No way," Scott said. But his voice betrayed his uncertainty.

"Why such an elaborate plan?" Mara said. "Whoever these people are, if they're so powerful, why not kill you with a simple hit?"

"He knows," Townsend said.

Scott's face was a mix of disbelief and awe. He was buying what Townsend was saying. "Because if I did it, the investigation would be one of the shortest in history," Scott said. "Rogue CIA agent who blames the ex-president for his wife's death gets his revenge in a bold assassination plan. Motive, means, and I always make my own opportunity."

"Only this time you've taken the opportunity to do exactly what Omega wanted you to do."

Mara saw the logic. "And if they hired an assassin, then it's all-hands-on-deck to solve the mystery," she said. "Over fifty years after JFK and we're still investigating."

A sense of dread wormed its way through her. She thought through the path that had brought them here. How she'd been given this assignment. Her dad's release from custody under the cover story of her assignment to kill him. Their escape from the prison parking lot. How they had evaded the manhunt up to that point. The relative ease of kidnapping the former leader of the free world. It was all too simple.

She made eye contact with her dad. She could tell he'd reached the same conclusion.

Nearly in unison, they said, "Oh shit."

"That's why getting in was so easy," Mara said.

"But you can bet your ass getting out won't be," Scott said. He turned to Townsend. "If this is true, then Jim Hawthorn is pulling the strings. Why does he want you dead?"

"Jim and I go way back," Townsend said. "Might be the best friend I have, even if he did abandon ship with the other rats when it all went to shit. You don't ask why Jim wants me dead. The real question is, who is Jim working for and why do they want me dead? Answer that question, and I think you find out who really gave the order to have your wife killed."

Scott grabbed Townsend. "Tell me. Tell me who it was."

Townsend laughed. "You think I was the most powerful man in the free world when I was president? There are far greater forces in the world. Behind the scenes. Staying in the shadows. They went through Jim. Always through Jim. He has the answers you need."

"Bullshit, you know more than you're letting on," he said. "I need a connection into Omega. Who do you know?"

Townsend shook his head, but he wasn't convincing. He glanced at the wallet and cigarette case Mara still held in her hand. It was only for a second, but both Mara and Scott caught it.

Mara tossed the wallet to Scott and he dug through it. She

opened the cigarette case. Five Marlboro Reds were lined up in a row, each secured by a small elastic hoop. She pinched the end off one and it crumbled into dry flakes. "These have to be a few years old."

"I kicked the habit a long time ago," Townsend said. "I keep them around as a reminder of my self-control."

She wasn't buying it. Quickly, she broke up each cigarette to see if anything had been stashed inside one of them. Nothing.

Rolling the case over in her hands, she looked for anything she might have missed. Townsend's body language told her there was something more there.

Then she saw it. A tiny button on the inside edge. She pressed it and the inside of the case levered open. She pulled out the thumb drive and held it out to Townsend.

"Pretty elaborate way to hide your porn," she said. "Or maybe there's info here about Omega?"

"You two don't know what you're dealing with," Townsend said.

"No, but I have a feeling based on how you're acting that what's on that drive will fill in a few gaps." He threw Townsend to the floor. "If I find out you lied and that you ordered Wendy's death, I will find you again. And I will make you pay. You got that?"

Townsend didn't reply, but met Scott's stare. He'd caught the implication just like Mara had that they were going to leave him alive.

"We can work together," Townsend said. "Think about it. They tried to use you to kill me. You don't think they'll just figure out some other way to do it? I want them found and destroyed as much as you do."

"Then give me the names. Or are they already on the drive?"

"I only have names of people who accepted the bribes from Omega, not the people who paid them," Townsend said. "Worth millions to a publisher in a tell-all book, but not so much to law enforcement. I'll tell the world that Omega exists, but I can't reveal who they are. I have some ideas, but no proof. My thinking is once I admit Omega exists, others will seek them out and find them."

"Or people will think you're a crank," Mara said.

"I am an ex-president. That still means something to people."

"Look what Jimmy Carter's UFO sighting did to that movement," Mara said.

Her dad nudged her to be quiet and she did so.

"If my name or my wife's name appears in that book," he said to Townsend, "I'll be at your first book signing. You got that?"

Townsend looked dismayed, but seemed to remember quickly that he was bargaining for his life. "I'll take it out. You have my word."

"Good, now when they find you, I want you to say you were taken by some protesters. Young guys with masks. They lectured you about climate change or animal rights or something."

"Why would I do that?"

"You said you wanted to help; that's what I need you to do," Scott said.

"Besides," Mara added, "if the headline reads ROGUE CIA OPERATIVES DETAIN PRESIDENT, then all your old scandals about the CIA during your administration get recycled. If it's climate protesters that kidnapped you, then everyone will just feel sympathy for you. Only the Secret Service comes out looking bad in this."

Townsend eyes lit up, liking the idea. "This one has a nose for politics. That's too bad."

"Why's that too bad?" Mara asked.

"Because you're not going to survive this. These people you're up against are everywhere. You don't stand a chance. Neither of you. Not for long anyway."

Mara pulled a syringe from her pocket. Another present from Harry.

"Thank you for your concern. Good night, Mr. President. I'm sure they'll find you in an hour or two."

"No, wait. You don't have to—"

Mara injected the entire syringe and then pulled the needle out of Townsend's arm, put the cap back on, and slid it back into her pocket. In only a few seconds, Townsend slumped to his side and Mara rested him against the wall.

"Let's get the hell out of here," she said.

Scott didn't need to be asked twice. He carefully opened the door and checked the hallway. They'd scoped the area out well and chosen part of the building that was under construction and so the least likely to have someone randomly walking the halls, especially on a Saturday afternoon. They left the storage closet, closing and locking the door behind them. There were five different egress routes from this point in the mission.

"Let's split up," Scott said. "I'll take exit one and fall back to two if it's blocked. You take three and fallback four."

"And five?"

"If the shit hits the fan, I'll meet you there."

"Rally point?"

"Field Museum, midnight. If one of us is detained, two-hour checks until noon, then clear out."

Mara didn't like the idea of separating, but she knew it was the right call. But still, right then, she felt like she needed to be by her dad. She was coming to terms with the idea that the man she'd hated for the last four years for killing her mother and betraying his country may have been telling her the truth. That he might have been innocent all along.

"Dad . . ."

He looked at her and gave her a smile. He knew.

"We'll talk about it later. Be careful. If they start shooting, duck." He struck off down the hall and took a right turn.

"Be careful yourself, old man," she said under her breath, then headed left to the exit, wondering just how foul the Chicago River was going to be for her upcoming swim.

Mara ran toward the back of the new construction area, letting the level of finish work be her guide toward the more unfinished area. Soon, she was running on bare concrete floors, the skeletal framework of hallways and rooms laid out in metal studs and what looked like miles of wiring. The lack of drywall was unnerving because it left her exposed to watching eyes anywhere on that level. But it was a necessary evil to get to her destination.

She pictured the building from the outside and recalled the position of the scaffolding. She cut to her right and ran that direction. The plan was simple. Crawl out onto the scaffold, shimmy down, and jump into the river. She pulled the rebreather out of the pocket on her hip. It was a small bottle, the size of a bottle of sunscreen spray. A rubber tube was attached the top, terminating in a mouthpiece the same as one found on a SCUBA regulator. The rebreather contained three cubic feet of air, enough for her to make an underwater escape away from prying eyes. Piece of cake.

Until she realized she'd make a miscalculation.

She was at the side of the new construction facing the river, and she could see the scaffolding set up outside. The only problem was that while the windows on the lower floors had yet to be installed, the ones on this floor were already in place.

She rapped her knuckles against the window. Thick safety glass that would take her firing her gun at it to get through in a hurry. The noise that would make would bring all kinds of unwanted attention. The place was certainly already crawling with law enforcement. She didn't want to bring them all to this spot while she was climbing down six flights of scaffolding.

There had to be a better way.

She spotted it just when the first voice shouted from behind her. Without looking at the direction of the sound, she took off for the end of the hallway. A shot rang out and sparks flew off the metal stud to her right. Another shot, this one to her left.

Either the shooter was making a point, or he was just a shitty shot. It didn't matter. Both ways it was a problem for her. She darted left and right, swerving through the metal studs, careful not to trip on the electric wire strung between them.

Another shot and the rebreather flew out of her hand, hissing from air rupturing through the breach. So much for her river escape plan.

She pulled her Sig from her shoulder holster, a smooth move that didn't cause even the smallest stutter in her step. Then she lifted it over her shoulder and fired off two quick shots behind her.

There was no chance she'd hit the shooter, but she wasn't trying to. It was the few seconds pause that came next as her pursuer took cover that she was after.

It was just enough for her to reach the end of the hallway, a rough opening in the concrete exterior wall that would one day provide a nice scenic view of the river. But right then it was lined with orange heavy mesh sheeting that opened like a monster's throat, a trash chute for the construction workers to toss debris to the bottom of the building.

Mara jumped into it at full speed, just as another bullet zipped past her head.

She scraped against the mesh and fell faster than she expected. She had a sudden panic that she was simply going to fall six floors and crush her legs and spine in the process. A miserable way to end an escape.

But once she reached out and dragged her hands on the side, thumping against the ribbed joints that held the chute open, she began to slow.

Then the chute curved, the rough material giving enough friction to stop the free fall. Still, when she hit the bottom, the force of the impact knocked the wind out of her. She rolled and landed in a rat's nest of excess telephone wire that she fell into like a pillow. She scrambled to her feet, gasping for air, seeing that a few feet to her right was a nasty pile of two-by-fours with nails sticking out of them like some kind of medieval torture device.

She pulled one of the boards, and a section of the pile moved with it. With a heave, she hauled enough of them over to the mouth of the rubbish chute to make for a tough landing for anyone who followed behind her. Not enough to do any permanent damage. As far as she knew, the men following her were Secret

Service just doing their jobs. She'd allow herself to be captured before seriously wounding one of them.

The area around her was fenced in with high chain-link covered with green tarp. A couple strands of barbed wire circled the top, but nothing serious. There was a double gate in the middle of the fence big enough to back a truck into. It was chained shut, but that wasn't a problem. They'd come down during their recon and cut the lock, carefully putting it back in place in case there were any workers grabbing double pay for working on a weekend. A second lock, this one uncut, hung open next to it.

Mara stopped at the trash can beside the gate. She picked through it, pulling out straws from the fast-food drinks she found inside, collecting five or six in only a few seconds. The lock slid off and she pried the gate open a few inches to see that she was alone. By ordinance, every building on the river had to provide public access to the water, so there was a chance she'd run into pedestrians in addition to Secret Service agents who wanted to shoot her dead.

Luckily, there was no one there.

A commotion behind her and then a yell in pain. One of the Secret Service agents had made the jump down the rubbish chute and found the boards with nails she'd left behind.

It was time to go.

She darted out of the gate and used the second lock to chain it shut behind her. At a full sprint, she ran to the river, half expecting a torrent of gunfire to follow her.

But none did. She reached the river's edge and dove straight down, trying to get out of sight as quickly as possible.

The water was colder than she expected and it took her breath away. Her clothes clung to her body and made her motion sluggish as she swam underwater downriver, using the current to give her speed.

She gave herself thirty seconds to add as much distance as possible from her entry point before she grabbed hold of the wall on the embankment, so that she was three feet underwater. Bracing herself with her legs to stay in place, she slid straws into one another to create two long straws. These she raised to the surface until they broke free. Once cleared of the river water, she was able to draw in fresh air and use the straws like a snorkel. She was counting on the Chicago River's notorious lack of clarity to give her the cover she needed. Even if someone was on the river's edge right above her, she doubted they would see anything of her in the water.

With new air, she let go of the wall and resumed her swim. Her eyes were shut as they wouldn't do any good in the silted water, so she kept a track of her direction by dragging a hand or a foot periodically against the embankment.

After the third time she'd stopped to use the straws, she heard a motor approaching. It was a steady, methodical sound, not the high-pitched whine she'd expect from a police boat or jet skis she knew they had available. She leaned against the dark, mossy riverbank and risked slowly rising to the surface for a look.

She was happy with the distance she'd made in the short amount of time. The current had carried her much farther than she expected. The motor was from a rusty barge carrying construction materials. Exactly what she wanted. Taking a deep breath, she dove back underwater and swam out toward it, using the sound of the motor as her guide. She chanced one more look as she got closer, worried that a misjudgment might put her into the motors.

Her timing was good and she crossed the bow of the barge just as it slid past her position, putting the hulk of metal between her and the Tribune Tower, where she figured all hell was breaking loose.

She dragged her hands along the hull just under the water line until she found an eyelet for a rope line, something that would be above the water when the barge wasn't weighted down. She clung to it and hitched a ride downriver, still using her straws to keep hidden from view. There was no way they were finding her now.

She just hoped her dad's exit had gone as well. Not only did she want him safe, but she still wanted answers from him. The talk with Townsend had raised so many more questions. She replayed the exchange between Townsend and her dad in her mind, trying to sort out what it all meant. She wanted to believe that her dad wasn't responsible for her mother's death, but she'd seen the footage. Heard him confess to it. She couldn't reconcile that with what she'd seen in his interaction with Townsend.

And then there was Omega. What was this organization that could infiltrate the highest levels of government? Had they really played both her and her dad so well that they'd almost assassinated Townsend on their behalf? The number of variables that had been at play was staggering, and yet whoever had masterminded the operation had almost been successful.

A sudden insight hit her. The Agency hadn't tried to kill her. And they hadn't taken Joey. It was Hawthorn. Working for Omega and using Agency assets, employing who knew what kind of disinformation and lies about her to explain why she had to be eliminated.

The thought gave her hope. The Agency had been her home for the last four years. They'd taken her in after Afghanistan and been her family after she'd lost her parents. Hawthorn specifically had taken her under his wing and given her a chance to redeem her name after her dad's betrayal.

His friendship had all been a lie. But it was clear now who the enemy was. It wasn't the Agency. It was Omega and Hawthorn.

As she clung shivering to the barge, doing her best not to ingest what was one of the most polluted rivers in America, she knew that one question was what stood between her and getting Joey back. She needed to figure out who was responsible, find them, and put them in the ground.

CHAPTER 13

Asset flinched when the fire alarm turned off. He liked it better when it blared throughout the building. The noise added anxiety and panic, two emotions that made people easier to manage, turning as they did to anyone in a uniform to tell them what to do.

His Chicago Police Department uniform had made it easy for him to infiltrate the building. Part of it was the uniform, but the other part was knowing how to look like you belonged. Asset knew how to blend in. He knew how to carry himself so that the keen eyes of the Secret Service didn't pick up on him trying to be too casual, or too stiff, or too anything. He was under no illusions that Townsend's detail was the second string. He knew these men rotated through. Any of them could be guarding the current U.S. president on his next duty.

Well, depending on how the day turned out, maybe not.

Asset had heard the calls go out on the communications line used by the Service. It was supposed to be isolated and unhackable, but it'd been easy enough for him. Not that he was any kind of tech genius. It was just that his current employer provided him with the best field gear money and espionage could acquire. It made up for the constant sense that the end of his contract would come with a bullet instead of a severance package.

He'd heard the sounds on the com-link when the attack happened in the elevator. It was subtle and hard to hear over the blaring fire alarm. But he'd been crouched down with his hand to his ear, knowing the alarm was only a cover for whatever Roberts had planned. When he heard the muffled coughs and thumps in his ear, he knew they'd taken Townsend on the elevator.

A brilliant move. Stunning really. A one- or two-person team abducting an ex-president was not only impressive, but Asset was unsure he could have pulled it off had the assignment been sent to him. He felt a pang of professional jealousy mixed in with a grudging respect for Roberts and his daughter. They'd accomplished the near impossible and made it look almost easy. But whether they would leave the building alive was another matter. Certainly Roberts couldn't have hoped to get Townsend off-site. And if he'd wanted to kill him, he would have left his body in the elevator. No, Roberts wanted to question the man.

But where?

While the remaining Secret Service detail engaged their operating protocols and called in reinforcements, Asset considered the options. There was no way they could hope to get Townsend out of the building. That meant either kill him in the elevator and then egress, or take him somewhere in the building. The new construction zone in the rear was the perfect choice. Abandoned. No surveillance cameras. It was a no-brainer.

It didn't take long for him to make his way over, instructing scared workers as he went in his official capacity as one of Chicago's finest. Whenever someone tried to slow him down, he barked orders at them and shoved them toward the nearest stairwell. Worked perfectly every time.

Now the fire alarm was off. Based on the chatter on the com-link, SWAT was on scene and outside the building had been turned into a holding pen for people streaming out, each one of them a suspect in the eyes of the Secret Service. He didn't have much time.

It took him three floors before he spotted what he was looking for. A barely discernible smudge in the thin coat of dust on the floor leading from the elevator.

He pulled his gun and followed the trail, entering the construction zone in the new building addition. The signs were harder here, mixed in with the footsteps of dozens of construction workers, but the occasional long streak looked like someone being dragged. He was guessing that was Townsend being none too excited by the idea of alone time with Scott.

The trail ended at a closed metal door. He leaned against it and listened. Nothing.

He turned the handle, expecting it to be locked, and surprised when it wasn't.

Asset flung the door open, counting on catching whoever was inside off guard.

The small room, a closet really, was empty except for rows of stack shelving, five-gallon buckets of paint, and the most recent leader of the free world. Townsend sat on the floor, his back against the bare concrete wall, his head lolled to one side like he was taking a nap. Blood trickled from his nose and lip, and his right eye was swollen, already darkening.

Asset thought he might be too late, although it wouldn't change his compensation package if Townsend was killed by Scott instead of himself. But the ex-president's eyes opened, glazed and disoriented. Asset realized they'd drugged him, but left him alive. Looked like he was going to have to earn his pay after all.

Townsend's eyes focused a bit, perhaps the uniform a powerful enough symbol to cut through his drug-addled mind, because he smiled and raised a weak hand toward him. Asset enjoyed the thought that the man would have some false hope at the end. He tended not to care about the marks he was hired to dispose of, but he'd voted for Townsend, using an alias of course, and the son of a bitch had given false hope to an entire country. It was a fitting end.

Asset raised his gun and aimed at the man's head. Townsend's eyes grew wide. His lower lip trembled and a line of drool slipped out, covering his chin. Pathetic.

"Lower your weapon!" a man shouted in the hallway to Asset's right.

More shouts followed.

Asset gritted his teeth. Ten seconds earlier and his job would have been done and he'd have been on his way. He figured the cop uniform had just saved his life. Without it, SWAT would have shot first and asked questions after.

He raised his hands over his head, making his voice shake as he called out. "I'm CPD. The president. He's in there." Asset carefully turned. The last thing he wanted was some overeager SWAT guy putting one in his chest. There were three of them, all in full tactical gear. He could have finished them off, even though they had weapons trained on him, but more men were visible down the hallway. In his ear, he heard the call for all men to converge on their location. There was no way he was shooting his way out of this one.

"Step away."

He did as he was told, moving slow and easy. "Room's not clear yet," he warned. I . . . I . . . don't know if someone else is in there."

"We've got it, fall back."

Asset did just that, leaning up against the wall opposite the SWAT team, pretending to hyperventilate from the excitement. A SWAT guy gave him a disapproving look, but then they rushed past him into the room.

"The president's secure," came the call in his headset. "Lock down the building."

Time to leave. He grabbed his chest and kept huffing. He grabbed the new SWAT guy who'd just arrived on the scene. "Gotta go down. You got this?"

The SWAT guy looked him over. "You injured?"

Asset looked embarrassed. "I get these . . . attacks . . . like a panic."

The SWAT guy had a disgusted look on his face. He waved him away. "Yeah, get the hell outta here." He called out down the hall. "Let this guy through."

Asset holstered his gun and stumbled past the row of SWAT in the hallway. Once he made a few turns, he stopped his hyperventilating and felt his pulse throbbing in his neck. It was high, but only because of the fake breathing. He didn't feel stress from his situation, although he knew he couldn't underestimate the cordon he needed to break to get out of the building. A legitimate attempt on an ex-president meant every law enforcement official in the city was likely en route. If the criminals in Chicago were smart, the next hour was the time to do anything they wanted. Asset just needed to get out of the building before the cops got organized. And then he had to contact his employer to see what she wanted done next.

He'd nearly gotten his pulse down to his resting rate when he thought of having to report his failure to her. His heart sped up at the thought before he willed it back under control. Asset, who could kill women and children without feeling a thing, hated the prospect of making that call. Few people in the world rattled his cage, but his employer had the uncanny ability to do exactly that.

He pushed that inevitable conversation out of his mind and focused on the matter at hand. Seconds later, Asset removed his hand from his carotid artery, satisfied he was calm and mentally ready to execute his egress plan.

He just hoped Scott and Mara Roberts had successfully escaped. They'd shown themselves to be worthy adversaries in a world filled with cheap imitators. He relished the thought of tracking them down and matching skills with them. He wanted the pleasure of killing them both himself.

CHAPTER 14

"Jesus, what a mess," Hawthorn whispered. His deputy, Shana Brooks, a young up-and-comer, a dangerous mix of genius and unbridled ambition, stood next to him.

"Yes, sir," she said. "A complete clusterfuck if there ever was one."

Hawthorn cocked an eyebrow at the language, but Brooks was focused on the scene playing out in front of them and didn't see it. He didn't say anything. Mostly because she was right.

The comms center was silent as the dozen or so staffers looked up from their stations at the images on the front wall. The screens were set up in a six-by-four grid, each of them able to either display an individual image or work together to create different sizes. Hawthorn wasn't allowed near the controls because he inevitably messed it up. Brooks typed away on a tablet. The display broke into four sections. Two of them were news channels, CNN and Fox News. One was the body cam of someone running down a hallway; the label on the bottom said: SANCHEZ, TEAM LEADER. The last screen was another body cam, labeled FRANKLIN. On this one, Hawthorn spotted Townsend in a room, sitting on a chair and being seen to by a doctor.

"That one," Hawthorn said.

"On it," Brooks said.

The entire wall turned into the body cam image. At that size, the resolution suffered, but it gave them a clear shot of Townsend's face. There was still dried blood under his nose, but it was his right eye that got Hawthorn's attention. It was red and so puffy that it was nearly swollen shut.

"That's going to hurt in the morning," Brooks said.

"And you'll see it on every channel."

"Of course, this is big news."

"No, I mean you'll see him live on every news channel. Starting tonight, probably. If there's one thing Preston Townsend loves, it's a chance to be in the spotlight playing the martyr."

"You don't like him much, do you?"

"Does anyone?" Hawthorn asked. He felt a pang of guilt at the comment. He'd once thought himself to be a surrogate for Townsend's father once his good friend had passed away. But that feeling had long since passed. Unless an overwhelming sense of disappointment could be considered part of the natural paternal relationship.

"Good point," Brooks said. "This might get him some sympathy points, though. People even came to like George W. Bush after he'd been out of office long enough. Americans like ex-presidents. If this was ISIL or some Al Qaeda–inspired attempt, then shit will get real in a hurry."

Hawthorn arched an eyebrow in her direction. When she'd started working for him six months earlier, she would have passed out from embarrassment if she'd cussed in front of him. She noticed the look this time.

"Sorry," she said.

"I think I'm rubbing off on you. That's not always a good thing."

She shrugged. "Not all bad either."

Hawthorn smiled. He liked Shana. She was intelligent and had good instincts, two things you couldn't teach. Her petite frame and round face with a tiny nose that barely kept her glasses from sliding off made her look like someone from the accounting department, but she used her looks to her advantage.

Being underestimated could often be as powerful a tool as being physically imposing. She was career CIA and knew nothing about his involvement in Omega. He liked to think that if he went down, the people he'd shielded from his actions would survive in their careers, but it was a fiction. Anyone close to him would be forever under suspicion, no matter the evidence. Their careers would be over. It was a shame, but such a small sacrifice compared to what was at stake. "About what you said, you don't think this was ISIL or AQ, do you?"

"No way. If it was, Townsend would be dead. But one of the dumb bas . . . one of these splinter groups might miscalculate and take credit. Hell of a recruiting video to say your guys smashed up the face of a U.S. president. Only problem is that Americans get angry when you mess with our top guy. We can hate him, but others better keep their hands to themselves."

"So, if not Islamic terrorists, then who?" Brooks didn't know about Scott and Mara. He'd purposefully left her out of the loop. Partially because he didn't know her well enough to trust her, but also to protect her career. Where he needed to go, she didn't want to follow.

"Issues group? Someone domestic. Trying to raise a cause profile. Watch it be PETA. Wouldn't that be something?"

"I suppose the president will be able to tell us." He gathered up his bag. "Monitor things here. Contact me with significant developments. I'm going to make sure our guys are whacking the weeds to shake loose whoever was responsible for this."

"If DCI Lewis finds out we're active on this, he's going to hit the roof."

Hawthorn winced. The reminder that he was no longer DCI hurt. Not that he missed the politics of the role. He was more than happy to be out of that rat race. And he was thankful Marty Lewis had, albeit reluctantly, accepted his request to create a small Special Operations Group within the existing framework of the Special Activities Division. A SAD/SOG in the alphabet soup of Washington jargon. But still he chafed under the idea of being beholden to Lewis.

He thought about the DCI, an ex-congressman on the Intelligence Committee who everyone in Washington knew was out of his depth. Not a bad man, but less than the country needed during these trying times. Hawthorn couldn't let such a man slow him down. "Probably not. But when did you think I started to care about what Director Lewis wanted?"

"Go get 'em, boss."

Hawthorn smiled. Scott had called him boss throughout their relationship. Even when things had gone sour between them, he'd used it as an epitaph. As he left the room, he found himself wondering whether his old friend had made it out of the Tribune Tower alive. He also couldn't help but recall the last time Scott had met the president of the United States had resulted in Townsend looking just about the same way.

Four years ago

"Get him out of here!" Townsend screamed from inside the Oval Office.

Hawthorn had Scott by the arm and neck as he shoved him into the anteroom that housed the president's personal secretary. Scott didn't resist. He allowed himself to be pushed across the room toward the door to the hallway. Before they reached it, a Secret Service agent burst in, gun drawn.

"No," Townsend shouted behind them, now standing at the door to the Oval. "Let them go!" The Secret Service agent blocked their way, his face clearly not registering the president's order. "Goddamn it, Rob. I said let them go."

At the use of his first name, the agent seemed to snap out of his daze. He holstered his weapon and stepped aside. Hawthorn pushed Scott forward and they passed by him.

As they did, Hawthorn heard Townsend shout, "Get Doc Samuels. Tell him I fell and hit my face on the desk."

Once in the hallway, Hawthorn guided Scott first left and then right, going as far from the press corps as possible. They stopped outside the chief of staff's office. The door was closed without a guard, so it was a safe bet it was empty. Hawthorn threw Scott roughly up against it.

"You just hit the president of the United States in the face," Hawthorn said. "Are you insane? That's the end of you. It'll take every ounce of capital I have to keep you out of Leavenworth."

"Don't do me any favors," Scott snapped. "How could you bring me to that meeting and not give me a heads-up? I can't believe you buy any of that bullshit in there."

"You have to—"

"Only thing I have to do is get out of here before I take your head off."

"Scott—"

"I'm serious. I swear to God, Jim. Step aside or Doc Samuels is going to have two patients tonight."

Hawthorn stepped back, but Scott didn't move.

"What Townsend told you in there. I have to pursue it, Scott. You know I do."

Scott's lips curled back from his teeth, making him look like a dog about to attack. "Go get 'em, boss." He slammed into Hawthorn's shoulder as he pushed by, striding down the corridor to the exit.

The next time Hawthorn saw his friend was the day Scott shot and killed his wife.

Hawthorn entered his office and closed the door behind him. The walls were spare, lacking the brag wall of framed photos with powerful members of the DC elite. He, more than most, understood the fleeting nature of power. And how quickly his own fortunes could turn, requiring that he give up his office to a younger man or some political shit-for-brains appointee. Packing an office was a miserable experience, an insult to add to the injuries he'd sustained over the years.

And for what? His country? He hardly recognized the place anymore. The politics had always been rough and tumble, but now it was abusive and intransient. Disagreements had turned to hatred. Dividing lines about tax policy, immigration, and defense spending now had the zealotry that used to be reserved for abortion and race relations. Both sides cloaked every issue in gauzy morality that was actually just rampant hypocrisy. Perhaps it'd always been this bad and he'd just been a stronger man when he was younger. Impervious to the sideshow while he focused on the security of his nation. At least that had been a success. Or at least he liked to think so.

If he hadn't been at work, would there have just been another man in the role who could have done just as well? Perhaps even better? Another man who would have sacrificed so much time? Put the job ahead of his marriage and his relationships with his kids? Who could have proselytized the importance of family, but still managed to have a two-year-old grandson he hadn't yet held?

Had it all been worth it? It was the question for an old man to ask. But lately he'd felt the years more and more, seen the effects of time with each glance in the mirror. Felt his motor running down from the wear and tear of the life he'd chosen.

It was why he was pushing so hard. Taking chances he never would have allowed himself even a few years ago. Desperation lent itself to mistakes. And in the game he was playing, mistakes could cost him everything.

He picked up the one framed photo on his desk. It was him and his wife, Margery, sitting on wicker chairs down at their place in Sanibel Island, Florida, a few years ago. God, she loved that place. Hunched over on her morning walk doing the Sanibel Shuffle, looking over the millions of shells on the beach for a new gem to add to her collection at the cottage. In the picture, their kids and their spouses stood around them, along with their grandkids.

Margery beamed in the center of it, the queen bee with her people. The light was just right so it was easy to imagine that her cheeks were not sunken, the dark circles under her eyes were not there, that the wig she wore was her own beautiful hair. He looked happy, too, he thought. Tan, rested, at peace. Holding her hand.

It wasn't an hour after that photo before his detail had appeared and whisked him off the island to the nearest heliport to manage a crisis. He couldn't even remember what the problem had been that had dragged him away. He did remember that a day later, while he was in the Situation Room, he'd gotten the call that Margery had died, making the photo he held in his hands the last he would ever take with the love of his life. He remembered that part with perfect clarity.

Had it all been worth it?

Damn if he knew. But this last thing he was doing was going to allow him some closure. Maybe even give him the license he needed to ride off into the sunset and spend his waning years bothering his kids and spoiling his grandchildren. Telling them at every opportunity what a wonderful grandmother they had and how much she loved them all.

He pulled his special phone from his suit jacket pocket and dialed the number. He waited as the series of clicks chirped in his ear, the call routing through dozens of exchanges to mask the location of the woman who answered on the other line.

"Townsend is still alive," came the voice over the line. Hawthorn listened intently for any ambient noise that might give away the woman's location. He'd never met her in person, and he had a feeling that if she had her way, he never would. "You said Roberts would complete the task."

"The daughter is the wild card. We never thought she'd go this far with him. She's having an unexpected effect."

"Use the boy. Send her his ear and see if the effect continues to be so unexpected."

"She hasn't made contact. There's no leverage there."

There was a long pause before she came back. "There has been an asset deployed. Restrict your actions pending instructions." The line went dead.

Hawthorn slipped the phone back into his jacket pocket, the photo still in his hand. Had it all been worth it? He planned to make damn sure that, in the end, it had.

CHAPTER 15

He was late.

Mara checked her watch again even though she'd done so less than a minute ago. Six past noon. In the real world, six minutes late meant a taxi hit traffic, or someone lost track of time while getting ready. In her world, six minutes late meant someone was likely captured or killed.

The Field Museum loomed over her right shoulder, its massive granite columns reminiscent of a Greek temple. One of the premier museums in the world, the Field Museum looked the part, with columned wings extending in either direction from the front entrance, each ending with another small entrance portico. Mara stood below the flight of white marble stairs leading to the main entrance, off to the side in the shade of the trees arranged in a row parallel to the museum. From her vantage, she could see the length of the building and everyone who came or left.

She checked her watch again, feeling foolish as she did so.

It wasn't lost on her that only a day before she'd been in a similar situation. Waiting for the great Scott Roberts to appear from the prison, ogling her watch like a teenager waiting for a date in her living room.

So much had changed since that last time. Her world was

upside-down. At the center of it was Joey, stolen and being held God-knew-where. Overnight, it'd taken all of her willpower not to call Hawthorn and demand his release. It wouldn't have done any good, she knew that in her gut. All it would have done is give the bastards holding him the opportunity to use him against her. One scream from Joey and she knew she'd do anything they told her to.

Beyond Joey, there was her dad. She'd fed her hate toward him so mercilessly over the years that it was hard to let it go. Hard to make the adjustment to the idea that he might not be guilty of the crimes of which she'd convicted him, serving as judge and jury in her own head.

And nearly executioner. She couldn't forget that.

She pulled the burner phone from her pocket and dialed the number from memory. The person on the other end picked it up so quickly that she wasn't sure if it'd actually rung.

"Lordy, you've stumbled into it this time, haven't you?" Jordi said.

"Did I make a mistake when I sent it?" she asked. Jordi had given her specific, albeit complicated instructions on how to send him the contents on the thumb drive they'd taken off Townsend. If she'd messed it up, then who knew who else could gain access to the files.

"No, I got everything all proper-like. That's not the problem."

"So, what's the problem?"

"This encryption. It's like, I dunno. It's almost better than the stuff I create."

"Almost better or better?" She turned in a circle as she spoke, scanning for her dad. Or for a SWAT team closing in on her if he'd somehow been compromised.

"Come on now, this is me you're talking to," Jordi said. "I'll break it. It'll just take longer than I thought."

She heard the hesitation in his voice. "But . . ."

"But what am I going to find when I open it? I see the news, Mara. I can imagine where this file came from. I mean, holy shit."

"Jordi," she said softly. "Listen. If you don't want to do it, I understand. But if not you, I don't have anyone else I trust." She paused for a few seconds, listening to him breathing into the phone. She had a sudden pang of fear that she'd pushed him too far with this ask. With an IQ off the charts, of course he would have figured out where the file had come from. "I can still trust you, can't I?"

"Ask me that again and I'll drain your bank accounts and ruin your credit."

"Whatever is on there," she said, "I'm not going to use it to do something you wouldn't agree with. I'm not going to compromise national interest."

"It's not you I'm worried about," Jordi said. "It's the company you keep."

She had no answer for that. "Then just trust me that I won't let him have anything unless it's absolutely necessary."

"It's just that—"

"I trust you more than anyone right now," she said. "All I'm asking is that you return the favor. I need this, Jordi. Please."

"Please?" Jordi sighed. "That's exactly the sort of thing that gets me in trouble. I'll call you when I have something. Bye, luv. Watch out for the men with guns. Seems like they're all after you."

He ended the call before she had a chance to reply.

She slid the phone into her pocket as she looked over the plaza again, trying to spot her dad's telltale swagger among the crowd of tourists. She found herself wondering if Jordi's concerns were founded. Maybe she'd already developed a blind spot when it came to her dad.

His attempts to get the identity of her mom's killer out of Townsend had seemed sincere. But it also could have been an act. A carefully orchestrated manipulation to gain back her trust. But to what end? It made no sense.

Still, doubts about him swirled in her head. She didn't know if it was from habit or if it was his bullheaded stubbornness not to give her the whole story. He knew more than he was telling her. He'd admitted it was the case, saying he wanted to protect her if things went wrong.

It sounded good, but it had the aftertaste of a lie.

And it wouldn't have been the first time he'd looked her in the eye and hidden a dark truth from her.

Mara and her mom hated fishing. It was Lucy's thing and her dad knew it. Still, he'd dragged all of them along on the float-plane trip to Canada. Mara thought it was just a ploy to get her and Lucy away from their boyfriends.

Her dad hadn't adjusted well to his daughters hitting the high school years, admitting that he still saw them as kids and that kids didn't need to go on dates, especially with guys who were older and could already drive. He was gone from home a lot, some kind of salesman for an international company called Rayco Technologies. Lucy preferred the title from his business card, global account executive, because it sounded cooler. But Mara didn't care what it was called. Traveling around the world was pretty sweet, but business and sales sounded as dull as mud to her. Almost as dull as her mom's job working as a cultural attaché with the State Department. She didn't even begin to understand what she did, only that she spoke a bunch of languages and was endlessly frustrated with Mara's inability to conjugate verbs in French.

All she knew was that her dad wasn't home much, but it was always fun when he was. Her sister didn't always feel the same way.

Mara had it a little easier than her sister, or so Lucy complained all the time. There were three years between them, so by the time Lucy was a high school senior and Mara was a freshman, Lucy had already fought most of the battles about boys and curfews and drinking. Their parents weren't a defeated enemy, they still put up plenty of obstacles to keep Mara from having fun, ruining her chances of being popular, but they were softer with her. She would never admit that to Lucy, but it was true. She didn't look forward to Lucy leaving for college the next year because she imagined that her mom and dad would make up for the empty nest by fixating on her every move. That was going to suck.

She was also going to miss her sister. Another thing she wasn't about to admit to Lucy.

"C'mon, boat's leaving," her dad called out.

He was dressed like he'd stumbled into an L.L. Bean store and was blindsided by an overzealous salesman. Hip waders extended from his feet to his midsection, held in place by suspenders that gave him an old-timey feel. He wore a plaid flannel shirt and a fishing vest with a dozen pockets. A floppy hat with flies burrowed into the brim completed the picture.

Her mom walked up next to her with a steaming cup of coffee in her hand. She slid her other hand around Mara's back and pulled her close. "He's like a little boy."

"More like a little dork," Mara said.

"Yeah, but he's our dork."

"Do I have to go?"

"There's no Internet out here. No telephone. No TV. You might as well learn to like fishing. 'Cause we're here for six days, whether we like it or not."

"Maybe you could fake an injury," Lucy said as she trotted by them, fishing pole and tackle box in hand. She had a way of doing that, adding a line into a conversation she wasn't part of and then scurrying off like a little rat.

"Maybe I could give you a real one," Mara called out. Her mom's arm squeezed around her waist sharply. It didn't quite hurt, but it got her attention. "I was just kidding around."

"How often do we get out together?" her mom asked. "Can you even remember the last time?"

She did. Disney World when she was thirteen. One of the best weeks of her life. "I dunno," she said.

"Exactly. Between my work and your dad's, we're never together. This trip is a way to catch up for lost time."

"Is that why you and Dad disappeared into the woods yesterday? Is that what you call it when you get older? Making up for lost time?"

"Mara!"

"I agree, Mom," Lucy said, passing by again on the way to the cabin. "Sound travels on water. Pretty gross."

"What's gross?" her dad asked, walking up, grinning like he was a puppy who was just told he got to go for a ride in the car.

Mara and her mom both laughed. "Nothing," Mara said. "Are we going to catch some fish today or what?"

"That's the spirit," her dad said. "Prizes for first fish, most fish, and biggest fish."

"How about a prize for the most tangled lines?" her mom asked.

"That person cleans the fish," he said. "The Roberts family is eating well tonight."

Lucy walked back to the dock, this time carrying a cooler. "If Dad and I catch the fish, that is."

She was right, of course. Lucy and her dad landed fish left and right. Huge walleye that stripped the line from the reel and bent their poles until they looked like they might break. She and her mom caught one every now and then, but switched to playing cards on the small pop-up table they'd brought with them. Her dad didn't seem to mind. He had them all on a boat together, and that appeared to be good enough for him.

A few hours in, Lucy hooked up with a monster fish. Her excitement, and then her dad's once he saw the fish break water, was contagious. Mara put down her cards and stood up to get a look.

"Careful," Lucy said, nearly losing her balance from Mara shifting her weight on the small boat.

Lucy's adjustment, along with Mara's, just made it worse and the boat rocked hard to the side.

Then they heard the gunshot.

Something zinged past Mara's ear.

Then her mom had a hold of her arm, dragging her down, sliding her body on top of hers. The boat surged forward, her dad applying full throttle.

"What is it? What's happening?" Mara screamed.

"Stay down," her mom said into her ear. Urgent but calm. That made her relax a little. If she was calm, then it probably wasn't a big deal.

The boat cranked to the left, then back to the right, the engine whining at full speed.

"There's a cove," her dad yelled from the captain's chair. "I'm getting off. Keep going down lake. You have coms?"

"I have coms," her mom said.

The boat barely slowed, but Mara felt it rock and she knew her dad had just jumped into the water. Her mom was on her feet and reached the steering wheel just as the boat was headed into a stand of tall grass. It cut through the grass and burst out into a narrow channel of water. Her mom cut left and took them back into the main body of the lake.

Lucy was crawling toward them from the bow, her face pale white.

"Are you hurt?" her mom yelled over the screaming engine.

Lucy shook her head. "Where's Dad? We can't leave him."

"He can take care of himself," their mom said. "You girls stay down."

"Mom! Don't leave him. You can't," Mara screamed.

Their mom, keeping a hand on the wheel, crouched down low out of the wind. "Your dad knows what he's doing. You girls want to worry about someone, worry for the idiot who just fired that shot at us. Now stay down. Not another word."

Lucy wrapped her arms around Mara and hugged her tight. Mara hugged her back and held on as they bounced down the river, running from whatever lay behind them.

Twenty minutes later, they pulled into a cove that twisted and turned into the marshy weeds. Once they were far enough back, the tree canopy reached out from both sides to form a kind of tunnel. Their mom cut the motor and told Lucy to throw out the anchor.

"Are you going to tell us what's going on?" Mara asked.

Her mom pulled a small walkie-talkie from her pocket and put it on the console above the steering wheel. "Now we wait."

They'd heard that tone before and knew there was no point in asking further. Lucy reached out and held Mara's hand. She hadn't done that in years, but she'd never been happier to have her sister by her side than at that moment. She clutched her hand and leaned into her chest, letting her stroke her hair.

It was over an hour that they sat anchored in the cove. A sickening wait, during which the small walkie-talkie her mom held in her hand refused to make a sound. Finally, her dad's voice rang out. "All clear. You ladies all right?"

Her mom, who'd gone from looking angry when they'd first anchored, to frustrated as the minutes stretched out, to scared as the time went longer, put her hand to her mouth and stifled a short sob. As fast as it was there, it was gone. She toggled the walkie-talkie and replied, "What took you so long, Roberts? You've got fish to clean."

She gave Mara and Lucy a wink as if to say everything was all right. Mara wasn't buying it.

"Had to tell this fool hunter that it wasn't duck season and that he wasn't alone on this lake," came the reply. To Mara's ears it sounded like the most obvious lie in the world. Like a bad actor saying some shitty line they hadn't even bothered to completely memorize.

But her mom ate it up. Or more likely, she thought, she was part of the lie.

"Was the guy hunting by himself?"

"He said he was. But he's outside waiting for me. I'm going to ask him again."

Her mom lowered the walkie-talkie, frowning. She thought for a second before answering. "Should I meet you?"

"The floatplane's coming for pickup. Tell the girls sorry, but when I came back to the cabin there was a message from work. I gotta go in. Vacation's over."

Lucy groaned. But all Mara could think was that her dad was telling another lie.

"Okay, we'll hold here until contact with the floatplane."

A long pause and then her dad's voice came back softer. "Sorry, Wendy. I wanted this time . . . I wanted, you know . . ."

"I know," she said. "Just be careful."

Lucy moaned about how unfair it all was, how both of them always had work things getting in the way. That the whole purpose of the trip was to have a getaway from work. Their mom just repeated that she knew and that she was sorry. Mara didn't say a thing. She was piecing together what her dad had meant on the radio, trying to read between the lies. She'd been to the gun range enough with her dad to know that the sound she'd heard hadn't been a shotgun. And why would the hunter be at their cabin waiting for her dad to ask him again if he was alone?

Then, as the breeze drifted toward them, Mara heard a new sound in the air. Her mother heard it, too, cocking her head to the side the second it came. Soft at first, then louder. Proving that sound did carry over water.

Especially when it was the sound of a man screaming in pain.

With sudden insight, Mara understood it was her dad *asking* the hunter if he was alone. And that the hunter hadn't been there for ducks. She made eye contact with her mom and they shared a look, confirming that they both knew the truth of it.

Her mom reached down and clicked on the boat's radio, turning up the music to drown out the man's screams. As they waited for her dad to be done getting answers, it occurred to Mara that she maybe she really didn't know what her parents did for a living. One thing was sure. Her dad wasn't a salesman. He was something else altogether.

Mara checked her watch again. Twelve minutes past. There wasn't a large crowd outside the museum, so she didn't worry that she'd missed him going inside. Even with her thoughts floating back through memories she hadn't dredged up for years, she'd kept her attention sharp. She decided to give it until fifteen after and then move on.

She tried to push away the flashes of the rest of the fishing trip. The fake smile on her dad's face when he'd met them at the floatplane. The way his change of clothes made her even more suspicious about what he'd been doing. The dark red fleck on his neck that her mom wiped off as she walked up to him. A fleck that looked like dried blood.

After that trip, she'd known the truth, or at least the version of the truth she conjured up in her head. On the way home, she'd played that day over and over in her mind. Not only her dad's reaction, but her mom's. Everything about her had changed the second the shot was fired. She'd turned cold and hard, focused only on their escape. She was barely recognizable. Such a different person that for weeks she found it uncomfortable to be around her. It was like a mask had been pulled back and once seen, the real person underneath it couldn't be forgotten.

It was a year before they came fully clean about who and what they were, and only then because she'd left them no choice in the matter. Her parents were out, a rare date night because they were both in town. She'd presented a good rendition of "bored teenager" as they left, flopped out on the couch with the TV on while talking on the phone with one of her friends. But once their car had cleared the driveway, she was on her feet, all business.

She started in their bedroom. Through their drawers, closets, under their bed. She didn't know exactly what she was looking for, but she felt a strange sense of certainty that she would find something. And that something wouldn't belong in the perfectly designed suburban life of Scott and Wendy Roberts.

Her first search came up empty. But that only made her more resolute. She started over, this time searching in the nearly impossible to reach places. The first thing she found were the guns. Back then she didn't know what kind they were, only that they were cold and black and taped to the back of the top nightstand drawer on either side of the bed.

After finding these, her search took on a more frantic pace. She stopped worrying about putting things back in their places. She didn't care if her parents, the liars, found out she'd rifled through their things. A creak in the floor under the area rug stopped her in her tracks. After rolling it back, an effort that required moving a chest of drawers and her dad's leather reading chair, she uncovered the spot. A tiny hole in the floor was her way in. Unbending a wire hanger, she inserted it into the hole, twisted it, and yanked. A small section of the floor lifted up to reveal a small lock box.

She stared at it for a few seconds, almost not believing the search had actually paid off, then quickly lifted it out. It was a combo lock with six digits on it. She set it to all zeroes. Nothing. She knew their ATM pin codes from when they'd given her their card to get money for them. She tried both of those. Nothing. She'd never get it. She needed to break the box open. She scoured the room for a tool to bash it with. Her dad kept an iron for his dress shirts in the closet. She ran and grabbed it, then positioned the box on the ground in front of her.

But as she lifted the iron over her head, her dad's voice, calm and soft, came from the bedroom door behind her.

"1-0-0-3-6-3," was all he said.

She spun around. Both of them were there, watching her. Their expressions confused her. She thought they'd be incensed. Angry at the violation. Instead they both looked sad and, oddly enough, just a little proud of her.

"If you want to open it, the code is 10-03-63," he said.

Saying the numbers that way, she recognized it as her mother's birthday. She spun the numbers and opened the box. Inside were stacks of cash. She knew dollars and euros, but there were some Asian currencies she didn't recognize. There were passports, a bundle for each of them. She flipped through, seeing different names for her mom and dad, different nationalities, different identities. Each had at least one credit card that matched the name inside.

She put everything back in the box and turned to her parents. Adrenaline pumped through her body. She felt a mix of excitement and terror. It came down to the next question she asked, the question she wasn't certain she wanted the answer to. With a shaking voice, she asked, "Are you the good guys or the bad guys?"

Her dad's expression turned pained. But the question didn't shake her mother. Mara never forgot her answer.

"We're the good guys," she said, walking across the room

and sitting next to her on the bed. "But we're the kind that have to do bad things to protect what we love."

Then the three of them had sat in the room together and they'd told her the truth. Her dad worked for the CIA. Her mom did as well, but described herself as more of a "diplomat with an extra portfolio." Of course, Mara had asked a million questions, apparently none of them answerable due to security reasons. By the end, the feeling of betrayal was gone, replaced by a sense of pride in her parents. And worry that they lived in constant danger.

From then on, whenever her dad was on a business trip, her stomach twisted as she imagined the danger he might be in. She, Lucy, and her mom had spent many nights watching late-night TV together, trying to block out the fear as they waited for a check-in phone call. Whenever the call was late, they all felt the anxiety as the minutes, and sometimes the hours, ticked away past the time when he was supposed to call. None of them discussing it, only watching show after show of bad TV until the phone finally rang telling them he was all right.

As she stood waiting for him, eyes searching the growing crowds of tourists heading toward the museum, she felt like a kid again, curled up on the couch and waiting with a cold dread that this time was going to be different. This time the phone would ring and it would be some stranger to tell her mom that something had gone wrong.

Only now she was waiting by herself. Her mom and sister were dead. And only two days before, she'd considered her dad dead to her, too. It'd been a long time since she'd felt anything but bitterness toward him, but that was changing. As she checked her watch again and again, she told herself the lie that she was concerned about him because he was still her path to saving Joey. That his safety was an operational necessity.

But it was more than that. Now that there was a chance he was innocent, even if it was still slight and unproven, she felt the possibility of having him back in her life. In Joey's life. She was worried because it was her dad who was missing. And she needed him.

She felt her eyes sting and she blinked hard against the tears that welled there, both surprised and angry at her reaction.

Then she spotted him across the plaza. He had a ball cap pulled low over his eyes, and he wore a Chicago Cubs windbreaker that looked two sizes too big for him, but she knew it was him. She let out a short sob and then turned away as if checking the perimeter to make sure no one was watching them. She used the movement to discreetly wipe her eyes. There was no way she was going to give him the satisfaction of knowing she'd been worried.

"Hey," he said as he walked up, as if they were just two people meeting for lunch in the park.

"What took you so long?" she said, trying to sound casual.

"Cubbies went into extra innings. Wanted to see the end of the game."

"Funny, it's not baseball season."

He smiled, but it turned into a grimace. Now that he was closer she saw he had a swollen lip and bruises down one side of his face and neck. "I should have given you the harder exit. You're younger. More agile."

"Nah, your old man immune system couldn't have handled the Chicago River."

They turned and walked down the row of trees, paralleling the museum and heading back toward the city. She noticed he favored his right side as he walked.

"We made a splash in the news," she said. "Wall-to-wall coverage of the global warming activists who kidnapped and roughed up the president."

"Imagine that. Who knew the tree huggers had it in them?"

"So Townsend is playing ball."

"We'll see. Who knows what story he told the Secret Service? That old saying about how do you know when a politician is lying—"

"When his lips are moving."

"Right. I'm not trusting anything from that man."

"Why'd he choose global warming activists? I thought he was a big environmentalist?"

"Every news channel is playing the highlight reel of Townsend's environmental record, making that same point. They're reminding America about the one good thing there was about the Townsend presidency."

"He wants to pull an Al Gore."

"A Nobel Prize is a pretty coveted piece of hardware. I bet he'll use this to launch a huge environmental campaign. Not because he gives two shits about the polar bears and their shrinking ice floes, but because it's something that'll draw cameras and coverage."

"Maybe he'll accidentally do some good along the way."

"I doubt he'll live that long. Whoever set us up to kill him isn't going to stop that easily." He waved a hand ahead of them. "We need to get the hell out of Dodge. The truck's up here."

She grabbed his arm and pulled him roughly to a stop. "We need to get Joey."

Scott's shoulders hunched forward. He looked suddenly tired and old. Whatever he'd been through over the last eighteen hours had done a number on him. She wondered for the first time if he was up to the challenge ahead of them.

"We need to regroup. Just a few hours to think and figure this out. Preferably with no one from either Omega or the Agency trying to kill me while I'm doing it."

"Joey—"

"Is all I'm thinking about, Mara. Trust me."

She let go of his arm. Did she trust him? She was starting to, and she realized that might be a problem. "Any ideas?"

"There's a safe house. A farm just over the Iowa state line."

"Hawthorn might be Omega, but he's still pulling the levers at the Agency. They'll be watching their own places."

"It's not an Agency location. They don't know about it." She must have looked unconvinced because he continued. "I'm going to fall asleep standing up if we don't go to the truck. Unless you're willing to carry me. . . ."

"Let's go, then. But you're going to fill me in on some missing details on the way there. To hell with deniability, I want to know everything. I've already defied direct orders, assaulted an ex-president, and probably another dozen things that could land me in prison, so I don't think I have anything to lose at this point."

He looked defeated and worn-out. Part of her wanted to press him right there and leverage his exhaustion to her benefit. It was what she'd do if she were on a mission. But she didn't. Instead, she slid her arm into his and took some of his weight. He didn't object, and together they walked slowly toward where he'd indicated the truck was parked.

She'd waited years for the truth. A couple more hours wouldn't make a difference.

Besides, a part of her buried deep inside knew something her conscious mind refused to acknowledge. She wasn't totally sure that she wanted to know the truth at all.

CHAPTER 16

Preston Townsend was enjoying himself more than he had in a long time. The entire nation was tuned in to his story, hanging on every detail that was released about his abduction. Every headline scroll on each network and cable news channel had his name on it. He was loving every minute of it.

He rested comfortably in his favorite leather chair in his den, a space designed to make him look learned and serious. He hadn't read any of the books that filled the shelves behind him, but he'd picked them out himself based on the titles and authors so that they conveyed the image he wanted. The cameraman and two producers were in the room with him setting up for the next interview. His chief of staff Mirren refreshed his glass of water.

"The last one was perfect," she said. "Can I get you anything else?"

"No, thank you," he said. "You've been great through this. I appreciate it."

She smiled, seemed to want to say more, but then gave way to the hair and makeup person and exited the room.

Townsend watched Mirren leave as the tech touched up his hair, wondering who her replacement ought to be. Did she really think he didn't remember how dismissive she'd been over the last few months when she thought she was on a sinking ship?

He couldn't wait to fire her and put a high-powered pro in her place. The fun was about to start, and he needed a better team at his side.

"Two minutes, Mr. President," one of the producers called out.

"Who is this one?"

"NBC. They are breaking into regular programming to carry it."

He smiled. This was the kind of treatment he enjoyed. He tried to remember the last time he'd felt this good and had a hard time coming up with something. No, this was his sweet spot. The eyes of the world on him. It was the way things were supposed to be.

Casting a shadow on his fun was the fact that he'd nearly been killed, a fact that bothered him more than he cared to let on. Whenever he closed his eyes, he saw the rage on Roberts's face when he'd held the gun to his head. Then, strangely, there was a second image. A police officer pointing a gun at him. But that one was hazy and confused. The SWAT team had explained to him that the CPD uniform cop had been the first to find him, so that must have been what he was remembering. He'd given instructions for the cop to be found and brought to him. What a photo op. But he was still waiting on them to figure out the name of the officer.

Omega worried him, too. Sending Roberts to kill him had been a bold move executed with subtle tactics. If Roberts was to be believed, even he didn't understand he was being played for a pawn in their game. If Roberts had been successful, then it never would have been traced back to Omega. The perfect alibi. Smart. But the fact that he was still breathing showed it hadn't been smart enough. Even the mighty Omega, with its tentacles seeming to spread into every organization around the world, wasn't infallible.

But they were tenacious. And he worried that they would try again.

Still, Omega's modus operandi was to stay in the shadows. He doubted an assault in the immediate future. Besides, Roberts had assured that his personal protection unit had been beefed back up to nearly where it had been while he was in office. The Secret Service's embarrassment meant he would be safe. For a while at least.

And during that time, he intended to have some fun. It'd been a while since he'd had popular support. Even the last two years of his presidency had been a real drag. The Democrats had wiped the floor with his party in the midterm elections of his second term, running the whole thing as a referendum on him. Once they retook control of the House, the oxygen had been sucked out from his entire legislative agenda. He'd been a lame duck from the day after the election until he left office as one of the most unpopular presidents in American history. Approval ratings even lower than Bush the Younger. That hurt.

No, he had to think back to his first days in office to remember a time when he'd had this much fun. That had been far better, of course. The media reporting on his every move. The entire world voraciously digesting every utterance from his mouth. The way entire markets rose or fell just from a sentence or two spoken to the press pool. The feeling of power had been intoxicating, and he'd reveled in it.

His kidnapping and assault had created a media buzz and an interest in him that felt very much like those heady early days. Roberts had been right about that. Reporters who'd come after him with knives and flamethrowers when they tore down his White House until it was no more than rubble, fawned over his condition, expressing admiration for his resilience and positive attitude. One of the anchors on Fox News actually choked up, live on air, at the sight of the ex-president with his bruised face and swollen eye.

The environmental angle couldn't have been working better. As a conservative Republican, no one in his party had seen it coming when he'd declared his support for climate change initiatives toward the end of his presidency. Of course, the punditry had decried it as a desperate bid for relevancy at best, or an attempt to distract from his administration's many scandals at worst.

Truth was, he'd never bought into the climate change deniers who filled the right wing of his party. But he loved the contribution checks they wrote, so he'd been happy to join the anti-science chorus throughout his career, calling into doubt the truth of climate change, even in the face of near consensus among the world's most brilliant minds. Once it was clear his presidency was going down the toilet bowl of history, especially once those same ignorant, science haters turned their backs on him, he'd taken off the shackles and committed the cardinal sin in politics. He'd told people how he really felt.

It'd gone well enough. Some commentators had even compared him to Nixon going to China back in the seventies. Just as it took a conservative to reach out to China, because a liberal would have been suspected of caving to socialism, a conservative breaking ranks and trumpeting climate change was enough to create a national conversation. Until the CIA scandal; then it was back to being compared to Nixon for other reasons.

But, thanks to the short attention span of the American people, that was ancient history now.

Today, he was an American hero again. And damn if it didn't feel good.

"Mr. President, I have to say, your willingness to excuse this outrageous attack is leaving some people surprised," the CNN anchor said. The camera was set up in the living room of his Lincoln Park home. A location suddenly with a much-improved security detail since the events the day before.

Townsend smiled and then winced just enough for effect. "I'm fine. It'll take more than a black eye to keep me down. Besides, I understand what these young people who grabbed me are so worried about. The Earth is in trouble and we need to take action to save it."

"You said young people," the anchor said. "Earlier you said your kidnappers wore masks and you were not able to determine any specifics about them. How do you know they were young?"

Townsend was sure that viewers watching the interview would be leaning forward, loving the feeling that a gotcha moment was about to happen on live TV. But the anchor had walked right into where he'd wanted. "I assume they were young because they weren't aware of everything I've done for the environment. That I was not only on their side, but actually an environmental activist. If you remember, during my administration, we . . ." And then he was off to the races on a hit parade of his accomplishments.

After the light went off on the camera, the members of his staff in the room broke out in applause. Townsend knew they were kissing his ass, and he loved it.

Mirren, his chief of staff, walked up and handed him a printout. "The media requests keep pouring in," she said. "National shows are lined up. The local shows are listed below for you to choose from. We also have to decide if we want to do late-night and who first."

Townsend stood, enjoying the adrenaline high he was on, and took the paper offered him. Another aide, a young man whose name he'd never bothered to learn, rushed forward to hand him a coffee. Townsend took a sip. Prepared exactly as he liked it. "We need that date for a climate conference. Something to announce on these shows."

"Greenpeace has a conference in Miami next month. Sierra Club has something in two weeks. Or we have the option to create our own if we don't want to piggyback on something already set up."

"Let's see what the capacity is for their events and then think through the pros and cons of both options."

"All that is in the briefing paper," Mirren said, clearly pleased with herself for anticipating his question.

And he was pleased. His staff had come to life the same way he had. Instead of sitting on retirement watch, they were standing, at least for a news cycle or two, at the center of the universe.

Townsend glanced at his watch. "When's the next interview?"

"You have a ten-minute break. Then it's MSNBC. Also, Patterson's staff called again to set up a call. You want me to put him off again?"

"I'm not talking to him."

"It's awkward for the sitting president not to be able to say he spoke to his predecessor after such a public attack."

"Awkward? Kind of like it was awkward when he asked me not to campaign for him? Asked me to not speak at his nominating convention? To hell with Patterson."

Mirren glanced over at the camera operator, then at the other staff in the room who were all studiously pretending they hadn't heard the outburst. "But we're trying to change—"

Townsend held up a hand to stop her. Under his breath, for her ears only, he said, "Tell them I'll say we spoke. He can say the same. It's good for both of us. And better for me that I don't have to talk to the son of a bitch."

"You got it."

His phone rang in his jacket pocket. He pulled it out and recognized the number. "I'll be in my study. No one disturbs me."

He answered the phone. "Hold on," he said, then lowered it from his ear as he walked out of the room, across the foyer, and into his study. His heart pounded in his chest. This was the phone call he'd been waiting for. He took a deep breath, then raised the phone to his ear. "You know who did this to me, don't you?"

Jim Hawthorn answered without hesitation. "I have a pretty good idea."

"Did you send him?"

"C'mon, Preston."

"Was it you?"

A long pause. Then, "I think we need to talk. It's time."

"So talk. This is a secure line."

"You don't really believe that, do you? I'll come out. Tomorrow."

Townsend hesitated, working through the optics of Hawthorn walking up to his front door in front of the press pool that had gathered on the street outside. He'd be able to work up some kind of excuse. Besides, an active government official coming to check up on his well-being only made him look more powerful.

"Okay, tomorrow. But if you don't shoot me straight and give me some goddamn answers, I'm going to tell my new Secret

Service detail to give you a body cavity search. Right now, they're not inclined to tell me no."

"The shiner looks good on TV," Hawthorn said. "Those global warming activists sure pack a punch."

The line went dead. Just like Hawthorn to get in the last word. Townsend clenched his hand around the phone and nearly hurled it against the wall, but he stopped himself. All of his favorite photos of himself covered nearly every square inch, and he didn't want to damage any of them.

A soft knock came on the door. It was Mirren. "I'm sorry, Mr. President. But we're one minute out from the MSNBC interview."

He smiled. Another dose of adulation and sympathy was just what the doctor ordered. He touched his fingers to the bruise around his eye and then poked at it violently. It hurt like hell, but he wanted it as angry-looking as possible on TV. He opened the door and grinned at Mirren, ready for his close-up.

CHAPTER 17

Finding the place hadn't been that hard even though Asset doubted the Secret Service would even look for it. The story told by Townsend had thrown them off the scent of the actual people responsible for his kidnapping and beating, and no one had questioned the ex-president's version of events.

Because what possible reason would an ex-president of the United States have for looking into camera after camera on the news programs to lie to the American people about who'd so easily defeated his Secret Service protective detail, beat him bloody, and then dumped him in the bottom of a closet? If the truth ever came out, Townsend was going to set a new record for least popular ex-president. A record he already held.

But Asset knew Scott and Mara Roberts had been the perpetrators of this particular crime. He also knew someone had to provision them for the assault, and that it had to be someone Roberts trusted. If it was some regular black-market purchase, a patriotic seller might have put two and two together after seeing the details of the attack on TV and decided it was their American duty to call in a tip to the authorities. Anonymously, of course. Patriotism only went so far.

As Asset got out of the car, he thought about his own love for his adopted country. Serbia held no part of his heart. But there'd been a time when Mother Russia had meant something to him. No, it'd meant everything to him. But that was a long time ago, in a different world where a nineteen-year-old version of himself wore a uniform without a shred of cynicism, only pride. That kid was gone, scoured faceless in the mountains of Afghanistan and deserts of Syria. Damaged by what he'd seen, then destroyed by what he'd done in revenge.

Still, after all the years of chiseling his psyche into its current perfect version of a paid killer, the order to kill a U.S. president had caught him off guard. He knew America. He'd studied her as he would any adversary, recognizing both her beautiful strengths and her terrible weaknesses. Americans failed to comprehend just how omnipresent the U.S. was in the world's psyche, but Asset understood perfectly. An ex-president, even one universally despised like Townsend, was part of not only the country's inherent fabric, but the world's as well. Killing him was going to be news that reached into every far corner of the globe. Parts of the world would cheer when they heard, but it was destined to raise a rage in America not seen since the attacks of 9/11.

The immensity of the act made him pause. Made him question. Made him doubt.

Made him feel weak.

And there was nothing he despised more.

He used his training to transform the anger he felt at his own emotions into fierce intention. This was a job, just like any other. The next time he had the president in his sights, he wouldn't allow such weakness to slow him down.

The street was empty except for some dogs digging through a pile of trash to his right. He took in the cameras positioned around the perimeter of the building and felt a small rush of appreciation for a fellow perfectionist. His contacts in the area had pulled Harold "Harry" Walker's name out of the air for him within an hour of his first inquiry. There were a couple other men in the city who could have provided the supplies, and a crazy lady who operated a gun hall out of Chinatown, but Harry Walker was the one who did it.

Ex-Marine.

Ex-contractor for the CIA.

Ex-friend of Scott Roberts.

Soon-to-be ex-weapons dealer in Chicago's South Side.

Only, he wasn't really a dealer. According to his sources, Harry bought guns to get them off the streets, paying top dollar for the real powerful, destructive stuff that had no place in an American city. Take the money and run. No questions asked.

But he still serviced a handful of high-end pros from the old days, agents who did private protection work or corporate espionage gigs.

Or helped an old friend kidnap a president.

He opened the door to the pawnshop and walked inside.

The place looked like any other pawnshop. Mostly junk that no one wanted or needed. A sad shrine to people's failing fortunes, a battlefield graveyard in their desperate fight to stave off hitting rock bottom.

"Can I help you?" a gangly young man spoke up from behind the U-shaped counter. He wore a jacket that was too big for him and he slouched, but neither of those fooled Asset. The smallest movements, the smooth glide of the man's hands across the glass countertop, tipped him off that the man was someone to be reckoned with.

"Here to see Harry Walker," he said.

"He's not here. What can I help you with?"

Asset looked up to the camera mounted on the ceiling nearest him. "Just a few minutes of your time, Mr. Walker. I'm friends with Cedric Rol."

"Look, mister," the young man said. "Maybe you don't hear so good, but I said Harry's not here. Now, if you're looking for some baseball cards or an iPhone 5 with a cracked screen, I can hook you up."

Asset remained staring at the camera, ignoring the man. He spread his arms and lifted his sports jacket to show his beltline.

"Whitey, check him," came a voice over an overhead speaker. The young man showed no sign he was embarrassed that he'd been caught in a lie. He deadpanned, "What do you know. Looks like Harry's here after all."

He walked out from behind the counter and motioned for Asset to raise his arms again. Asset complied and Whitey gave him a rough pat down. When he felt up his groin, Asset whispered, "Shake it more than twice means you're playing with it."

Whitey stepped back and nodded to the camera.

The back door buzzed and a tall African American man with a white beard stepped out. He didn't look too happy to see him. "Cedric usually lets me know if he's sending someone over. He didn't mention you."

"We both know Cedric Rol is dead, Mr. Walker," Asset said. His eyes danced over the wall behind the old man. He spotted a hole where a gun muzzle appeared, trained on him. This was going to be more difficult than he'd planned, but nothing he couldn't handle. "But I believe we both knew him."

Harry made a show of leaning back against the counter, his arms spread wide. To most people it would look like he was making himself vulnerable as a sign of trust. But it was an easy gesture with two other guns backing him up. One behind the wall. And the young kid, Whitey, had taken a position behind him. Still nothing he couldn't work with. He'd kill the two back-ups and then take his time with the old man. If there were more men in the back, they might prove a complication, but he didn't think there were. Otherwise there'd be a third gun on him.

"Maybe we did," Harry said. "Maybe we didn't. Still not a fan of someone comin' in my store without a little heads-up about it. Makes me feel, I don't know, a little nervous."

Asset didn't like this man. He was arrogant. Disrespectful. He felt a small rush as he clicked through the options he'd employ to get him to talk. Even after he told him everything he knew about Scott and Mara Roberts, Asset promised himself a little extra time with the bastard to make him pay for his disrespect. It was an indulgence, but all work and no play, as the saying went.

He searched the walls around him until he found what he

needed. A mirror, half covered with the Pabst Blue Ribbon logo, hung at just the right angle to show him the young man behind him. His eyes darted there for only a second, but it was enough for Harry to notice.

"Whitey, watch out for—"

But he never finished the sentence.

Asset had his phone out of his pocket, spun, and hurled it at Whitey's head. The kid's reflexes were good, but not good enough. Instead of hitting him square between the eyes, the phone hit his right temple and careened off.

Whoever was behind the wall either had slow reflexes or much better ones than his friend, because no shot was fired. Whitey was lucky either way. Asset had already dropped to the ground, so a shot at him would have struck the guy he'd just beaned with his phone.

Using the second of confusion, Asset launched himself forward across the ground, sweeping the man's leg and then crawling over him like a snake wrapping up its prey.

As he did, he felt a bulge on the man's waistline. A second later he had Whitey's knife held up to his throat.

The man tensed and then went still.

Good. He didn't want to kill the man. Not yet anyway. A corpse made a terrible bargaining chip.

"Hey, hey, hey," Harry said. "Chill out now. Hold on."

Asset grinned. The old man obviously had affection for the man under his knife. That was helpful.

He pulled Whitey to his feet, knife at his throat. He whispered in his ear. "I know you're trained, but nothing has prepared you to fight me. Struggle and I'll open your throat. Understand?"

Whitey made a soft, gurgling sound that Asset took for agreement.

"That's a good boy." Asset forced the man to stand in front of him, a human shield between him and the now two guns pointed at him. He hadn't even seen the old man pull the gun, but there it was, a very serious looking Model Smith & Wesson

500, a hand cannon if there ever was one. Asset had the feeling Harry Walker knew how to use it, too.

"Let's try this again," Asset said.

The old man showed no sign of nerves, only resolve. Ex-military for sure. "You might just be the stupidest sumbitch who ever walked in here." He put up his hand. The door behind Asset made a hollow *thunk*. Locked.

A smile creased Asset's face. The door didn't matter. He hadn't plan on going anywhere.

"I just wanted to make certain I had your attention," Asset said. "Do I have it now?"

"Oh yeah, you got it."

"Good," Asset said. "I need information about Scott and Mara Roberts. I need to know where they've gone."

The old man barked out a short laugh. "That's what you're here for?"

"You find it amusing?"

"Yeah, I find it *amusing*," the man said, emphasizing the last word in a mocking tone. "'Cause you're gonna die trying to get information I don't even have."

"Shoot this asshole," Whitey said.

"Shut up," the old man said.

"Yes," Asset agreed. "Shut up, Whitey."

Asset looked back to the old man, calculating the steps to reach him, the different cover he could use, the items on the walls of the pawnshop he could use as weapons. He needed Harry alive to interrogate him, which made the whole thing more complicated. But only barely.

Harry's intuition was strong because he seemed to sense he was about to make a move. "Why don't you let Whitey go and we'll let you just get the hell out of here? Chalk this as just one big cluster of a fuck?"

"Sorry, but I don't—"

Asset stopped. His second phone rang, vibrating in his pocket, a very particular cadence that he recognized.

He turned his knife blade so that the point was jammed under his prisoner's throat. If the men in front of him had any training at all, they'd know taking a shot at him would end up with the knife four inches in the man's neck.

Slowly, with his free hand, he pulled out his phone.

"What the fuck?" the old man said. "Are we keeping you from something more important?"

Asset glanced at the screen and smiled.

"Yes, you are," he said. "Your information is no longer necessary. I'm going to leave, but maybe I'll be back later to see you. We can finish this little standoff then."

The old man grinned, showing a mouthful of metal teeth. "Maybe I'd like you to stay a while. Visit. Drink some sweet tea together out on my porch. Then you can tell me who you are and why you came by," Harry said.

Asset lifted a hand to the side of his neck, feeling his quickening pulse. He took a slow breath and it immediately settled. He needed to call back the person who'd just reached out to him, but if he needed to kill these three first, he needed to make sure he didn't miscalculate. Nothing made you later for a meeting than getting shot in the head.

"I need to leave. I can kill the three of you first, or you can unlock the door and let me walk out of here. Your choice."

"That's it?"

"Unless you want there to be more, Mr. Walker. The choice is yours."

Asset half found himself hoping the old man's pride would get the best of him. But the man must have seen something he didn't like, because his eyes opened wider for a split second. Just a microexpression, but enough for Asset to know what was about to happen.

"Open up, Drey," he called to the wall behind him.

"C'mon," Whitey said. "Kill this asshat."

"I told you to shut up, boy," the old man said. "Open the door." The door unlocked.

Asset backed up toward it. He pointed to the phone he'd first thrown at Whitey. "Pick that up."

Whitey glanced at Harry, clearly unhappy, before bending down to the floor and then handing the phone over.

Asset opened the door behind him, then bowed his head to Harry.

"It's been a pleasure."

"Pleasure, my ass. Don't bother coming back, all right? I don't serve weird motherfuckers here."

Asset grinned at the insult. If he had the time, he'd come back and pay a visit to Harry Walker and his two sidekicks, Whitey and Drey. He wouldn't charge for it. He'd do it for fun.

Weird motherfucker? He thought as he slipped outside. *You have no idea.*

"What took you so long?" the Director said.

Asset pulled away from the curb, checking his mirrors for any sign of a tail. "I was meeting a new friend."

"Hawthorn is en route to Chicago. He's your way in to finish your original assignment. If he leads you to the Roberts, terminate them, then use Hawthorn to get to your target."

So, Townsend was still in play this quickly after yesterday's attempt. He was trained to follow orders. He was trained to never look at a situation as impossible. But even he knew this was new territory for him in level of difficulty. Still, his response was automatic.

"Affirmative."

"Hawthorn's flight details have been sent to you. He's not aware of you. Use your discretion for when you approach him. Don't fail us again." Then the line went dead.

CHAPTER 18

The Director liked neither uncertainty nor surprise. While others spent their resources analyzing trends, studying personalities, and parsing historical information to tease out a prediction, she'd risen to her position by exerting her will on events. Hers was an ethos based on action, not reaction. Strength, not accommodation.

And yet she felt like she'd been on her heels since the day Scott Roberts was let out of prison.

She walked through the sleek hallway, her steps echoing against the bare walls. Her most trusted assistant stayed half a step behind her. She was a tall, muscular woman who knew better than to say anything while her boss was in one of her moods. The Director noticed the woman type quickly into a tablet, wait, and then fold the cover over it.

"They're ready," she said softly.

The Director slowed a step; it was all she needed to do to show her displeasure. Her assistant lowered her head and dropped back to follow behind.

Of course they were ready. They had an appointment. An appointment to which she would be precisely on time.

An appointment during which they would second-guess her judgment and her ability.

But she intended to have none of it. The whole thing had been the Council's plan. While her underlings thought she was the ultimate leader of Omega, she was only the face of a much more powerful group of people. True, they gave her wide, nearly unlimited discretion to achieve their goals. But in this case the orders that had come rumbling down the mountain had been clear and specific.

She would have chosen a different route if she'd been left to her own devices. For one, she wouldn't have ordered the assassination of a U.S. president. Even a despised rodent like Townsend. She knew the American people too well. They liked to throw eggs at their presidents, but they wouldn't stand for it if one of them was killed. The effort that would be mounted to uncover the perpetrators of an assassination would be immense. And there was always the chance that someone in Omega's own ranks would break. Patriotism could hit at the strangest times and for the most peculiar reasons. A dead POTUS created all kinds of variables.

Still, she agreed that Townsend had become a problem for them. He'd tried backchannels to reach out to join them at first, searching for power and relevance after his fall from grace. Normally, the group would have welcomed an ex-president as a new recruit, but not this particular ex-president. His unquenchable desire for the limelight was a liability that they couldn't tolerate.

They'd played him along, trying to keep him in his box. But while the man was a lot of things, stupid wasn't one of them. He knew he was being iced out, so he let his pride get the better of him.

Once they discovered his memoir would name Omega and the few details he knew about the organization, they were forced to deal with the issue. She'd argued for subtler means— leverage, blackmail, threats to his family—but the Council wanted a more permanent solution. And that was when Roberts had been brought into the mix.

Despite its flaws, the plan had its merits. They'd been trying to track down Scott Roberts since he'd gone off the grid four years earlier, knowing that he was spending his considerable talent trying to hunt Omega. They hadn't been able to catch him, he was too good for that, but he hadn't been immune to the disinformation put out there that Townsend had ordered his wife's death. The town where Roberts had been arrested had been on Townsend's schedule the next day. It was a Podunk town in the middle of nowhere. The only reason Roberts would have been there was to take his revenge of Townsend. That fact had started the wheels in motion within Omega.

The plan had been to use Scott as the patsy to kill Townsend. Using his daughter had seemed overly complicated at first, but gaming out every other scenario ended with Roberts likely uncovering Omega's involvement.

Surprisingly, it was Hawthorn who'd pushed for using Mara in the end. He'd balked at taking the kid as an insurance policy, but he'd done as he was told in the end.

Roberts killing Townsend did have a sense of poetry behind it. He might have even thought it a worthwhile reason to die given what had happened to his wife. And if he did die, shot by the Secret Service was the thinking, then really how far would the intelligence agencies need to look for their motive, means, and opportunity. The case would be closed and Townsend would be silenced. Not only that, but it would serve as an important reminder to other world leaders that any interaction with Omega was never to be revealed.

Only things didn't work out that way. She'd try to tell them that with a Roberts involved, things seldom went as expected. With two of them, the plan was almost guaranteed to go off the rails. They ought to have taken Scott out in the prison when they'd had the chance and left the girl alone. The CIA had qualms about killing a man in plain sight, but Omega did not.

But the chance was gone now, and the Director had a strict personal ethos against dwelling on the past.

She entered the communications center, a Sensitive Compartmented Information Facility or SCIF, with tech that outmatched even the rigorous NATO SDIP-27 Level A protocols. It was a circular room with a curved screen covering the walls. A podium stood in the middle with a microphone and a small video camera rising from its center. The security the room afforded gave the White House Situation Room a run for its money. But since Omega had that room bugged, the thought didn't fill her with a lot of confidence.

The Director stepped to the podium as her aide closed the door. The room darkened, and one by one the Council members arrived to the meeting. Their faces appeared on the screen surrounding her, but each was so strongly backlit that their features were cast in shadow. The Director thought the whole thing overly theatrical, as if whoever had organized it was living their fantasy of being in a James Bond movie. Regardless, once all ten members arrived, surrounding her on all sides, it had the desired effect. A shiver ran down her spine.

"Hello, Council," she said. "I understand you have some questions for me."

"Based on this meeting," she said, "am I to believe the Council has lost confidence in me?"

The questioning had gone on longer than she had expected. Most of the questions had come from one of the women on the Council. For all the cloak and dagger, the Director had uncovered the identities of eight of the ten members. It was Sweena Mehta who was coming after her the hardest, the wealthiest woman in India. Not an heiress either, but a rough-and-tumble entrepreneur who'd beaten the boys at their own game and cobbled together a near monopoly of the cell phone market in the billion-person country.

The Director admired her, but that hadn't stopped her from acquiring compromising photos of her with more than one lover. Of both genders. She hadn't been surprised to discover that her sexual appetites had run to the extreme. Mehta wasn't one who did anything average. She had been surprised when that appetite included her submissive partners sometimes ending up in the hospital. And even the morgue. The Director wished she could pull her aside mid-meeting and show her some of the video in her possession to block her line of questions.

"Surely you don't begrudge this Council's desire to determine whether your judgment has been impeded, do you, Sheila?" Mehta said.

The Director swallowed hard, hoping her temper didn't show. She hated that name, she hated more that it was used to show the Council's power over her. They could unmask her at any moment. She fought down the impulse to call the woman by her first name. One didn't survive as Director long by being impertinent. Her predecessor had taught her that lesson by getting himself killed for that very transgression. "Impeded?" she said, letting the word drag out.

The ten faces stared at her, all of them letting the silence weigh on her like a physical thing.

"I assure you that there is nothing about this mission that has impeded my judgment. My position about assassinating even an ex-president has nothing to do with leftover vestiges of patriotism, if that's what you think."

"And what about—"

"None of the other circumstances around this mission have given me pause," she said. She realized she'd never cut one of them off before, but she was growing tired of this. Still, she realized this was a sign of weakness and girded herself for more questions.

"I believe our director has acquitted herself on this issue," a man said behind her. He'd been the easiest one to unmask because he didn't seem to care who knew he was there. Marcus Ryker was a tech billionaire who'd parlayed an Internet fortune into a conglomerate that included self-driving cars, genetically modified foods, immunotherapy cancer drugs, and the world's more reliable transportation into space. He was easily the man on the Council with the purest vision of what Omega was trying to accomplish.

"Thank you," she said. She looked at the others in turn, as if daring them to speak. None did. "I have a clear path forward.

Townsend is more dangerous now than before. I will see him silenced and remove the loose ends."

"I don't like it any more than you do," Ryker said. "But what we're fighting for is greater than the lives of a few men. We're fighting for the survival of humanity itself. And in that fight, sacrifices and casualties are inevitable."

Just not people close to you, she thought to herself. These powerful people had joined for what could be considered the most altruistic cause in human history. But they were still just people. Flawed. Egocentric. When the end of the world came, they and those they loved would be safely ensconced in luxury bunkers, protected by personal armies and stocked with enough provisions that they would want for nothing. Sacrifice was what other people did.

"It's not about like and dislike," she said. "It's about completing the mission. I've not failed you yet. And I don't intend to now."

CHAPTER 19

Mara drove. She didn't ask what her dad had gone through to escape from the Tribune Tower, but whatever had gone down had sapped his strength. He slept in the passenger seat for the first two hours, making her wonder whether all of his partners had been glorified chauffeurs so the great Scott Roberts could catch some shut-eye between adventures. It certainly felt like it'd become her full-time job since picking him up at the prison.

She started the drive flipping between news channels on the radio. Townsend was keeping to the script and adding to it. Now he'd called for some massive climate conference, of which he would of course be happy to chair, to "refocus the nation's attention on this important issue that the current administration has seemed to have forgotten."

Mara imagined the new occupant of the Oval Office was going to get a kick out of that sound bite. Especially since they belonged to the same party.

But she'd turned the radio off as the city gave way first to suburbs and then to farmland. The silence of the road was what she wanted. Time to think things through and make sure she wasn't missing something important.

As the miles ticked away, she thought mostly of Joey, allowing herself to feel her fear over what was happening to him. She knew he had to be scared out of his mind, but she also knew there was a possibility he'd been hurt. Even killed. If that turned out to be the case, Jim Hawthorn would be the first person on her list to visit.

"Where are we?" her dad mumbled from the passenger seat. " 'Is this heaven?' "

It was a tee-up to a line from the Kevin Costner movie, *Field of Dreams*. It was one of her dad's favorites, and they'd done the line a thousand times together. Surprising herself, she played along. " 'No, it's Iowa.' "

Her dad sat up in his seat, rubbing the sleep from his eyes. "I thought I felt better. Iowa always does that."

Her dad loved the Hawkeye State. Always had. He'd been born in Des Moines, but left when he was just a kid. Still, he'd always maintained a sentimental tie to the state, enjoying his one-liner that he was, "Iowa-bred and corn-fed," when people asked where he was from. It didn't surprise her that he had a safe house in the state.

"Want me to drive?" he asked.

"I'll drive. All I want you to do is start filling in the gaps. I want to know everything."

She expected him to protest, but instead he looked resigned. "I'll tell you. I promise. We're an hour out from the farm. Let me tell you there."

"Why?"

"I don't think either of us want you driving when you hear what I have to say."

She wanted to argue the point, but she figured she wouldn't get anywhere with him. He was going to make his case that he was innocent of killing her mom and betraying his country. She decided if he needed some time to lay it all out, she could wait another hour.

But there was something else bothering her. Something that couldn't be explained away even if he were able to convince her of his innocence.

"Lucy," she said.

"Yeah?"

"Did you know? You were on the run, but did you know she was sick?"

He looked out the window. "I knew."

"Your guy on the inside?"

"Yeah, he knew how to reach me."

Mara fumbled for the bottle of water in the cupholder, her throat suddenly constricted. It was empty, but she still tilted the bottle back anyway, getting a few drops out of it.

"Let's do this when we get to the farm."

"She asked for you," she said. "Toward the end, she asked for you a lot. And Mom. She asked for her, too. Sometimes she was so out of her head from the pain meds that she was sure she'd talked to you."

"Mara, please."

"She'd tell me whole conversations. How you'd held her hand. Sang her a song. Told me a story about me and her on adventures together." She gripped the steering wheel so hard she thought she might crush it. "I played along with it. Why not, right? It was only a matter of time. What was the harm in pretending, right? If it made her feel better?"

"What are you asking?"

"If you were out in the world and you knew, why didn't you come see her? Why didn't you come and actually hold her hand? Actually sing to her? Tell her one of your shitty stories? How could you stay away when she needed you?"

"I couldn't," he whispered.

Mara's heart skipped a beat. She hammered the brakes and the truck skidded to a stop on the side of the road. She faced forward, unable to look at him. "What did you say?"

"I was there, Mara. I visited her when I could. When you weren't there."

"Bullshit."

"You decorated the room. Photos of your mom and you. Lots of pictures of Joey. His crayon drawings. The big one from his school that said: *Get Well Joey's Mom*."

"You son of a bitch," she said, tears streaming now. "And you didn't tell me?"

"Lucy needed me. I had to be there."

"I needed you!" she wailed. "Joey needed you. How could you do that?"

He reached out to take her hand, but she batted him away. "Don't touch me. Don't you dare."

"It was for your own protection," he said. "If you knew I was there, you'd have either had me arrested or killed me."

"If you were innocent, you could have told me what was going on."

"I didn't know then who was involved. Shit, I still don't know for sure. It was too dangerous. I wore a disguise. Cleaning crew mostly. You said hi to me a few times. You were always nice to me, even when you were at your saddest."

She tried to recall any of the cleaning staff, but that whole time was a blur. "You were there?"

"I was. Saw her the day before she passed away. God, I loved her so much, Mara. The both of you."

Mara wiped her tears and took a breath. "You should have told me."

"Maybe," he said. "But the explanation for this, all of this, isn't easy. And things were already hard enough. You see that, right? I couldn't . . ."

He faced the window, his shoulders jerking as he tried to contain his emotion. She knew her pain at losing a sister. She realized she'd never stopped to wonder at the pain of losing a daughter. Her worry about Joey gave her a glimpse, and it was terrible.

"I'm glad you were there," she said. "It meant a lot to her. It's why I played along when she told me. It made her so happy."

"Can we drive? Please?" he asked, barely getting the words out. "Can we move on from here?"

Mara pulled back onto the road and considered the question. She thought, for the first time, that it was a real possibility.

* * *

The farmhouse was right out of a movie. A long, gravel road bordered by tall, swaying stalks of corn. Several outbuildings came into view first. A red barn, trimmed with white boards so it looked like a little kid's version of what a barn ought to look like. Two metal grain silos with a rust patina that matched the scattering of farm equipment beside them. A couple of old plows. A horse trailer. A rusted, vintage John Deere tractor covered with so many weeds that it looked like the fields were strangling it as payback for all the times it'd gone to work on them.

The homestead was a squat two-story house. There was a central door flanked by two windows on either side and matching windows on the top floor, giving the place a sensible symmetry preferred by Midwesterners. A wing extended off the back of the house, probably the kitchen, Mara guessed. The most welcoming feature of the entire property was the wide, covered porch that stretched across the front of the house. A bench and two rocking chairs stood ready for hours of sitting and rumination about the nature of the world and the quirky species that inherited it.

There were livestock pens and a chicken house, but no sign of any animals. It made sense if there was no one to tend the farm, but it gave the place a barren, lifeless feel. Instead of feeling like a home, it felt like visiting a graveyard.

"Who farms this place?" she asked, nodding toward the corn.

"I lease the fields out to a local guy. Corn mostly. Some soybeans. He looks in on the place."

"Does he know we're here?" She didn't like the idea of some old-timer coming around and accidentally getting himself shot for the trouble.

"He knows to stay away for a few days. Thinks I'm a writer who uses this place as a getaway. I've been here a bit over the last few years. Never a problem."

She parked the truck inside the barn, nudged up against some old, moldering hay bales. When she got out she heard movement in the loft above them, dozens of tiny feet. A fat cat looked up from its perch nearby and regarded them with suspicious, disdainful eyes, as if to say, *Yeah, I hear 'em. What of it?*

"Lazy ass," she said to it. The cat looked away and went back to sleep.

They took what little gear they had—groceries from a truck stop on the highway, a cooler of beer, a change of clothes, and a bag of guns, explosives, and other toys from Harry Walker—and carried them inside.

There was a room on either side of the entrance and a center staircase that led upstairs. Around the stairs, Mara saw the kitchen in the back. The furniture was sparse and broken in, perhaps left by the previous owners, or picked up from the nearest Goodwill.

"Place gets a nice breeze in the summer," her dad said. "Bathroom's over there, one upstairs, too, by the bedrooms."

Mara dropped her bag on the floor. "This isn't summer camp. You told me to wait until we got here and I have. Now it's time to tell me what's going on. Tell me what really happened with Mom."

He flipped open the cooler, took out a beer, and cracked it open. She was about to refuse it when he took several gulps of it for himself. He picked up the cooler and headed back to the front door. "Let's sit down. I'll tell you what happened. Starting with the meeting the first time I punched Townsend in the face."

CHAPTER 20

Four years ago

The Oval Office didn't disappoint.

Scott felt every muscle tighten as he stepped through the French doors leading from the colonnade. The bravado he'd felt seconds before as he picked up the president's cigarette butt and shared a look with the Secret Service agent on duty was gone. The immensity of the office of the president hit him over the head like a shovel.

He'd heard the Oval Office referred to as the greatest home court advantage in the world, and he finally understood what that meant. Although he'd seen the room so often from live shots in the White House, not to mention in TV and movies, stepping into that hallowed space impacted him more than he imagined it would.

He walked past the *Resolute* desk, a gift from Queen Victoria, made from wood from the Arctic exploration ship of the same name. Unable to help himself, he reached out and touched the carved surface, hesitating slightly to sense the weight of history in the room.

"Have a seat," Hawthorn said.

Scott refocused and collected himself. "Thank you." He crossed to one of the twin couches that faced each other by the fireplace. He waited for the president to sit on one of the wingbacked chairs first and then followed suit.

"Scott, the president wanted to be here when we discussed what I have to tell you. I would have preferred to do this just between the two of us . . ." He paused and looked at Townsend. The president was stone-faced, staring at Scott, sizing him up.

"It's not like you to dance around something," Scott said, feeling a pit open in his stomach. Whatever was coming couldn't be good.

"No, it's not," the president grumbled.

Hawthorn wrung his hands. Scott watched them closely. They had a basic sign language worked out, for use if an agent was captured and held hostage. If the operative was filmed for ransom or propaganda, they could signal messages without their captors knowing.

But there was no message. Besides the obvious one that Hawthorn was nervous.

"Nearly a year ago, we began working a path through Kahlil Al-Saib."

"I think you had an interaction with Al-Saib recently," the president said. "At the Four Seasons in Georgetown, if I remember correctly."

"Yes, sir," Scott said. He addressed Hawthorn. "I was on Al-Saib for years. Are you saying there was intel about him that wasn't shared with me?"

"There was something we came across in an intercept, something that we assumed was misinformation. But when a second source corroborated, someone we trusted, we had to look into it."

"Jesus, Jim. Get to the point, will you?" Townsend said.

A flash of anger crossed Hawthorn's face. "You said you'd let me do this."

Townsend waved his hand, a king waving his subject to continue.

"I have to say I agree with the president," Scott said. "What are you getting at here?"

The hand-wringing again. "We followed the evidence. I did it myself. A small team that I picked personally. I should have recused myself, but I didn't trust that it wouldn't leak if I didn't control the process."

"Jim, what in the hell are we talking about here?"

"Your wife," Townsend said, unable to contain himself anymore. "There was a problem with your wife."

"I don't understand," Scott said.

Hawthorn glared at Townsend, but softened as he turned to face Scott. He placed a hand on a folder on the table between them. "Wendy was implicated in a series of communiqués. High-level Russian intelligence."

Scott laughed, incredulous and bitter. "You think Wendy's a Russian spy? That's ridiculous."

"No, it's worse than that. The Russians were hunting her," Hawthorn explained.

"If they were after her it was because of her work for us."

"That's what I was hoping," Hawthorn said. "But it was soon clear that they knew about her activity for us, and that wasn't what had them in an uproar. She was working for someone else."

"Who?"

"We don't know," Hawthorn said, sliding the files toward Scott. "But we're working on it."

Scott reached for the file, only then noticing that his hands were shaking. He opened the dossier and leafed through it. Phone transcripts. Photos of Wendy meeting with men in parks. Computer screenshots. It was impossible to distill the information into anything usable at a glance, but the sheer abundance of it told him what he needed to know. This was no casual accusation. But it didn't matter. They were talking about his wife.

"You're wrong," he said.

"I wish we were," Hawthorn said. "At every point, I tried to twist the information to excuse her behavior. But it's all there. Off-book meetings with known operatives from China, Russia, France. Lies in her official record of her movements to cover them up. A virus inserted into her phone captured encrypted transmissions that our techs can't break. The encryption signature is unlike anything we've seen from any intelligence group we've run up against."

"Show him the readout," Townsend said.

Hawthorn hesitated. He pulled the second file toward him and opened it up. "This is from six days ago."

Scott took a paper from him.

ROBERTS: I NEED OUT.

UNKNOWN: ARE YOU COMPROMISED?

ROBERTS: I THINK SO. I CAN'T BE SURE.

UNKNOWN: YOUR HUSBAND?

ROBERTS: (LAUGHTER) NO, HE SUSPECTS NOTHING. HE'LL NEVER BELIEVE THEM NO MATTER WHAT THEY SAY. (PAUSE) THE AGENCY. I THINK THEY SUSPECT.

UNKNOWN: ONE WEEK.

ROBERTS: SOONER.

UNKNOWN: ONE WEEK. PRAGUE.

Scott stood up, smashed the paper in his fist, and threw it on the floor. "This is bullshit. It's a setup. Russians have tried to do this before to us."

"It's not that," Hawthorn said.

"I want to see the raw intelligence. I want to talk to the analysts myself. Get them over here."

"Where's your wife?" Townsend asked. "Right now, where is she?"

"At a conference. In Boston. World Affairs Council, I think. Left yesterday."

Townsend snorted a short laugh. Dismissive and smug. Almost enough to make Scott want to take a swing at him. But it was what Hawthorn said next that rocked him.

"I'm sorry, Scott. She boarded a flight at Dulles two hours

ago," Hawthorn said, the sadness clear in voice. "Destination Prague."

Townsend stood and Hawthorn followed suit. Scott wished he could sit back down. His legs suddenly felt a lot less stable than they had seconds before. He couldn't think straight. The room's walls seemed suddenly taller, like the room was stretching higher. The walls throbbed in time with the piercing headache that had started behind his right eye.

None of this could be true. Out of all the things that were wrong in the world, Wendy was the one good thing. Her and the kids, but they'd come from her, too. Everything he believed in, everything he valued, was wrapped around her. Hawthorn had to have it wrong. There had to be an explanation.

"I know this is a lot to take in," Hawthorn said. "But we don't have much time to make our next move here."

Scott looked at him and the movement sent him a little off-balance. He reached out to the sofa to steady himself.

Townsend was right in front of him when he said exactly the wrong thing. He let out another of his smug, snorting laughs and said, "You look like a man who just found out his wife is a treasonous, lying whore who sold out her country. I just wonder whether you're just as dirty as she is."

Scott's fist flew without even the barest hint of hesitation.

It connected with Townsend's face right under his left eye.

The man dropped to the floor. A result that saved the right side of his face from a punishing left hook that glanced harmlessly off the top of his head as he fell.

"Enough!" Hawthorn yelled, jumping in between the two men. He shoved Scott in the chest. "Out, now."

Scott towered over the president as he crawled back to his feet. "How dare you?"

Townsend stammered. "I could have you locked up for the rest of your life for that."

"On what charge? Hitting an asshole? Three-fourths of the country would throw me a parade."

Hawthorn held him by the arm and neck, steering him toward the door like a perp being put into a squad car. He allowed himself to be pushed along and through the door into the small office where the president's secretary sat.

Townsend shouted behind them, "Get him out of here!"

But Scott barely heard him. All he could think about was his wife. And how fast he could get on a plane to Prague.

CHAPTER 21

"This isn't true," she said. "This is some kind of sick manipulation."

Her dad didn't argue. He didn't say a word. With a beer in his hand, he scanned the cornfield like he was searching for something hidden there that he'd once lost. Not the steely-eyed look of an operative seeking out danger, more the distant gaze of an old man seeing memories mixed in with the landscape. A home movie reel playing inside his mind's eye while the real world passed by unnoticed.

"Tell me it's not true," she whispered. "That that's why you were in Prague with her the night she died. To prove that what they said was a lie." She pulled in a shuddering breath, wrapping her arms around herself. "Or did you go there and find out it was true? And that's why . . . that's why you killed her? Because you found out Hawthorn was right."

"I didn't kill her," he whispered, taking a long drink of his beer. "Not the way you think anyway."

"What the hell's that supposed to mean? What happened in Prague?"

He didn't respond, lost again somewhere in his own head.

"Hawthorn's in on this," she said, finding an edge to hold on to. "He's the one who recruited me to kill you. He abducted

Joey. If he's in on it, he must have steered you wrong with the information on Mom. He was the mole on the inside, not her."

"It's not that easy, Mara," he said. "I wish it was."

"You know more than you're telling me. I can see it in your eyes," she said. "You can't do this to me. Not after everything else. You can't tell me only that much about Mom and then just . . . just . . ."

She wiped away tears, her memory flooding with images of her mom. Kind, gentle. Her comforting fingers stroking her hair. Soft words of encouragement that were always on the edge of her mind, whispering to her whenever she was scared or nervous. Even when she was mad at her, there was always an undercurrent of wanting her to be better, wanting her to learn from whatever mistake she'd made so she could be stronger.

She sensed her dad tense next to her, his head jerk up. Something had caught his eye. She didn't turn to see what it was.

"Tell me. What happened in Prague?"

Scott stood up, tossing his beer can to the side. "I'll tell you everything, I promise."

"I'm not waiting. You'll tell me now, goddammit."

Scott jerked his head toward the front of the property. She finally turned and saw a black SUV hauling ass down the gravel road, a rooster tail of dust spiraling into the sky behind it.

As charged up as she was about what she'd just learned, the operative in her compartmentalized all of it and locked it away. The threat was in front of her. And if it was in front of her, there was a chance it was coming at them from all sides. An entire platoon of Marines could be crawling through the cornfields surrounding the house and they wouldn't know until they were right on top of them.

"I'm guessing your farmer friend doesn't drive a black Escalade."

"Nope."

Mara went inside for a few seconds, then came back out with a 9mm Glock in one hand and a DX-12 Punisher snub-nosed double-barrel shotgun in the other. She tossed the shotgun to her dad, who caught it with one hand. He walked to the far end of the porch, adding some distance between them. If whoever was in the SUV came out shooting, there was no reason to give them an easy shot at both of them.

But when the Escalade stopped and the door opened so she could see who stepped out, she nearly pulled the trigger herself. It hardly seemed fair that the person she most wanted to kill just pulled up and delivered himself to her.

The question was, how the hell had Jim Hawthorn found them?

CHAPTER 22

Asset watched Hawthorn exit the vehicle on the tablet screen he held in his hands. The mini-drone he'd launched had an effective range of half a mile, so he was an entire county road over from the farmhouse where Hawthorn had gone.

He had to admit that the old man was good and that without a little bit of luck, he would have lost him at the airport. Hawthorn landed on the flight Asset had been given, but he'd taken pains to leave the airport in the most circuitous way possible, using old-fashioned craft to shake any tail he might have picked up.

Hawthorn had started in the taxi line, waiting patiently for his turn. Once in, he rode the cab only halfway around the terminal, jumping out right next to a bus for Avis, the rental car company, and jumping onto that. Once at the remote off-site rental center, he left the shuttle and reboarded another shuttle to return to the airport. This time, he got off nearest to the subway station, quickly heading downstairs and then boarding the first train into town. Even then, he switched trains a few times, each time scanning the crowd for familiar faces.

Asset lost him twice during all of that. Both times he'd guessed a direction and just gone with it. Both times, he'd guessed right. Every mission had an element of the unforeseen, but having so much left to chance so early had unnerved him.

Once he'd seen Hawthorn pick up the parked Escalade with the keys in it, he'd quickly found a motorcycle and relieved it of its driver. After that, he hadn't let the old man out of his sight.

He wanted to see what Hawthorn did before making any kind of move. He wanted to see him enter Townsend's house normally, so if he had to do it under duress for him, Asset would be able to tell what was normal behavior.

He was glad he waited. Because instead of driving to Townsend's home in the city, Hawthorn drove straight out of town to I-88 and never looked back. Once they were into Iowa and the Escalade turned north toward Dubuque, he hung back farther. Things got really difficult once he turned on the farm access roads, miles and miles of gravel cutting the farmland into massive grids.

Fortunately, his backpack had a few tricks in it. He pulled over long enough to deploy a mini-drone, no larger than a child's toy, but with all the highest end surveillance equipment on it that money could buy. Using a tablet to see the drone's video feed, he sped it ahead until the Escalade appeared on the screen. He painted the target with a laser from the drone and then set it on auto-follow mode at a quarter-mile distance and 200-yard altitude. After that, he just had to stay within a half mile of his target and he was golden.

Now the drone was serving an even greater purpose. He had a front row seat watching who Hawthorn was meeting. He toggled the controls to fly the drone closer, hoping his guess about who was at the farmhouse proved to be correct.

CHAPTER 23

Mara ran off the porch, gun drawn, pointed right at Hawthorn's head. She saw her dad sprinting toward her in her peripheral vision, but she had a lead on him.

"Where's Joey? If he's hurt, I'm going to shoot you right here, I swear to God."

She reached Hawthorn first and clocked him one right in the jaw. Hawthorn took the punch, didn't fall, but bent over to steady himself.

Her dad grabbed her arms and pulled her back.

"Stop," he said. "He's with us."

She froze, her brain playing catch-up. It took several long beats for her to realize she was holding her breath. She spun around to look at her dad, his expression guilty, maybe even apologetic.

"Hawthorn's your guy on the inside?" she asked. "But Joey . . ."

"He's safe," Hawthorn said. "They were going to take him either way, so I made sure I was the one to do it."

She felt a surge of relief, but it was pushed aside quickly by the rage returning. Everything was moving too quickly for her. She raised the gun again. "Tell me where he is."

"No matter how this turned out, I wasn't going to let anything happen to him. Men I trust are watching him. CIA, not

Omega. They've been told they're on protective detail. These men will die before they let anything happen to him."

"Put the gun down," her dad said.

"Not until this asshole tells me where I can—"

"I have a shadow," Hawthorn said. "I thought I lost him, but I saw him across the field on the way in here, too late to stop. A half mile to the east. Maybe less."

"I don't care if you have a whole SEAL team tracking you, I want to talk to Joey," Mara said.

"I have an extraction plan when we're ready. Not before," Hawthorn said.

"Extract him now."

"Omega will know we're on to them. Jim will be exposed. We need to see this all the way through."

"You knew this whole time," she said, finally piecing it together. "You let me worry about him. Do you know what that's been like? Do you have any idea? What's wrong with you?"

Her dad took a step back, as if worried he'd be the next one to get punched. "Jim and I have been on this since your mom died. He's worked his way into the group, so he had to be careful. He took a big risk getting the information to me about Joey."

"That call to the school didn't help," Hawthorn said, rubbing his chin where she'd hit him. "I'm just glad you resisted the temptation to put a bullet into Townsend. That would have been a mess."

"You should have told me," Mara said.

"And if I had?"

"He's just a little kid. You should have—"

"Would you have waited if I'd told you?"

"Of course not."

He put up his hands. *See, there you go.*

"But I wouldn't have gone with you either. You didn't need me to go after Townsend."

"But you would have gone charging after Joey, maybe killing

some of the innocent men guarding him. The situation was under control."

"You don't get to make that call," she said, her voice trembling with anger. "I'm responsible for Joey. Not you. You weren't there, remember? You lost the right to make any decisions when it comes to him."

"Sorry to break up the family fun, but can we focus here?" Hawthorn said.

Her dad held her stare for a few beats, his eyes filled with both anger and hurt. Finally, he turned to Hawthorn. "Who's the trail? Internal CIA or Omega?"

"I don't know for sure. Omega is my guess. Whoever it is, he or she is good. I used every trick I had." For the first time, Mara took stock of Hawthorn. His face was drawn, pinched by anxiety. He looked like he hadn't slept in days. She had a good guess why.

"Who do they have of yours?" she asked.

His expression changed, something akin to acknowledging an equal. She'd guessed correctly. "Everyone," he said. "If we don't cut the head off this thing, they'll kill every single person in my family."

"Oh shit," her dad said. He indicated with his eyes without moving his head.

Mara spotted it, too. A glint of sun off metal a hundred feet in the air, hovering over the corn. A drone.

"We're on TV," she said. "A surveillance drone. Coming at us."

Hawthorn's shoulders sagged forward. "I was afraid of this. I'm sorry. This changes everything."

He pulled out his Sig Sauer service revolver, told them one last secret, and then shot them both.

CHAPTER 24

The farther the car drove her out from Vienna, the more the Director realized that she may have made a mistake.

She hadn't been completely surprised when the phone call came. It wasn't permitted for members of the Council to contact her directly, an internal policy designed to prevent any of them from feeling left out of the decision-making process. And yet one had broken that established protocol to not only call, but to suggest a meeting.

The act was so brazen that she had to consider whether it was a loyalty test. Perhaps it was. But she sensed it was an opportunity. Especially given her read of the person who'd called her. As the car sped through the night, she wondered whether her instincts would prove to be correct. If they were not, and if it was a loyalty test, she entertained herself speculating what the punishment would be for taking the meeting.

The curiosity wasn't whether it would be death, only the manner in which the sentence would be carried out.

But she held on to the hope that her evaluation of Marcus Ryker's psych profile was correct. Bold, risky, ego-driven, brilliant, visionary, all accurate descriptors of the man. But she didn't think that it told the entire story. There was more to him, something he didn't put on show for the rest of the world to see.

She'd combed both the public literature and the private dossiers on the man, trying to uncover his secrets. His bio was one of the most well-known on the planet. From street urchin on the streets of Rome to a Silicon Valley entrepreneur to an angel investor with a Midas touch, Marcus Ryker was not only one of the wealthiest men on the planet, but one of the most respected and well-known.

The Director hoped it wouldn't prove necessary to kill him once the meeting was over.

"Were you surprised I called?" Ryker asked as she walked into the cavernous room. She was in a magnificent home on a lake, private except for a few outbuildings that blended into the pine forest, still visible in the light of the full moon rising over the mountains. Even without the light, she knew where the buildings were located. She'd done her reconnaissance on every residence Ryker owned.

Ryker stood next to a floor-to-ceiling window that stretched across the entire room and beckoned her to him. She obliged, scanning the room for cameras, points of egress, and any sign of backup. There was nothing obvious, but she knew the man who developed autonomous cars, reusable space vehicles, and crops that could be grown in the desert could likely position a camera somewhere she wouldn't be able to see it.

"You didn't answer my question," Ryker said.

"I don't respond to questions to which the asker already knows the answer," she replied, trying to mark off some territory early in this interaction.

Ryker laughed. "You give me too much credit. I don't know the answer. I imagine you thought it was a possibility, but not a probability. If the other members of the Council knew—"

"What makes you think they don't?" she snapped.

This took him by surprise and she had to suppress a grin. He was scared of the Council as much as she was. Perhaps more. After all, she had only her life to lose. He had the chance to change the world.

"Unless you told them," he said, "then they don't know. And I don't think you told them."

"Why do you think that?"

"Curiosity," he said, his voice echoing in the room. "You're not the only one who can read people. Some would say that the ability to find the right people is my greatest talent. To my detractors, they would say it is my only talent. The rockets that will lift the manned mission to Mars say Ryker on the side of them, but they were designed by men more brilliant than I could ever hope to be. Men I found and funded and encouraged."

"I don't design rockets," she said. "So why am I here?"

The grin returned, a self-satisfied look that said he knew he was back in control. He was right. Curiosity was getting the better of her.

"Come, I want to show you something."

Her ears popped as the elevator plunged down into the mountain. Ryker watched her closely, not saying a word. She locked eyes with him, refusing to look away and resisting the temptation to ask any more questions. It was clear he had a plan of how to show her what he wanted her to see. Either that, or the bottom of the elevator was where they'd dispose of her body after executing her for violating the rules of the Council.

But she felt more confident that Ryker didn't care about the rules. He had some other reason for her to be there.

The elevator hissed as it slowed and then stopped. The doors opened to an immaculate white room, brightly lit with recessed lighting in the ceiling. The back wall was the exception, shrouded in darkness. Then the lights turned on in the next section, showing the room to actually be a hallway. One by one, sections came online, revealing a hallway that stretched out into the distance, curving in a wide arc.

"Impressive," she said. "You've built a hallway."

Ryker laughed, shaking his head. "You're everything I'd hoped," he said. Then his smile disappeared. "Let's see how you handle the rest of it."

They walked together through the hallway, their footsteps echoing off the walls, giving the place an eerily abandoned feeling. There were doors along the hallway, each of them with a security pad next to it.

"When I was approached to join Omega, I thought it would be fun," Ryker said, not turning to look at her as they walked. "A billionaire's club that got to complain about the world and use its resources to throw wrenches into the machinery when it suited our aims. But soon, I realized the full potential of the group."

"And its limitations," she said.

Ryker stopped and she did the same. He regarded her closely, as if seeing her for the first time. "I'm not sure if that sort of comment shows your value to me or shows you to be a threat."

"Perhaps my value to you is that I could be a threat?" she suggested.

He cocked his head to the side. She'd seen that trait in videos she'd watched of him. He was recalculating. Absorbing new information. Processing.

"Perhaps," he said. "But so we're clear, in my current work, in my *mission*, I don't tolerate threats. I destroy them."

She saw something in his eyes at that moment that made her shudder. Gone was the rational scientist, the charmer, the billionaire philanthropist as at home on the world's fashion magazines as on serious scientific journals. For a moment, she saw the eyes of a killer. And it unnerved her.

"You brought me here to show me something," she said.

He snapped back into his easygoing smile. "Yes, this way."

They stopped at a door that looked no different from the dozen or more they'd passed. Ryker placed his hand on the screen. The Director watched as the reader scanned Ryker's hand. She thought it likely the device was also taking a DNA sample. She committed every detail to memory in case she ever needed to infiltrate the compound. Old habits.

The lock clicked open, but Ryker hesitated. "Why are you part of Omega?" he asked.

"Because mankind is on a collision course with—"

"No," he said, holding up his hand. "Not that answer. The real one."

She took a deep breath, doing her own recalculation. How far down the rabbit hole was she willing to go? Judging by the elevator ride she took, she guessed she was already deep enough that there was no going back. She disassociated herself from the things she ought to say at that moment and did her best to clear the way for the truth.

"My parents died when I was thirteen. A gas explosion and fire while I was at school. Just one of those everyday tragedies. But I had no other family. No aunts or uncles or grandparents. So the state took me in, which is where I was selected for the intelligence program and trained. But before that, before they took me away, the social worker let me visit the rubble to try to find something to remind me of my parents. But there was nothing. Not a single thing to show they'd been alive. Made an impact. Lived a life of any consequence."

"And that idea scared you," Ryker said.

"Survival isn't good enough," she said. "I want what I do to matter a hundred years from now."

"A thousand years?"

"Yes," she whispered.

"Then we're kindred spirits," he said. "I could tell that about you. Your strength in front of those fawning prima donnas on the Council, the way you manipulate them without their knowledge. You're meant for great things."

"And Omega isn't accomplishing those things?"

"The Council is the problem. They talk about the need to reset civilization, but it's bluster. They still pursue short-term profit for their companies, using the group to create wins for themselves. Like this whole business with President Townsend."

"They don't want to be unmasked."

"We could launch the reset tomorrow," he said. "It wouldn't matter who knew about us."

"But my understanding is that we're not—"

"We're not ready?" he said. "No, not for the entire plan. But the broad strokes are there. We will be completely ready for a global rollout in less than a year."

She digested that information. Everything she'd been told by the Council predicted a seven- to ten-year time horizon. A year? Could it be that close? "The Council knows this?"

Ryker stared at her and she felt his eyes evaluating her. "You know something now even they do not. Only me. And my scientific team, of course. But they are sequestered in labs under lock and key."

She felt a rush at knowing something so monumental. But with the adrenaline came a bout of nausea. A year. It was so soon.

"You see?" Ryker said. "Even you feel it. When the new beginning is that close, people will react in unexpected ways. I predict half the Council will get cold feet when it's time for action. That's why they can't know."

She sensed this moment was why she'd been summoned. This was the test. "What do you want me to do?"

He smiled, apparently pleased that she'd realized the moment had arrived. "I want you to bring this Townsend business to a conclusion. Show me that you're not conflicted about any of the circumstances inherent in this situation."

"That won't be a problem."

"And I'll need another demonstration of loyalty from you."

She steadied herself, her internal alarm ringing. The real ask was here.

"I believe we need clarity to achieve the task ahead of us. A singular voice to set objectives, dictate the precise actions Omega needs to take to achieve its goals. Leadership by committee has taken us this far, but it won't suffice as we do the hard work ahead."

"Each member of the Council controls their own levers of power. Decentralized by nature."

"But you know how the dots are connected, don't you?" Ryker said with a sly look. "Sometimes out of necessity when you run an operation. But you've been doing digging on your own, too. Unmasking the Council one by one. Gathering leverage on them."

The Director tried not to show the pulse of fear that she felt at the words. The accusation was akin to reading out charges right before summary execution. It was all true, of course. But she thought she'd been clever enough to hide her activity. She wondered who besides Ryker knew. She glanced at the door in front of them, imagining that a small squad of men were on the other side, waiting for Ryker's signal to take her. If that was the case, then the stairs behind her were probably also guarded. What a fool she'd been to come here.

She turned to Ryker, dropping the subterfuge of the submissive underling reporting to her superior. She let her anger show. "If you're planning on taking me down, you'll be dead before anyone puts a finger on me."

Ryker appeared shocked at first. She wondered when was the last time someone had spoken back to the billionaire, let alone to threaten his life. But he recovered quickly and responded in a way she hadn't expected. He laughed.

"I'm not here to *take you down*," he said. "I'm here to elevate you. Give you a promotion. Recruit you to my cause, if you will."

She was puzzled, and it must have shown on her face because Ryker continued.

"I have my own resources to achieve my vision, but it would take years to do it on my own. With Omega, we can transform the world in less than a year. I need you to help me marshal the resources of Omega. Share with me the dots you've connected. I'm the strategy, but I need a tactician. And I believe that's you."

"And the Council?"

"You and I both know there are members on the Council who don't possess the backbone to finish what they've started. They lack certainty at a time when it's the most required trait to possess."

"And you possess that certainty?"

"I see humanity's one chance for salvation. I've never been so certain of anything in my life."

The Director pretended to think over the proposition. She really had no choice but to accept. If he'd caught her working behind the scenes to unmask the members of the Council, he already held her life in his hands. She was buying herself some time to think through how best to make Ryker understand that her acceptance of his offer was genuine.

She'd come with the hopes of forging an alliance with Ryker. Instead, she was being offered a front row seat in his insurrection against the Council. She couldn't have imagined a better outcome.

"I dedicated my life to this mission as a young girl," she said. "I've sacrificed all semblance of a normal life so I could be here at this moment. I have clarity on what needs to be done. You're not the only one who possesses certainty."

Ryker clapped his handed together. "Good. Very good. But remember my two caveats. Finish this business with Townsend and the loose ends with the Roberts agents."

"And you mentioned one other test of loyalty," she said. She was curious what was waiting for her on the other side of the door. She was rarely surprised by anyone, but she couldn't get a read on Ryker. It felt dangerous, and she liked it.

Ryker invited her to open it. On the other side was a small room, set up like a prison cell with a cot and a toilet in the corner. A prisoner was tied to a chair, a gag in her mouth.

Sweena Mehta.

One of the most powerful women in the world and one of the most vocal members on the Council. The one who had challenged the Director the most in the last meeting.

When Mehta saw her, she struggled against her bindings, desperate guttural sounds filling the small room.

"The culling of those who lack pure intention begins now. Do you need a weapon?" Ryker asked.

The Director stepped into the room, stopping right in front of

Mehta. She stared down at the woman for several seconds. Mehta looked back up at her, her eyes pleading.

"No," the Director said, pleased that the loyalty test being asked of her was something she was actually going to enjoy. "That won't be necessary."

Mehta screamed through her gag as Ryker shut the door.

CHAPTER 25

Asset didn't like what he saw.

He'd hoped for a while that Hawthorn was leading him to Scott and Mara Roberts. His employer had made it clear that even though Townsend was primary, the Robertses were to be eliminated if found. Since the Tribune Tower, he'd been occupying his mind by devising ways to torture them. He knew the emotion was unwise and it ran counter to his training, but the two had ruined his perfect record. They'd interrupted his operation and forced him to retreat from the field without a kill.

For the first time in his career. And for the most important of clients.

Asset didn't like losing. Something drilled into him as a boy when his Serbian masters had savagely beaten him each time he lost in the cage matches where he'd earned his keep. Some of the boys shut down after a few months, unable to take the abuse. Asset's reaction had been different. He simply stopped losing.

Even since his training with the FSB, where his handlers had taught him to control the rage when it threatened to overwhelm him, losing still provoked a visceral reaction in him. Only a few months earlier he'd lost to a stranger at pool in a roadside dive bar. He'd almost been able to walk away until the man taunted him, trying to get Asset to play again. He broke both of the man's arms and nearly ripped the man's lower jaw from his face.

And Asset didn't even consider himself any good at pool.

But he was the best in the world at killing. So the Robertses deserved more than broken arms for ruining his perfect record. And they would get it.

At first, he'd been ecstatic when he'd seen the two of them on the screen, allowing his heart rate to increase by ten beats per minute before forcing it back under control. But he didn't like the way Hawthorn allowed the girl to hit him. That didn't make any sense. Unless he was trying to convince them to come in alive.

That's not what his employer wanted.

He wasn't certain his employer wanted Hawthorn alive much longer either. Asset wouldn't mind killing the old man. He'd do it free of charge, paying him back for nearly making him look like a fool when he was tracking him from the airport.

But then the totally unexpected happened. To Asset's disappointment, the old son of a bitch pulled a gun and shot both Robertses dead.

The drone was close when it happened. Probably nearer than was advisable to avoid detection, but the directional microphones weren't picking up the sound, so he'd been forced to fly in tight.

And now he was looking at two bodies on the ground.

The old man had even more surprises in him than he'd thought.

Asset pulled the drone back and higher. There was no audio to be heard, unless Hawthorn was in the habit of talking to himself. But Asset wanted to watch.

Hawthorn took off his suit jacket, rolled up his sleeves, and then pulled one body at a time over to one of the small livestock sheds. Then he disappeared into the main barn and came back with a gasoline can. He spread the fuel outside the shed and then appeared to dump the rest inside. Hawthorn bent down, and seconds later wide swaths of flame leapt up the shed walls. It was old wood, dried out after decades of Iowa summers and winters, and it caught fire with ferocity.

Asset looked up from the tablet and spotted the thin column

of black smoke rising in the distance. He wondered whether it would draw attention, but decided it likely wouldn't. Farms burned trash all the time. That was all Hawthorn was doing, burning the trash.

Back on the screen he watched Hawthorn stare at the blaze for over a minute. Just standing there like he was lost. Asset wondered whether he'd been injured. Maybe one of the Roberts had gotten a shot off after all. Or maybe a knife wound.

Or maybe he was just a confused old man.

Asset chided himself for the thought. He underestimated Hawthorn at his own risk. The man had evaded him on the way out here and then taken out two top operatives by himself. He had to stop thinking of him as an old man. The guy was still able to take the fight to the enemy.

Finally, Hawthorn climbed back into the Escalade and drove back up the road. Asset rolled the motorcycle into the cornfield and waited for him to pass. It was easy to track the progress with the mini-drone, but that was about to come to an end. The battery alert flashed in the corner and soon the drone would automatically return to its base. He wished he had a backup, but it wasn't necessary. He imagined Hawthorn had to go back to Chicago to see Townsend. With the motorcycle, it'd be easy enough to catch up to him on the open road. He wanted to take a look down at the farmhouse first.

The fire still burned hot by the time he parked the motorcycle in front of the livestock shed. The roof caved in as he watched, sending a whirlwind of sparks and smoke into the sky. The metal grain silo next to it was coated black on one side, but the fire had nowhere else to spread.

He tried to get in closer, knowing his employer would like a photo of the bodies as proof, but the heat kept him at bay. He had the recording from the drone, so that would have to suffice. It was Hawthorn's kill. He had no problem giving credit where it was due. He got paid either way. Besides, the real target was Townsend.

Asset went inside the farmhouse and did a quick look around. He didn't think the Robertses would have picked up a third person for their team, but he stayed alive by being thorough. He explored the small house, appreciating its Spartan furnishings and pure functionality. It was the kind of place he could live in.

He found a bag of guns and small explosives. After a quick inventory, he zipped up the bag and hoisted it on his shoulder. Maybe when he had time, he'd return the guns to Harry Walker and give him a little lesson in manners.

On the porch, he spotted a cooler. He opened it up and groaned. Bud Light. Who in their right mind would drink Bud Light?

A floorboard creaked inside the house.

Asset instantly had the bag off his shoulder and gun out, his body pressed against the outside wall.

The floorboard creaked again. Unmistakably. Right inside the front door.

He aimed the gun along the wall. Head high.

The screen door edged open. Only an inch. Then it closed again.

Did the person inside know he was here?

He crouched lower and turned to the side, reducing his profile in case someone came out shooting.

The screen door edged open again, wider this time. Six inches or so.

Then it slammed shut.

The fattest cat he'd ever seen strutted across the porch.

Asset lowered his gun and laughed. He looked around, a human impulse when embarrassed, as if someone else might have seen the whole episode.

Little did he know, someone had.

CHAPTER 26

UNKNOWN: I DIDN'T EXPECT YOU TO CALL.
HAWTHORN: WE NEED TO SPEAK.
UNKNOWN: WE ARE.
HAWTHORN: NO, IN PERSON.
UKNOWN: YOU KNOW THAT'S NOT POSSIBLE.
HAWTHORN: SCOTT AND MARA ROBERTS ARE DEAD. OR
    DID THE ASSET YOU PUT INTO THE FIELD TELL YOU
    ALREADY?
PAUSE.
UNINTELLIGIBLE. VOICES HEARD IN THE BACKGROUND.
UNKNOWN: THAT CHANGES NOTHING. IF YOU HAVE INFOR-
    MATION, TELL ME.
HAWTHORN: IN PERSON.
UNKNOWN: WHY?
HAWTHORN: ROBERTS TOLD ME SOME THINGS BEFORE HE
    DIED. THE GROUND TRUTH HAS CHANGED. I WANT TO
    MAKE A FINAL DEAL.
UNKNOWN: YOU REMEMBER YOUR FAMILY LIVES ONLY BE-
    CAUSE I ALLOW IT.
HAWTHORN: HARD TO FORGET SOMETHING LIKE THAT. DC.
    TOMORROW NIGHT. I'LL SEND YOU THE LOCATION VIA
    ENCRYPTED TEXT TOMORROW.
UNKNOWN: WHAT MAKES YOU CERTAIN I'LL COME?
HAWTHORN: BECAUSE I HAVE THE INFORMATION YOU
    WANT. YOU'LL COME.

"Think it through. If you go out there, we lose our advantage. We reveal that Hawthorn just staged our deaths and is working with us. What do you think happens to Joey then?"

She strained against his grip, but it was like being caught in a vise.

"Let me go."

"Emotion can't drive action," he said. "That's how you end up dead."

She wrenched her arm free and eyed the silo door. But they both knew she wasn't going to walk through it. She was trapped. Both by the situation and because he was right. The safest thing to protect Joey was to stay in the silo and follow his plan.

She returned to her spot on the floor and watched as the man left the house with their duffel bag of weapons. Something spooked him and he took a defensive position against the outside wall of the house. Her first thought was that Hawthorn had circled back to get the drop on the man, but that didn't mesh with her dad's plan for Omega to keep trusting Hawthorn.

Then she saw the cat and nearly laughed. The man glanced around, as if to see if anyone had spotted him going head-to-head against the tomcat. This made her grin even more. She filed it away for later. This guy had an ego and it could be used against him someday.

A shot went off and she jerked back from her spyhole on reflex, losing sight of the man for a second. She was back in position in time to see him kick the cat's lifeless body off the front porch.

Mara pushed her emotions back down, knowing the swell of anger inside her was counterproductive. Still, what kind of asshole shot a cat just for making him look bad?

The man jumped on his motorcycle, revved it up, and kicked up a tail of gravel as he hauled down the drive.

Mara sat up and leaned against the wall of the silo.

"I hope you're right about staying put," she said. "Because I would have loved to introduce myself to that guy."

* * *

They resolved to wait inside the silo for another hour. There was no way to know whether the man had left a drone in place to monitor activity. Most of the drones had a max battery life of an hour, and those were the advanced versions. If they waited it out long enough, anything out there would run out of power and land harmlessly out in the corn.

Mara decided to use the time and the forced proximity to get the rest of her answers.

"I'm still pissed at you," she said.

"For not telling you about Hawthorn?" He spoke in a low voice, but more than a whisper. There'd been an unspoken acknowledgment that the drone outside, if there even was one, would probably be far enough away to permit them to speak.

"That. And for everything else you aren't telling me."

There were enough holes in the old silo that shafts of light crisscrossed the wide column of darkness, dust motes dancing in the air. Her dad leaned against the wall directly opposite from her, light hitting his chest and reflecting his face in a way that drew deep shadows, the way he used to hold a flashlight under his chin when he told her and Lucy scary bedtime stories.

"Maybe I made some mistakes," he said. "But always to protect you and Joey."

She remembered what he'd said outside. She'd been so angry that it was a little blurry, but it was there. "You were right. If you'd told me about Hawthorn, I would have made us go get Joey. I wouldn't have been willing to wait."

He leaned his head back and closed his eyes. "I know. But maybe we should have gone right away. We might have even gotten him out. Even if we had, you'd never have been able to stop running after that. Ever."

"Who are these people? Who are we fighting against?"

"Omega. I heard the name once from someone I interrogated, right before he threw himself off a roof to keep from being captured. I don't even know if that's what they call themselves. It was either call them Omega or keep calling them *those assholes.*"

"I guess either would work. Are they Russian?"

"Yes. And Chinese. And North Korean. And Syrian. And American. Nationality means nothing to them. Power is all that matters."

"To what end?"

"Jim and I have been trying to piece that together," he said. The best we can tell, they're some kind of doomsdayers. They believe the world is on a trajectory toward failure. Toward societal breakdown. Anarchy."

"Doesn't take much to reach that conclusion. Just the nightly news."

"There's a difference between thinking it might happen and being certain of it. Between thinking of ways to avoid the end of civilization, and seeking out ways to manufacture it."

"So they are destabilizers?" she asked. "Funding the anarchists at WTO meetings? That sort of thing?"

"That's amateur hour. These people, funded by some of the wealthiest families in the world, have infiltrated every level of government and institutions. They believe the apocalypse is inevitable. The only way to ensure they survive it is to control exactly how and when it happens."

The implications slowly sank in for Mara. "If an aircraft is going down, better to pick the spot for the crash landing than just fly it until it falls out of the sky."

"They're not preparing for the end of the world in case it occurs," he said. "They're preparing for the end of the world because they're going to be the ones that set it on fire." He drew in a deep breath. "And your mom was part of it."

Mara felt her throat constrict. Her stomach turned over at the easy reference to her mom as traitor.

"It's time you tell me," she whispered. "Tell me what happened the night she died."

CHAPTER 28

Four years ago

Prague was beautiful at any time of day, but sunset made it one of the world's most perfect sights. Called the City of a Hundred Spires for good reason, the Gothic churches and baroque buildings of the Old Quarter created a spectacular silhouette as the sun descended behind Scott as he walked out onto the Charles Bridge.

Getting to Prague had required him to cash in more than a dozen favors. After his run-in with Townsend in the Oval Office, he was put on administrative leave with his travel rights revoked. There were more than a few people who owed their lives to him, so there were allies more than willing to look the other way and ignore the flag on his file when he asked for a covert flight into the Czech Republic. He warned them that there might be hell to pay for helping him, but that hadn't stopped any of them. They'd regret the decision later.

The Charles Bridge was a fifteenth-century pedestrian bridge, a popular tourist attraction in the city, providing postcard-worthy views of the Vltava river, Old Town, and the other bridges connecting the two parts of the city. Scott had been there during the summer and walked the bridge with hundreds of people, enjoying the views and basking in the sun, but there were only a few other people on the bridge that evening. A light snow had fallen earlier in the day and then frozen in the frigid temperature that followed, keeping the bridge mostly empty. He assumed Wendy had known that would be the case. A public meeting place, but somewhere they wouldn't be disturbed by too many people.

After the Oval Office, Scott had first gone back to Langley and gone through Wendy's file. He'd read it all. Then he'd called analysts he knew who had worked on the brief and quizzed them ruthlessly on their methods and conclusions. He'd given them scenario after scenario that might have explained the paper trail in front of him, but they refuted each in turn. By the end, he wasn't willing to admit his wife was a traitor. But he accepted that she was involved in something he couldn't explain.

Just as he was trying to determine how to reach out to her, she called him on his cell.

"Scott, it's me."

He could tell immediately that something was wrong. He tried to answer, tried to play along as if he didn't know anything of what he'd learned over the last twelve hours, but the words caught in his throat when he heard her voice.

"I think you know why I'm calling," she said.

"I need to see you," was all he could manage.

"I can explain everything."

"I need to see you, Wendy. Tell me where and I'll be there."

"Will you come alone?"

"Yes."

There was a long pause. He could hear her breathing on the other end. He waited.

"Do you promise?" she finally asked.

"Yes."

She gave him the time and location for their meeting. When she was done there was silence, long enough that he was worried she was gone.

"Wendy?"

"I'm here."

Neither of them wanted to get off the phone, but neither of them knew what to say either.

"Whatever this is, I can help you," he said.

"I wish that were true," she whispered; then the line went dead.

Now, on the bridge as the hour drew near for their meeting, his feet crunching through the icy crust on the thin layer of snow, he wondered if she would come. And what he would do if she didn't.

A few people were on the bridge, braving the cold weather for the beautiful sight of the last glow of the sunset reflecting off the Vltava. He scanned them for any sign of danger, but saw none. Their body language all seemed natural enough. Then again, someone well-trained could easily pull that off. He tried to ignore it. Even if there were agents on the bridge, he wouldn't turn around.

The time came for their meeting, and he looked up and down the length of the bridge, the row of life-sized statues of the saints turned into dark shadows. He began to worry that his fear had been warranted. Something had stopped her from coming.

But then, on the far end of the bridge, he spotted a single person walking toward him. He knew immediately by her walk it was the person he'd spent the happiest years of his life with. He hoped with all he had that those years were not about to be proven to have all been a lie.

Wendy was wrapped in a heavy coat, snow boots, and a wool cap, walking slowly toward their meeting place, the statue of St. John of Nepomuk near the middle of the bridge. He'd considered whether her choice of meeting spot had been a message to him or just a point of convenience. Not only was he familiar with the story of St. John, the saint of Bohemia, but she would have known he was aware of it.

St. John of Nepomuk had been the head priest in the court of King Wenceslas in the fourteenth century. He was also the chief confessor of the queen. When the king demanded his priest divulge the secrets of the queen's confession, he refused. Enraged, the king had the priest tortured and then thrown from the Charles Bridge, where he drowned in the Vltava.

He and Wendy had both enjoyed learning about St. John the last time they had been in Prague together. They liked the story because their own lives in the CIA were ones where secrecy was valued above all else. The willingness to die to protect a secret was often at the heart of duty and responsibility for those in their line of work. He hoped that if there had been a message intended, it was their shared appreciation for keeping secrets, not the need to die to keep them.

"I didn't want this to happen," she said, stopping three steps from him.

He wanted to embrace her, but he sensed there were new rules in place. In an embrace, a knife could be thrust or a gun discharged without warning. They were on new ground here. He stepped closer and she retreated the same distance. The reaction tore into him.

"Whatever you've gotten into, there's a way out. Let me help."

She shook her head. Her lower lip trembled. "My handlers told me to marry you. But I would have anyway. That part was real. I want you to know that."

He bit the inside of his mouth, trying and failing to keep his emotions in check. He had a thousand questions to ask. The analysts at Langley had communiqués between Wendy and her Russian handlers going back ten years, but they were far from complete. The questions his superiors had were all who and how and what. He didn't have a single question that didn't start with the word *why*. But he didn't want to ask them there. He just wanted to get away, just the two of them, somewhere he could protect her. And, eventually, find out why.

"C'mon, let's get out of the cold. Go sit somewhere and talk. It's just me."

She wiped the tears from her cheek and took a shuddering breath. "I don't want Lucy or Mara to know. No matter what happens. I don't want them to know. Can you do that for me? Can you promise me that?"

He didn't like the way she sounded. He held out a hand to her. "Whatever they told you, we can fight it. It's not stronger than we are."

"They'll kill the girls," she said.

"I won't let them."

Wendy pulled her hand out from her coat pocket. In it was a Beretta M9. "They're watching. If I don't kill you, they'll kill the girls. They have people positioned near them right now."

Scott stared at the gun, thinking it had to be a play of light. Some shadow that just looked like a gun. But it wasn't. One look at the pained expression on her face and he knew she meant to use it.

"You don't have to do this," he said, dismissing the instinct to grab his own gun, to fire first as he rolled to the side. He'd be hit, but it would give him a chance for a nonfatal wound. His shot would hit its mark. But there was an instinct at work greater than his training. He could never hurt Wendy. Not ever.

She was crying now, shuddering so that the gun shook in her hand. "We can't both leave this bridge alive," she said. "They made it clear. I have to kill you, or die trying. Otherwise our girls—"

"We can protect them."

"No, we can't," she said. "You don't know these people. You don't know what they're capable of doing. What I'm capable of doing."

"That's where you're wrong. I do know you. You're smart enough to know we can work this out."

"I gave them nine of our agents," she said, meeting his eye as if daring him to judge her. "I gave them up to try to save you."

Scott opened his mouth to speak, but no words came. He blinked hard as if that might erase the nightmare he was in, but it made no difference. The woman he loved was still standing in front of him and admitting to sending nine men to their deaths.

"But it didn't make any difference. They want you gone.

Dead or discredited to embarrass the U.S., doesn't matter to them. I half expect they're the ones who exposed me just so we'd end up on this bridge. You don't understand who you're dealing with here."

"No, they don't understand what it's like to deal with me. Come in. Help me set this right. It's not too late."

Her eyes turned down, staring at the gun in her hands. "Only one of us can walk off this bridge. If we both leave here alive, our daughters will die, Scott. I couldn't live with myself if that happened."

Scott spread his arms wide and stepped toward her. "If you think that's the only way to save our girls, then go ahead."

She backed up until she was against the stone railing. "Stop."

But he didn't stop. "Go ahead, shoot me if it's the only way."

He closed the last few steps between them, pressing the gun against his chest. Then he pulled her into an embrace, feeling her sag into his arms.

But then she whispered, "I didn't say it was the only way. Please don't tell the girls what I did. Not ever."

BANG!

The gun went off between them. He felt heat and pressure on his chest and pushed backward, thinking he'd been shot.

But he hadn't.

Wendy held the gun still, turned so that it was pointed at herself. A dark stain spread across her chest.

He reached out for her, the most important thing in his life. He had barely touched her when another shot struck her in the shoulder, slamming into her with such force that she fell back against the stone rail, tipped over, and fell into the river below.

Scott yelled and scrambled forward, first at the spot where she went over, then across the bridge to the downstream side. "Wendy!"

"Get down!" a man shouted. "On the ground!"

There was a man with a gun to his left. One of the tourists he'd spotted on the bridge earlier. Another closing in to his right. How had he missed them earlier as operatives?

He ignored them and climbed up onto the railing to dive into the freezing, dark water below. It was all instinct. Jumping into the water would likely kill him, but losing Wendy was the same as dying. He felt like he was outside his body, witnessing the scene around him instead of living it. He refused to believe he'd lost her. Couldn't believe. He had to jump to try to find her.

Fierce pain exploded in his right leg as a Taser pumped thousands of volts into him. He tried to fight through it. Tried to get over the railing to save his wife. But he couldn't.

Strong arms pulled him off the railing and back onto the bridge. He struggled and shouted every obscenity in the world at them, but still they held him down.

Then Jim Hawthorn was there to tell him it was all over. That they had to leave. That he was sorry about Wendy, and that he would do everything in his power to make sure that whoever was responsible paid the price.

Scott didn't respond at first. He was numb to the world, unable to process what had just happened. He replayed it over and over in his mind. The feel of her in his arms. The last words she'd whispered in his ear. The sound of the gun. The sight of her falling backward.

When he finally spoke, he turned to Hawthorn and said the words he'd repeat over and over during the days of interrogations ahead of him. "I killed her, Jim. I didn't have a choice. I killed her."

"No, I know what happened," he said. "I saw it."

Scott grabbed his friend's wrist and pulled him in close. His teeth bared like an animal as he spoke. "I killed her, you got that? I don't care what you think you saw."

"But—"

"I don't need you to understand, I just need you to agree. Can you do that?"

Hawthorn searched his face like he'd gone crazy. "Scott, why would you—"

"You've got to trust me. I killed her, that's the story." Scott's voice shook. He was right on the edge. "I'm begging you. I can explain why later, but I need this. Please, Jim. Just this one thing."

Hawthorn held up his hand. He would do it.

"Thank you," Scott said, barely able the get the words out.

Hawthorn reached out and placed one hand on either side of Scott's face, forcing their eyes to meet. "She loved you, you know," he said. "Despite everything, I'm sure of it."

Scott lowered his head into his hands and cried like a child.

CHAPTER 29

Mara was glad the sun had softened over the last hour, making it hard to see her dad's face in the silo's dim light. She didn't want to see his face, and she didn't want him to see hers.

She dragged the heels of both hands across her cheeks, sure the dust and grime of the silo was mixed in with the tears that had been streaming down her face.

A mix of emotions churned inside. Her dad's voice as he'd told her the story had almost been too much to bear. The pain of the loss was so raw that he'd had to stop for long stretches to compose himself before he could continue.

Then she had to sort through how she felt about everything he'd told her. Her mother as a deep mole in the U.S. intelligence agency, a double agent. Told by her handlers to marry her father. That meant that her own birth had just been part of her cover.

"Everything about her was a lie," she said to the darkness.

"That's not true."

"Of course it was. How can you say that?"

She heard movement on the other side of the silo and saw his shadow change position. "Because I've had longer to think about this. You'll see it once you think about all the pieces."

Her sadness was fading, quickly replaced with anger. "She was a Russian spy. Of course all of it was a lie."

"What was her last wish?" he said. "The last thing that meant something to her?"

"That you lie to us, too," Mara said. "That if we lost her, we ought to lose you, too. Now that's some real selfless shit right there."

"You're angry."

"Hell yes, I'm angry. Aren't you?"

"I was. For a long time. Then I imagined what her life must have been like. Always in fear of being caught. Thinking she'd put you and Lucy at risk. In the end, she had to choose between killing me and taking her own life. She chose to save me."

"So you could be framed for her treason?"

They both knew the history. Immediately after Prague, the Kremlin announced nine CIA agents had been arrested in Moscow, publicly revealing internal Agency documents that proved their guilt. Moscow proposed an exchange in a communiqué that was leaked to the press. Nine CIA operatives for the return of their agent, Scott Roberts.

"I knew about the nine agents," Scott said. "But the offer to exchange them for me was a master stroke. I never saw it coming. Neither did Hawthorn. It was an outrageous move, even for the resurgent post-Putin FSB. Through back channels we found out that the strategy was coming from outside the normal FSB chain of command. That was when we first understood Wendy had likely been part of Omega. Hawthorn begged me to let him testify about what had really happened on the bridge, but I couldn't."

"Why?" Mara asked, the exasperation making her sound and feel like a teenager again. "What loyalty did you owe to Mom at that point? Me and Lucy, we were alive. We'd just lost our mother and you let them take you away from us, too?"

"It wasn't supposed to be for this long. My plan was to get the proof that exonerated me without having to reveal your mom's role," he said. "You asked what I owed her. Everything. I owed her everything. So I intended never to reveal her secret."

"Then why now?"

"I've justified not telling you for too long. You're in the middle of it now. Risking everything. You had to know."

"Is that it?"

He shifted position again as if answering the question was physically painful for him. "And because maybe I was wrong," he said. "Maybe you deserved to know from the beginning."

"The nine agents died," Mara said. "Because you stayed silent."

"No, the Russians wanted them dead either way. Or Omega did. It didn't matter which in the end. Leaking the whole thing discredited Townsend, especially when the people around him tried to cover it up. It essentially ended his presidency. The Russians won because they destabilized the West. Omega cut off my operation to expose them. Only there was one problem."

"Hawthorn helped you escape," Mara said, putting it all together.

"Yes, even with the fabricated evidence and the Russian request to exchange for me, he knew I wouldn't betray my country. We created a plan to infiltrate Omega."

"He went inside and you worked on the outside."

"It's taken longer than I imagined. Omega is better than any organization I've gone up against. Decentralized. Firewalls between operating units. No one breaking ranks. But we're close."

"And if you get them, would it have all been worth it?" she asked. "All the lies. How about the nine agents who were executed? Would their families think it was all worth it?"

"Your mom gave the Russians the evidence. Or she gave them to Omega, who gave it to the Russians. Not that it mattered in the end. If I'd blown the whistle on her, that wouldn't have changed the fact that they were spies. They knew the risks."

"But you let everyone believe . . . you let me and Lucy believe . . ."

"I let you believe your mother was innocent," he whispered. "Your sister died knowing her mother was a good woman who loved her. I kept the promise I made to the love of my life." He looked away, his eyes closed as if the pain of memory was too much to bear. "Maybe someday you'll forgive me. I just hope your mother will, too."

They exited the silo once it was dark. Most surveillance drones were equipped with infrared to track heat signatures, but unless the operator tracking them had special gear, the battery would have already drained by this time.

Mara waited by the truck while her dad went into the house. She was still reeling from the revelations over the last hour. She was glad to be out of the stifling claustrophobia of the silo, and wished that she could somehow leave behind what she learned while in there.

She couldn't stop rifling through every memory of her mom, wondering what was real and what had just been part of her cover. Had it all been a lie? When she'd cared for her while she was sick? The long talks at night when her heart had been broken in high school by Mitch Gainer? The tour they'd taken together of colleges in the summer between her junior and senior year?

All of her favorite memories of her mom came rushing at her, the same ones she replayed in her mind whenever she missed her the most. Only now they felt diminished, cast in a shadow. False, counterfeit experiences designed to sell a long-term cover.

She didn't want that to be true. She wanted to believe that that part of her mom's life had been real. But wasn't that foolish? How could she accept that for most of her life, her mom lived in deep cover, betraying her adopted country, burrowing deeper and deeper into the intelligence apparatus, but somehow believe her maternal instincts had won her over in the end and made her love her children? Maybe even love her husband?

No, it was just sentimentality. It was what she wanted to believe and she was just rationalizing the pain away.

One thing was for certain. If she thought she was messed up in the head before with parent issues, she'd reached a new level in the last couple of hours.

"You all right?" her dad asked. He had a new duffel bag slung over his shoulder. Judging from the apparent weight of it, there'd been no shortage of guns and equipment to choose from inside the house.

"No. You?"

"I've had years to think about this. Digest it. You're hearing it for the first time."

"So you're all right?"

He threw the duffel in the back of the truck.

"Hell no," he said. "But I've had time for scar tissue to build up all my broken parts."

"Yeah, well, I don't have time for that."

"You will. After we finish this."

"And how do you suppose we do that?"

"Hawthorn's drawing out the leader of Omega for a face-to-face. It's going to happen in DC. And we're going to be there."

"We need to get Joey."

"Once we capture or kill the leader, Hawthorn's guys are ready to relocate Joey to a safe location."

"Why not do it now? You said Hawthorn has his own men watching Joey. Men we can trust."

"Omega might be watching the site. It's how they operate. Multiple layers. Everyone wondering if they are being watched."

"And how do you know all this? That secret hand language you and Hawthorn have?"

Her dad grinned. "He whispered it in my ear when he dragged me to the hut. Why do you have to make things all complicated?" He jumped in the truck, the wisecrack remark signaling the end of the emotional bonding. Back to the safer ground of sarcasm and being a smartass. It was fine with her.

Mara climbed into the passenger seat. "Are you all right to drive?"

"Sure. I got some good rest."

"Didn't realize rest was a cure to being old as shit."

He fired up the engine. "There she is. Ms. Congeniality. Welcome back."

They tore down the gravel drive, leaving behind the farm-house, and headed east toward DC.

They were in Ohio when she called Jordi on a burner phone she picked up at the truck stop.

"What do you have?"

"Thank God."

She put the phone on speaker. "What's going on, Jordi? You okay?"

"Am I okay? You're updated in the system as terminated. And in the kind of files I was looking at, that doesn't mean you were caught stealing office supplies and asked to report to HR. I hear an echo. Am I on speaker?"

"Yes, my dad's here. This is Jordi. Jordi, Scott Roberts."

"Hello, Jordi."

"Hello, sir. Up until a few hours ago I would have told you to piss off."

"And now you called me 'sir' like I'm an old man. You must have read my date of birth in my file."

"I saw more than that," he said. "Townsend is one messed up mother-effer, but he can tell a hell of a story. This has bestseller all over it. I mean, it might get him killed, but it'll make good copy."

Scott cast her a sideways glance.

"I need you to focus, Jordi," she said. "Short version. What'd you find?"

"Don't you want to hear what it took to break the encryp-tion? Mind-melting algorithms. Nonsequential diffusion. Real transcendental work."

"Can we stipulate that it was absolutely brilliant and get into what you found?"

"Give me fucking brilliant and I'm good."

"Done. You're fucking brilliant."

"Damn right I am." He took a deep breath.

"The drive had some financial information on it. Offshore

accounts. Dummy corporations. The usual low-grade super-wealthy bullshit. Less than ten mil. Kind of sad, actually."

"What else?"

"His memoir. The first two hundred pages or so anyway. He's more James Patterson than James Joyce, if you take my meaning. A lot of action packed into those pages, not a lot of time spent on scenery."

"What does he say about Omega?" Scott said.

"Quite a bit, actually. But not what I think you want. He calls it the greatest existential threat to civilization since the Cold War. If you believe him, they have people positioned in every power center across the world, keeping tabs on things, pulling strings when it suits their interest."

"Sounds like something the tinfoil hat crowd will love," Scott said. "Don't tell me he thinks it's the Illuminati, or that he goes all anti-Semitic on us saying it's a Zionist cabal."

"No, what he describes is more practical. It crosses political and even religious lines. It's all about the accumulation of power and control."

"You just described all politics," Mara said.

"Only these guys stretch across international borders, use whatever methods they want, and have zero accountability. Jordi, what does he give for proof?" Scott asked.

"Not much. He tells stories of meetings with shadowy power brokers, conduits to something he calls the Council with offers to bring him on the inside. That it was prior to his fall from grace. And he talks about your mom, Mara." His voice trailed off.

"She was part of it," Mara said. "I know." She hated saying the words. For some reason it felt like a betrayal. She knew it was ridiculous, but that didn't change the emotion she felt.

"He talks about you, too, Agent Roberts," Jordi continued. "Did you really punch the president in the face in the Oval Office?" The respect in the man's voice was evident.

"Mara recently punched the same guy," her dad said. "He said she hit harder than I do."

Jordi laughed into the phone loud enough that the speakers distorted the sound.

"What else, Jordi?" Mara said. "Specific names. Contacts."

"No, and I know that's what you want," he said. "That's why he says he's writing this. That once the world knows Omega exists, they won't be able to hide in the shadows any longer. Well, that and the book is bound to make a shit-ton of money. There are some smut-filled chapters about his affair with what's-her-name. Like I said, bestseller."

"Thanks, Jordi. Keep your head down. If this doesn't go well for the two of us, then you release the manuscript."

"To whom?"

"Everyone," her dad said. "But do me a favor."

"What's that?"

"Redact the sections about Wendy," he said. "Mara knows, but there's no reason the world needs to know what she did. Joey doesn't need that."

There was a long silence on the line. Finally, Jordi asked, "Mara?"

She looked over at her dad and saw his pleading eyes. Even with everything that'd happened, he still wanted to protect her. At first she couldn't understand why, but then it struck home.

He still loved her.

"Do it, Jordi," she said. "Release it wide if they get us. Keep her name out of it."

"Yes, ma'am," he said. "But I have a better idea."

"What's that?"

"Just don't let these bastards beat you."

Mara looked at her dad. He had his game face on. "That's plan A. If there's a way, we'll figure it out. I promise you that."

CHAPTER 30

Marcus Ryker worried that he'd made a mistake. He wasn't a man accustomed to self-doubt, so the feeling weighed on him as he drove his Lamborghini Veneno through the mountain roads above Salzburg.

Driving fast was one of the few things that cleared his mind. The Veneno's zero to sixty in 2.9 seconds and its 221 miles per hour top speed fit that bill. The mountain roads, tree lined and perched on ravines that plunged hundreds of feet into darkness, gave him the challenge he needed. Enough to pull his mind away from the thousand voices clamoring in his head for attention.

But as he downshifted to take a hairpin turn, he lost control temporarily of the machine's backend, fishtailing wide. Headlights greeted him on the other side of the curve along with a blaring horn from a delivery truck. He made an adjustment and slid the Lambo back toward the inside lane, missing the truck by inches. He supposed the truck driver might have also adjusted, maybe even overcompensated and lost control into the guardrail. Ryker didn't know because he didn't even bother to check the mirror to see.

As he drove, he thought through his recent successes. He'd brought the Omega Director into his orbit, a goal he'd set for himself nearly a year earlier. On top of that, he'd removed Sweena Mehta, the most vocal voice on the Council, the one most likely in his estimation to oppose his accelerated time line. Things were going exactly to plan.

Then why did he feel so wrong-footed?

He had answers to that question. One of the plaguing faults of genius was to always have multiple answers to every question. Even in the sciences he'd proven there were always solutions beyond the most likely, even beyond those long accepted as doctrine. It'd been the strength that had built his monumental fortune, making him one of the top ten wealthiest men in the world according to the various lists published every year. And those lists didn't account for the significant resources he'd secreted away in caches around the world, the value of which exceeded his paper worth.

He knew what many of his fellow billionaires did not, those not on the Omega Council in any case. Soon, money would be meaningless. Ammunition, shelter, power generators, fuel. Those would be the hallmarks of wealth in the new world he planned to create. And he was ready for it. Which made his uneasiness that much more unnerving.

Clearly part of it came from his new relationship with the Director. Although he'd vetted her as thoroughly as humanly possible, she was still new to him. He'd carefully watched her rapid ascent in the organization, been impressed with her Machiavellian methods to push her predecessor aside, and enjoyed her ambitious attempt to generate intel on the Council members. She'd shown a deft hand at taking the reins at Omega, wielding the power with subtlety when it was called for, and ruthless violence when subtlety wouldn't do.

What she'd done to the body of Sweena Mehta had been proof of that.

The Director was qualified, that wasn't in question. And due to the decentralized command structure of Omega, she alone possessed control of far-flung corners of the Omega enterprise. He needed her.

But he didn't trust her.

Not completely anyway. Of course, there wasn't a soul he trusted in absolute terms. He was too much of a student of human behavior to make that mistake. People were prone to be unreliable, irrational, and inconsistent. They had the unfortunate habit of acting completely against their own self-interests for the most foolish of reasons. The degraded state of the global environment was a clear testament to that.

Question: What kind of animal would destroy its own home?

Answer: The kind that mustn't be left to its own devices.

None of the character traits possessed by human beings made for a good partner in the greatest scientific project in human history. But he knew he needed the help if he wanted to expedite his plan within the year, and the Director had exactly the resources he needed.

So why had he insisted on this last test of loyalty?

There it was. The root of his unease. He'd allowed his doubts about trusting the Director push him to demand she demonstrate that she could separate herself from her old emotional attachments. The new world he imagined went so much farther than the original Omega idea that he assumed there would be some deserters. He needed to test how people dealt with the sentimentality of patriotism and personal connections. When Hawthorn's message had come in, he'd insisted the Director go to DC for the meeting and not come back to him until Townsend had been removed from the equation.

She'd agreed without complaint.

But now that she was gone, he realized the nagging self-doubt he felt was not whether she was willing to do the task assigned to her, but whether it was worth the risk. If she were killed or captured, he'd lose a valuable new asset. One that could even out him if interrogated long enough. He'd recover from the loss, but it would set his plan back a year or more.

All because he lacked trust.

He accelerated through the next turn, loving the feel of the machine's power radiating through his hands. He slammed the gas pedal down and sank into the leather seat from the g-force. He felt his uneasiness melt away as the miles per hour ticked higher.

The Director would simply have to accomplish her task. If she couldn't, then she would have proven to be a liability in the long term anyway. If she didn't come back, he wouldn't waste time looking in the rearview mirror.

When one was planning on the destruction of ninety-five percent of the world's population in order to save an entire planet, a delay of a year or two wasn't the worst thing that could happen. Still, he hoped for the best and for the Director's safe return.

The sooner he could save the world from itself the better.

CHAPTER 31

Hawthorn hoped the plan was airtight, but he couldn't stop second-guessing himself. Too many missions under his belt to believe there wasn't a curveball he hadn't foreseen looming on the horizon. His mantra through his professional life was that no battle plan survived first contact with the enemy. And it had served him well.

But he couldn't think of any way to make the plan better.

At the heart of the problem was not knowing who to trust. Omega had its tentacles reaching throughout the national security apparatus, or at least they'd done so enough that it gave the appearance that their eyes were everywhere. He wasn't sure who to trust in his own shop, let alone reaching out interagency. He'd spent the last twelve hours racking his brain for some angle he hadn't spotted yet, and had come up with nothing.

And that scared him.

He sat at his desk, thinking through the lifetime of experience leading up to that point. He'd done battle both with and against presidents, kings, and the heads of foreign intelligence services in his time. There'd been more victories than defeats, but those were the ones that came to him now. The missed opportunities. The lives he didn't save were the ones that haunted him most of all.

But those weren't the only ghosts that haunted him as he counted down the time to his rendezvous.

"It's me," he said into the phone.

"Hello, me," his daughter Anne said. "Where in the world are you today?"

"In DC. Got back this morning."

A pause. "This morning?"

"Yeah."

"How bad?" Anne had been through the trenches with him for too many years. In her forties, she had taken over his wife's role as the family's matriarch. She knew there weren't many things that could have kept him away from at least a quick stop to say hi to his two grandkids.

"You know how it goes. There's never much good news around here."

"Do you want me to cancel my trip up to Bangor?"

"No, of course not. Megan needs you there."

"More like Travis needs me. The twins are more than he can handle. I got a video today of them running through the house. Looked just like two pigs had gotten loose in a peach orchard."

He smiled and closed his eyes. It was one of his late wife's sayings. He pictured the twenty-five-year-old version of Margery, one hundred percent Southern girl, a debutante armed with a thousand homespun sayings that she dished out with abandon. They always brought a chuckle and a comment from him, but not today. Today he felt a sting in his eyes as tears rose there unexpectedly.

"Is that right?" He let out a short cough to mask the tightness in his throat, but he knew she was too sharp for that.

After another pause, Anne's voice was lower, the tone she took with him when he didn't take his medicine or ordered a cheeseburger instead of the rabbit food she was always forcing on him. "Are you being careful?"

"As careful as I can," he said, not happy a lie had snuck into what might be his last conversation with his daughter. "You know me."

"That's why I'm worried."

"There's something else I can tell you."

"What's that?"

"That I love you. I love the family your mother gave me. And I couldn't imagine a version of life without all of you."

"Oh, Dad," she said, now her turn to grow emotional. "What did Mom used to say? Don't bullshit a bullshitter? What's really going on?"

He smiled. His wife had said the same thing the night he'd proposed to her. The response had taken him so off guard that they'd laughed about it for a half hour together. And then another four-plus decades after that.

"I've got to go. I'm going to call Megan before this meeting I have coming up."

A long pause this time, both of them breathing softly into the phone. He closed his eyes again, knowing she would find the call suspicious, hoping she would leave it alone. He imagined her sitting on the edge of her bed, phone cradled in the crook of her neck, looking out the window into the English-style garden, where she spent most of her mornings.

"They'd like to hear from you," she said finally.

"Goodbye, Anne," he said.

"Mom felt the same way," she said, catching him as he was about to hang up. "You were the great love of her life. Remember that."

"I do," he said. "Thank you."

They said their final goodbyes and hung up the phone. He sat at his desk a few minutes to collect himself. This wasn't the first time he'd made these types of calls to the girls—the *just in case* insurance policy. If something did happen, if the contact that night was an ambush, he didn't want his last conversation with Anne to be about which of them was going to pick up the dry cleaning.

But when he'd made that type of call before he'd been a younger man, going into danger for his country with a clear mission and the firepower to back it up.

This felt different.

These calls felt like saying goodbye.

He picked up the phone and dialed the first number from memory. "Hey-a kid," he said. "Heard you're about to pop any minute."

CHAPTER 32

"We have four hours," Mara said as they pulled onto Interstate 495, the Washington Beltway. "I say we get Joey's location from Hawthorn and I get him while you cover the meet."

Her dad dug into his pocket and pulled out a piece of paper. He hesitated, then handed it to Mara.

"What's this?"

"The address where Joey's being held." He pointed north. "He's in a basement holding area. Three guards. We're less than thirty minutes away."

She couldn't decide if she was thankful he'd given in to her or pissed that he'd had the address in his pocket the whole time. "How long have you had that information?"

He hesitated, and she knew she wasn't going to like the answer. "Hawthorn slipped it to me back at the farm."

Mara yanked on the wheel, cut off two lanes of traffic, and turned north.

"You know we can't get him right now," he said.

She pressed the nav button on the car's dash. "Give me directions to—"

He slapped his hand on the nav button, resetting it. She glared at him. "Don't try to stop me."

"Think, Mara," he said. "You're better than this."

"I'm warning you."

"The second you use the navigation system to get you to that address, alarms go off at NSA, and this car might as well be a tracking beacon. You know that."

She took a deep breath. He was right, if it was a CIA safe house, then any search would get flagged.

"At least pull over, for Chrissake," he said. "Let's take a minute."

Mara hammered the gas and they sped through traffic. "We're getting him now. I don't care about the meet tonight."

"Yes, you do," he said. "Because if you get Joey now, they'll know Hawthorn is working against them and we lose the head of Omega. Not to mention they'd kill Hawthorn. These people won't stop. They'll track you and Joey down no matter where you take him to hide just to get at you. Is that what you want? Is that what Lucy would have wanted?"

She slowed the car down. She hated the idea of Joey alone and afraid, but she knew he was right.

"Hawthorn told me he has Joey handled. That he'll be safe."

"You might trust him, but I don't. Not with Joey's life. I'm going. I'll wait until the meet is happening before I move in, but I'm not waiting."

He stared out the window, thinking through it. "You're as stubborn as your mom."

"I'm starting to get the feeling she was only that way from being around you all the time."

That made him laugh, releasing the tension in the car. "You might be right about that. I have two conditions."

She gave him a hard look.

"Okay, two favors to ask."

"Better."

"First, that you don't kill everyone at the house. Some of those guys, maybe all of them, are friendlies posted there by Hawthorn."

"That seems reasonable. What's the second favor?"

"That we eat at Ben's Chili Bowl. On the off chance things go wrong, I don't want my last meal to be a microwave burrito from Bob's Trucking Center."

Ben's Chili Bowl was a local spot that'd been serving up hot dogs and chili since the forties. It wasn't much to look at, but every president since Nixon had been there, along with every senator and congressman who gave two licks about food and tradition.

The place was too popular to risk one of them being recognized, so they parked down the street and found a teenager on the street willing to make a food run for twenty bucks. They got the food and then parked on a side street and dove into the split hot dogs smothered in chili and cheese. Mara didn't think she'd be able to eat anything, but once it was in the car, that all changed. She had to admit it'd been an inspired choice.

"Your mom loved Ben's Chili," he said, wiping his mouth. "Would have eaten it every day if she could."

Mara choked down the bite she was chewing and sipped her drink. "How can you do that?"

"What?"

"Talk about her like that?"

"Like how?"

"You know, like she was actually the person she pretended to be."

He lowered his food and studied her. "She pretended to be a State Department official who worked with the Swedish embassy. She pretended to be a CIA case officer. She pretended to be an American patriot. But she didn't pretend to be your mother, Mara. That was real."

"How about being a wife?"

His expression changed at the question. He put down his food as if his appetite was gone. "I like to think that wasn't part of the act either. At least she said that much at the end. She didn't have to tell me that, but she did."

"And that's supposed to be enough?" she said, feeling the anger rise in her. "Enough to make up for what she did to you? What she did to us?"

He wrapped up the last of the hot dog and fries, stuffing them in the bag. "Nothing can take away the betrayal. But there was so much good, you know? So many moments that . . . that can't be faked. Like when you and Lucy were born. The nights your mom and I stayed up late together when one of you were sick. The mix of pride and fear we felt when you deployed overseas as a Marine. There's a depth to those emotions that only a parent can feel. And they were all real. I know they were."

"Or maybe you just want them to be real."

"Yeah, I need them to be real," he whispered. "Besides, last time I checked my trophy case there weren't any medals for Dad of the Year in it."

"You did okay."

"I wasn't there as much as I wanted."

"As a little girl, I hated when you were gone," she said. "When you were home it felt like vacation, though. A thousand miles an hour, activity after activity."

"And a lot of ice cream," he added. "The guilty dad's secret weapon."

"Then when I was older, when I understood why you were gone, you'd think that would have helped. But it didn't. It actually made it worse." Her dad adjusted himself in the passenger seat so he faced her more. "You'd think that knowing my dad was out saving the world, protecting America from her worst enemies, would have made me proud. All it did was make me jealous."

"Mara . . ."

"I couldn't figure out why all of those strangers were more important to you than your family. More important than me."

"They weren't," he said. "All those missions were about making a world where my little girls could grow up safe. So that my grandkids would live in an America that I still recognized."

Mara looked out the window, not trusting herself to meet his eyes. "I know that now. I'm talking when I was growing up. I loved you, but sometimes I wanted to hate you, too. For all the times I looked in the stands at my basketball games and didn't see you there. For the activities at school where other kids brought their dads and I had my grandpa. For the father-daughter dance in ninth grade where you left an hour before it started. I had my hair and nails done. I was so goddamn excited. My dress was . . ." Her voice cracked and she tried to cover it by clearing her throat. "This is ridiculous . . . Why are we even talking about this?" She stuffed the debris from her lunch into one of the bags, as if having a clean car was suddenly of vital importance.

He reached out and put his hand on her forearm. "No, it's okay. I learned the hard way with your mom. You can't keep it in. You have to say the stuff that's inside. Otherwise, one day, you realize you missed your chance."

She stopped, took a deep breath. "When you killed . . . when you made it seem like you killed Mom and betrayed your country . . . there was hate waiting for you. For what you did, but also because if what they said about you was true, then all that time away from us hadn't been for some greater good. It'd all been a lie."

"And now you know it wasn't a lie," he said. "I was doing it all for you. And your sister." He looked out the window and an uncomfortable silence stretched between them. "Your dress was yellow," he finally said. "For that dance. I drove all over town with it to match the color perfectly for my tie. When the call came right before, I did everything I could to at least take you for a little bit. Even just one dance. But men's lives were at stake. I knew some of those men wouldn't have seen their own daughters ever again unless I went and did my job."

"I know that," she said. "I even knew it then, but it still hurt."

"I'm sorry," he said. "For all of it. This wasn't the life I wanted for our family."

She wiped a tear from her cheek. She turned and looked him in the eye. "When this is all over, you owe me a dance."

"As many as you want, kid. I'm all yours."

CHAPTER 33

Night in DC. For the casual observer, the nation's capital accomplishes the goal the architects set out for themselves. Monuments of white marble bathed in light give a sense of pedigree and permanence for a nation still an infant by history's measuring stick. The pillared edifices and grand neoclassical pediments purposefully recalled the great Greek and Roman civilizations, as if the American Empire were a natural continuation of these traditions. The clear intention was that two thousand years into the future, people would still walk among the buildings. And not as ruins, but as the center of a proud and powerful nation.

Even for those who lived in DC, the sight of the National Mall at night was enough to bring up a memory of their less cynical selves. The person who had sought out government service out of a sense of honor, responsibility, and patriotism.

As Mara walked down the graveled walkway toward the Washington Monument, the U.S. Capitol lit up behind her, she felt the power of those ideas. But she felt the sense of responsibility to Joey even more strongly.

She thought about the conversation with her dad earlier. About the balance between the desire to be with your family and the sacrifice needed to do what was necessary to protect them. To protect the world they would one day inherit.

These were the same ideals that had driven her to serve in the Marines. That and a healthy dose of wanting to impress her dad. Only she discovered quickly that the world was more complicated than good guys and bad guys. The battle lines of yesterday's wars were replaced by confusing layers of shifting alliances and hidden enemies. By the time she'd been medivacked off the battlefield for the last time, ending the tour right before she was recruited in the CIA, she carried wounds that were deeper than physical from her time spent protecting America.

Like most soldiers, in the end she was fighting for the man next to her more than anything else. That at least always had a purity to it, even when it felt that everything else was subject to interpretation.

The desire to save Joey held that same level of pure intention. But it was clouded by the fact that she'd be leaving her dad with his flank exposed.

She was second-guessing her plan to part ways with her dad. The operative they'd seen in Iowa was likely still in the field. Or a dozen others like him. If she left her dad to take down the leader of Omega on his own and he failed, then where would that leave them? She'd have Joey, assuming the three men at the house wouldn't be a problem for her, but then they'd be on the run. And her dad and Hawthorn would likely be dead.

"How much do you trust Hawthorn?" she asked.

Her dad, wearing a ball cap to thwart the facial recognition software that might be at work in the area, gave her a side glance. "I trusted him not to tell you about me, even though he thought it was the wrong call. He never gave me up. Not even to the president."

"And he helped you escape after Prague."

"He cracked open a door, but it was all I needed."

She worked through the calculus. There was no reason for Hawthorn to do any of that unless he could be trusted. They couldn't contact him prior to the meet, so anything he had lined up to secure Joey couldn't be changed. There was the possibility that she might even make it worse by injecting herself in his plan without coordination. Or kill an innocent man if one of Hawthorn's men got between her and Joey.

"I'm staying with you," she said.

"Are you sure?"

"No," she said. "But I want this to end. So leaving it up to a couple of old farts like you and Hawthorn seems risky."

He smiled. "You're probably right, but it's your call."

She set her jaw, all playfulness gone, the pre-mission routine of mentally preparing herself already starting. Once a decision was made, she was all in. There was no other way. When she gave her answer, there was no doubt left in her voice.

"Let's get these assholes."

CHAPTER 34

Hawthorn left the W Hotel across from the Treasury Building just after eleven o'clock. He checked up and down the sidewalk, looking for tails out of habit. He hoped Scott and Mara were there, somewhere, but he had no illusion that he would be able to spot either of them. Not unless they meant for him to see them.

He wondered whether the operative deployed in Iowa was there. Maybe. Maybe others, too. His fingers drifted to the gun in his pocket, a reassurance he wouldn't have allowed himself in his younger years as it tipped off anyone with sharp eyes where at least one of his weapons was located, but he needed the touch to steady his nerves.

He'd been on hundreds of meets before, often in foreign countries with governments that hated the United States. This one in the middle of his home turf ought to have been a walk in the park, but it certainly didn't feel that way. And he had a good idea why.

He always knew his adversary, often better than they knew themselves. Armed with a psychological profile, Hawthorn could understand why a zealot claimed to love their country even as he betrayed it, or why a man was willing to kill for money even if he had more than he might ever spend.

But he didn't know the woman he was about to meet. Not really.

He only knew that she was ruthless. That she'd demonstrated time and time again that Omega for which she spoke had incredible reach and resources. He didn't know how deep they were burrowed into his own people, but he'd taken no chances. The few people he felt he could trust completely were on guard detail with little Joey. He owed at least that to Scott and Mara. He hoped they'd repaid the favor by coming to DC and backing him up.

He needed the help because he needed to take the Director alive. Even if it cost him his life.

The meet was at the Korean War Memorial. He'd chosen to walk to give Scott and Mara a chance to see if he picked up any tails. And just in case things didn't go well, it gave him one last time to see this city that he both loved and hated.

It was a town filled with good and evil, altruism and cynicism. The brightest minds came hoping to make a difference, but even the strongest of them inevitably ran aground against the rocky shoals of DC politics. Broken and changed, most fled after a few years, heads shaking as they ran back to life in the private sector to cash in on their time in the cesspool. Those who stuck it out were changed, too, evolving into survivalists in a dystopian world of zero-sum politics and power struggles that rivaled any science fiction novel.

But it was the life he'd known. And he'd done the best he could with it.

He cut through the Ellipse in front of the White House, across Constitution, and entered the World War II Memorial. He stopped in front of the Freedom Wall, where four thousand sculpted gold stars commemorated the over four hundred thousand American lives lost during the war. His father was one of those casualties, and he wondered what his dad would have thought of the world he'd died to save.

Same shit, different day, was what came to mind. His dad had loved saying that. Hawthorn remembered clearly feeling like a man the first time his dad had said it around him.

And he was right. All of it was same shit, different day. But that was the only way the nation was going to survive. Fighting the good fight over and over. Playing relentless defense. Men and women willing to give their all to make a more perfect union even if it felt impossible at times.

Hawthorn smiled as he imagined the saying carved into the granite on the U.S. Capitol building. *Same shit, different day. And ain't it grand?*

Movement to his left drew his attention, and for a fleeting second he saw a man walk behind a pillar. But it was enough of a look for him to know it was Scott. And that meant Mara was somewhere nearby. If Scott had been able to convince her to let his men take care of Joey, that was. He breathed a little easier knowing he had backup.

He looked at his watch and realized he'd lingered longer than he'd meant, a foolish old man lost in his thoughts.

Hawthorn struck out toward the Korean Memorial, forcing himself to focus on the matter at hand. If he was going to survive the next half hour, he needed to be sharp. And damn lucky.

CHAPTER 35

He saw Hawthorn. The old man hadn't taken any measures to disguise his appearance or lower the profile of his approach. He walked down the middle of the gravel path next to the reflection pool that stretched from the Lincoln Memorial toward the Washington Monument like a man out simply to catch the night air.

Asset raised his Mk13 Mod7 and acquired the old man through his optics. With the magnification and the improved light-gathering properties of the Nightforce ATACR riflescope, he could clearly make out Hawthorn's face. He took aim at the man's head, imagining the red spray explosion if he chose to pull the trigger. The .300 Winchester magnum-caliber round wouldn't leave much of Hawthorn's head for the United States Park Police to piece together once they found him.

But his orders were specific. Townsend was on hold. His employer had set up a meet with Hawthorn, one that could impact his mission to kill the ex-president. Without a signal from his employer, he was only to observe the meet and ensure Hawthorn had come alone, as promised.

Asset shifted against the tree where he'd taken position and scanned the area behind Hawthorn for a tail. He'd already inspected the memorial and the area directly around it. He'd located the few cameras that covered the area and easily hijacked their feeds to play a loop of the empty memorial. He doubted if the precaution had been necessary. With thousands of videos canvassing the mall, it wasn't like a human being was reviewing the footage.

But his employer didn't like cameras. And if he ended up having to shoot Hawthorn during the meet, every security agency would be digging through the videos.

He was about to turn back to Hawthorn when he spotted another man on the far side of the reflection pool. He had a ball cap on and a windbreaker. He walked with his hands dug into his pockets, slouched over like a man who'd had a bad day. There was something about his walk that bothered him. A normal person would have missed it. Even he had trouble figuring out exactly what his instinct was telling him.

Asset increased the magnification on his scope, trying to get a closer look at the man's face. The ball cap kept his features in shadow and he had his face just slightly turned away, as if knowing he was being watched.

Then he passed beneath a light and turned just enough for him to get a look.

Asset smiled at what he saw.

CHAPTER 36

Hawthorn approached the memorial carefully, his hand grazing across the gun in his pocket. Unlike the Vietnam Memorial, which sank below ground level as visitors followed along the black wall of names, the Korean War Memorial drew focus to the statues of nineteen soldiers on patrol. They were slightly larger than life, each over seven feet tall, recreated in haunting detail. Thirteen U.S. Army soldiers, three Marines, a Navy Corpsman, and an Air Force Forward Air Observer. Muscles tensed. Eyes scanning for danger. Their worn uniforms showing these were men who had seen action. Their expressions made it clear they knew the horror of what war meant.

Hawthorn felt that he was one of them.

There were a few tourists lingering at the far end, past the black wall that lined one side of the monument that held the etched likeness of men and women who had served in the conflict. They were young, maybe early twenties, and posed for photos in front of the statues. One of them copied the stance of the man on point, giving his friends a good laugh. The act bothered Hawthorn. On a different day he might have marched over to them and had a conversation about sacred ground and sacrifice, but this wasn't the time.

He looked over the area, wondering where she would come from. Wondering if she would come at all.

"Hello, Jim," a voice with a slight English accent came from beside him.

He turned, shocked that she'd been able to get so close to him without him knowing. She was tall, younger than he'd imagined, although her dark skin may have simply covered any signs of age. Her proud bearing was unmistakable. Confident, coiled tight but cocky, a cat walking among mice. She wore black tight running clothes and a hooded sweatshirt that she left up.

"Director, nice to finally meet you," he said.

"Is it?" She cocked her head as if truly curious.

"Not really," he said. "Just being polite."

"Why don't you worry less about being polite and instead tell me why you needed to meet?"

The tourists near the fountain at the far end of the monument were moving on. Hawthorn considered that they might all be operatives, working for this woman. If so, they were good. He walked along the path on the opposite side of the row of statues from them and the Director followed.

"I killed Scott and Mara Roberts," he said.

"Yes, I know."

He allowed himself to look surprised, careful not to overplay it. "How could you know?"

She squinted as she looked at him, and he worried she'd caught some tell that he was playing a part. "Have you really forgotten who I am? Who I represent? We're everywhere. We know everything."

He slouched his shoulders just enough to look resigned to the truth of what she was saying.

"They were my friends."

"You have a message from Townsend?"

He stopped and turned to her. "He wants in."

"In where?"

"Omega. Life on the outside of power doesn't suit him. He craves to be part of it all again. To be relevant. The book was a ploy to get your attention."

"You could have told me this over the phone."

"He wanted the message to go to only you."

"What does he know about me?"

"That you can act on your own discretion, but that really you're just a conduit. There are others behind you, men who tell you what to do, how to do it."

She showed no reaction to the bait. The Director he knew wouldn't have accepted the comment. The woman in front of him was too controlled. Too much into her performance. She was good, but Hawthorn's power of observation was better.

The woman continued to walk. "What is Townsend willing to do to prove his intention?"

Hawthorn stopped and waited for the woman to do the same. "He wants that only to be communicated to the Director herself," he said.

When she saw his face, her expression changed. She took a step back, a hand disappearing into her jacket. He had no doubt that he now had a gun trained on him.

"Is the real Director nearby?" he said. "Or has this just been a waste of time?"

The woman tried a flicker of indignation, but then gave up on it. Her expression turned hard, but she said nothing.

Hawthorn felt the energy drain out of him. It was all for nothing. The woman hadn't come.

"Where is she?" he demanded.

"I'm here, Jim," a new voice said.

As he turned, he felt something hammer his chest. Not a heart attack, or a blow from a fist. A shock so great that he felt he might lose his balance as he tried to make sense of it.

A woman walked up from the shadows behind the fountains and Hawthorn found himself looking at a ghost.

Wendy Roberts.

CHAPTER 37

The old man's head was still in the crosshairs of the Nightforce scope. Asset watched as the black woman turned and left the scene, taking position to the west of the monument. Asset didn't like that there were players on the field he didn't know about, but he wasn't paid to like things. He was paid to kill.

He took three slow breaths and checked his pulse against his neck. Too quick. The professional in him demanded that he focus on the matter at hand. The hunter in him couldn't help but feel the excitement.

Seeing Scott Roberts alive brought with it a rush of emotions. Clearly, Hawthorn had spotted him back in Iowa. How, he didn't have a clue. But he had; then he'd staged the death of the other two for his benefit.

He'd been played for a fool.

But now he would set things right. Not only with Hawthorn, but with Scott Roberts and his daughter. He drifted his sniper rifle to his left and centered his scope on Scott crawling up toward the edge of the monument, where Hawthorn talked with his employer. He moved his finger to the trigger and felt its comforting cool metal against his skin. An easy shot. Too easy. Not nearly the sport he'd hoped for from an operative as renowned as the great Scott Roberts.

But wasn't that just an indication of how much better he was? That he could take out his adversary so easily?

His orders were to kill anyone who appeared to violate Hawthorn's promise to come alone, but to only shoot the old man on a signal.

He settled the entire weight of the rifle on the shooting sticks so it felt weightless in his hands. A deep breath. His heart slowed on command.

The world ceased to exist around him except for what was in the sight.

He envisioned the shot, then pulled the trigger.

CHAPTER 38

Mara followed in a flanking maneuver for the entire walk to the monument. She only spotted the sniper by chance, and with the help of one of Harry's toys.

The sniper had passed on the most obvious positions to cover the meet and instead chosen a copse of trees on a small rise, where he took a prone position on the ground. Using a pair of thermal binoculars, she caught the barest trace of him, a heat signature that might have been a squirrel in the trees.

But staying on the position proved fruitful as the man made a movement, his hand to his neck from what she could tell, allowing her a quick look at his position before he covered back up with a thermal blanket.

She completed the scan, looking for a second sniper or any kind of support, but found none. But she knew from experience that not seeing something didn't mean it wasn't there. She needed to proceed with caution.

A look at the Korean War Memorial, where Hawthorn had just been joined by a tall woman in a hoodie, told her she didn't have much time.

Taking a wide arc around the sniper's position, she worked her way through the trees, coming up directly behind him. The ground was wet from rain earlier, otherwise she doubted the approach would have worked.

She was only a few feet away, behind a tree, when she saw him adjust the rifle on the shooting sticks.

He was about to fire.

Mara lunged forward and kicked the barrel just as the rifle discharged with a muffled *thumph*, its suppressor stifling the shot's sound.

She dropped her body mass straight down at the lump under the thermal blanket, leading the point of the knife in her hand.

The man was gone, rolled out to the side an instant earlier.

Pain exploded in her right shoulder. She kicked and twisted her body as a knife sliced the air inches from her face.

She countered with a blind thrust, risking the exposure to buy time.

Her knife found flesh and dug in, eliciting a grunt of pain from the man.

She didn't press the attack. She had no blade awareness of her opponent, and the opening she thought was there might have been a trap. Bait designed to get her to gamble and try to end the fight early.

Her instinct told her that it would end if she lunged forward, but not the way she wanted it.

Instead, she pushed back, rolled, and climbed to her feet. She reached for her gun, but it wasn't there.

She'd lost it on the ground, somewhere in the leaves.

The man was on his feet in front of her, favoring his left leg, where she'd stuck him. He didn't reach for a gun either. She wondered if he didn't have one, or if his ego had the better of him and he wanted the knife fight.

Either way, it showed overconfidence. A weakness she might exploit.

She recognized him from the farm in Iowa. He seemed to know her as well because he grinned and inclined his head, as if they were acquaintances enjoying a chance meeting on the street.

Her shoulder ached, a slashing wound through the muscle. Not bad, but enough to give the man in front of her an edge in a fight.

She shifted her knife to her left hand. She preferred her right, but not by much. Purposefully, she assumed an awkward grip and posture, as if fighting left was a foreign idea to her.

If she was correct about the man in front of her, she was going to need every advantage she could get.

CHAPTER 39

Wendy.

It couldn't be. But there she was, walking toward Hawthorn. Alive. Her mannerisms unmistakable even from a distance. The tilt of her head. The movement of her hands. The way she glided instead of walked. The proud, confident bearing that had always made her stand out in any room she entered. It was her.

His wife.

Back from the dead.

He choked back a sob at the sheer surprise of it. The years of pain and false grief pouring off him like layers of accumulated sediment. The reality of seeing her slamming him forward into the moment.

Into the truth of what her presence meant.

Betrayal. All over again.

The shock passed through him and left behind a new emotion. It started as disappointment, grew to anger, and then ended in rage.

He climbed up from his hiding spot, snipers be damned, and set out to confront the woman who'd broken his heart all over again.

CHAPTER 40

Mara lunged with her left, leaving her right shoulder open to attack, trying to draw the man in. He didn't take the bait. Instead, he retreated and circled her, first left and then right. Too cautious for her liking.

"The great Mara Roberts," he said. "It's a pleasure."

"The pleasure's all yours, asshole."

He grinned. The overconfidence showing again. Or was he good enough to fake that weakness to lure her into a trap?

"It's a small world you and I inhabit," he said. "I know of you."

"I don't know anything about you."

He grinned again, maddening in its casualness. "I believe that makes me better than you, yes?"

"We'll see."

She pressed the attack, feigning a stabbing motion at his abdomen before switching to a slash up to his chin.

He blocked her with his forearm, but it was what she expected.

She rolled in, her right fist slamming into his face. Then she sprang back, just as his right hand cut through the air with the knife.

Her hand ached, it was about as good a punch as she could land. And it had barely fazed him.

A small trickle of blood from his left nostril was the only evidence she'd landed on the attack.

He licked his lips, tasting the blood.

"My turn," he said.

The man came in fast, a whirlwind of jabs and feints. He started high, but then crouched low to the ground, stabbing up at her.

She was on her heels, backing up on unsteady ground, but she blocked him again and again. She made a few weak counterattacks just to slow him down, but they were ineffective against the onslaught.

Her lungs burned, but she ignored it. Adrenaline brought everything into high focus. She knew one mistake and someone was going to die.

No sooner had the thought come to her than it happened.

The man lunged, leaving an opening. She reacted to it on instinct, even as another part of her brain screamed that it was a trap.

Once she stepped into her attack, the man closed off the opening and twisted into a plunging motion, the point of his knife directed at her neck.

But her right hand rose to block it. The knife skewered the center of it, the blood-covered blade sticking out of the back of her hand.

Her hand that had not been holding her knife.

The man's eyes opened wide in recognition of his mistake. Mara had sacrificed her hand to lure him in. And he'd fallen for it.

Mara's left hand slammed her knife into the man's rib cage.

He cried out, gasping as if amazed at the intensity of the pain.

Mara twisted her right hand, the man's knife still in it, and ripped it away from him.

He staggered backward, fear in his eyes.

"I guess you weren't better," she said. Then kicked him in the groin like she was a World Cup soccer player.

*　*　*

Mara felt satisfied the man was tied well enough. As an extra precaution, she found a thick branch on the ground and smacked him over the head with it. She wanted the man alive when this was all over. He wouldn't break easily, but he would eventually give up the answers she wanted. They always did.

Once he was secure, she rewrapped her hand with a strip of cloth she'd torn from her shirt. It hurt like a son of a bitch, but being dead would have been a lot worse. From what she could tell it'd been a clean puncture through the meat of her hand. She hoped there'd be no permanent damage, as it was the hand she liked to kill bad guys with.

She grabbed the man's rifle. She'd lost her binoculars in the fight and she wanted to see what was going on down at the meet.

Using the shooting sticks to balance the gun so that she could get a clear view with the high magnification, she took a look.

First, she saw her dad and Hawthorn, standing side by side. That wasn't the plan. Something had gone wrong.

Then she turned to the right, going too far at first so that the person they were speaking to was only in the frame for a split second.

She edged the gun back to the left, centering the scope on the woman.

Mara blinked hard, trying to clear her vision, because there was something wrong with her. The woman below looked exactly like her mother.

CHAPTER 41

Scott walked toward her, hands out to his sides, unable to say anything. He felt numb. A buzzing sound filled his ears. Hawthorn turned toward him and then looked away, as if the sight of him was too much to bear.

Wendy had no such problem. She stared at him, chin thrust out as if challenging him to look her in the eye.

"Hello, Scott," she said. "I heard you were dead."

"I heard the same about you." He pulled his gun from his jacket and aimed it at her head. For a second, his anger and his pain nearly proved to be too much. But his need to have his questions answered stopped him from pulling the trigger.

"We need her alive," Hawthorn hissed.

"What the fuck is going on?" was all Scott could manage. He hardly recognized his own voice. It sounded like someone was strangling him.

He swore there was a flicker of doubt in her face, not fear of the gun he held, but a softening. The barest sign of the woman he once loved. Then, just as fast, it was gone. "Nice that you haven't changed much. Then again, Townsend's still alive, so maybe you have. Maybe you've gone soft."

Scott regripped the gun like it was trying to squirm out of his hand. "Maybe I learned from that mistake."

"Scott," Hawthorn said. "We take her in. We'll have years to question her."

"I want answers," Scott said. "Now."

"What do you want me to say? I'm sorry? Well, I'm not." She pointed to them both. "Think of the things the two of you have done for your country. The laws you've broken. All the people killed in the name of national security, both targets and collateral damage."

"I saw you die. I saw you go over the bridge," Scott said.

"The first shot was staged. My gun, remember? I just needed a clean way out. I knew Hawthorn was on to me."

"How did you know?" Hawthorn asked.

She smiled as if talking to a little boy. "There's little Omega doesn't know."

"And the second shot?" Scott asked.

"That was a little surprise gift from my employer. Shoulder wound to make it even more convincing. There were divers in the water waiting for me." Her eyes burned as she recalled the memory. A shudder passed through her, maybe a recollection of the freezing waters.

"You went into the water as Wendy Roberts and came out as the Director of Omega," Hawthorn said.

"No, that took a while to work up the food chain once I was out of deep cover." She smirked at Scott. "But you know how competitive I am."

"Why?" Scott hated how weak his voice sounded. Waves of nausea crashed over him as a lifetime of belief and identity collapsed in on itself. Even the words she'd said on the bridge had been lies. She'd never loved him. She hadn't kept the charade going to protect their daughters. None of it was true. And that left him with nothing to cling on to.

Then a new thought hit him even harder. Mara couldn't know. It would crush her. He refused to have her endure the betrayal all over again. As Wendy spoke, his brain rifled through a way to protect his daughter.

"Omega is more important than us. More important than any one country. It's the future of humanity."

"How can you say that?" Hawthorn said.

"The world is failing. You can see the signs everywhere. When nations crumble, there has to be something there to rebuild it from the ashes. Omega will be there, even when everything else is gone."

"Do you really believe this bullshit?" Scott said. "Or is someone listening in on us? Because this is class A looney bin prepper talk here."

Wendy expression changed, adopting the look of a teacher speaking with the slowest student in the class. "You don't get it. We're not waiting for the world to end. The cataclysmic fire that would come on its own might destroy everyone. No, like good stewards, we intend a controlled burn. Destruction of only what is necessary for new growth to take root."

Scott heard the certainty in her voice. Saw the seething fire in her eyes as she spoke. It was the look of madness, found in messiahs and zealots, priests and penitents alike. This was her new religion. Or maybe it had been her religion all along.

"Our family," he whispered. "Our two daughters. You just left them. You left me. You left Lucy to die alone."

Wendy blinked hard twice, but that was the only outward sign she gave that his words made a damn bit of difference to her. He realized he didn't know this woman. That he never had.

She turned to Hawthorn. "I know you met with Townsend. Was there a message for me, or was it all subterfuge to get this meeting?"

"No, he had a message he wanted me to deliver to you and the Council."

"And it is?"

"That you and the hairy bastards you serve can go straight to hell."

Wendy inclined her head, as if in resignation. She raised her right hand and then lowered it, quickly. If it was a signal to someone, that someone wasn't watching.

Scott's reflexes twitched as he anticipated gunfire. But when none came, he knew there was only one likely explanation: Mara had neutralized whatever threat had been out there. But that meant she might have seen whom he was talking to. He couldn't bear that thought.

Wendy raised her hand again and snapped it down.

Fear replaced the smug look on her face.

"Expecting someone?" Scott said.

"How about me, Mom?" Mara said, walking out from the darkness. "Were you expecting me?"

CHAPTER 42

Asset squinted his eyes open, feeling like he had to crawl out of a dark hole trying to pull him back down into unconsciousness. A burst of pain in his side and in the back of his head took his breath away. Light flashed, exploding into a million points of pain that cascaded through his body.

There was comfort to be had if he just let himself slip back asleep, but he fought against it. The person who'd hit him was still alive. And he needed to take care of that.

Even in his urgency to get loose, he knew the importance of calm. He closed his eyes, focusing on his breathing. On his heartbeat. And he slowed them both down, clearing his head of both pain and panic.

Once he was in control, he tested his bindings. His hands were zip-tied together behind his back, then connected by a short rope to his feet, forcing him into a prone position with his back arched.

The pain radiating from the knife wound in his side threatened to make him black out again. The way he was tied pulled his rib cage taut, making it hurt even more.

But he knew that if he didn't concentrate that he'd be spending the rest of his life in some CIA interrogation hellhole. He had to escape, and he had to do it now.

He took inventory of the area around him and the state of his bindings. There was some play in the rope between his feet and hands. The woman had been in too much of a hurry, or had relied too much on his staying unconscious. Either way, the mistake was going to cost her.

He rolled three full times over to a metal fence surrounding ground under repair, each rotation sending another shock wave of pain through his rib cage. It took only a few seconds for him to find a sharp area on one of the posts and set to work on the rope. The first binding snapped clean, and his arms and legs were no longer connected. His shoulders screamed with the release. He pressed his forearm against the wound on his side, wincing from the pain.

The zip ties on his wrists were harder to break. The burr on the metal post kept slicing into his wrist. After his hands were slicked with blood, he decided to try a different tack. He leaned against a tree, resting his shoulder against it. Lifting off only a few inches, he slammed his shoulder, popping the joint out of its socket. He was amazed at the next level of pain his body was able to deliver. He clenched his teeth, his training reminding him that pain was purely biology. Fear brought by the pain was what hurt performance. And fear was all mental.

He took a deep breath, willing the pain to disappear into his body. Carefully, he rotated his arm around until his hands were in front of him.

He sat on the ground and untied both of his boots. He pulled one of the laces through the small gap between his wrists and then tied it to the lace on his other boot. Once the knot was tight, he rocked back so that his legs were off the ground, tension on the laces. Carefully, he moved his legs in a bicycle motion, working the laces back and forth like a saw. Within seconds, the zip ties popped, freeing his hands.

He stood, unsteady on his feet at first, but quick to stabilize. He didn't bother feeling his pulse. It was jackhammering. For once in his professional life, he didn't give a shit.

He went back to the same tree and leaned against it, kneading the muscle around his shoulder socket. With a sudden thrust, he jammed it back into place.

Next, he searched the area for his rifle. She'd taken that, of course. His knife was gone, too.

But under a nearby bush, he found his backpack of supplies. She'd missed that. He pulled out a Sig Sauer handgun and the extra clip, shoving it into his pocket.

Then, holding his side and gritting his teeth against the pain, he struggled toward the Korean War Memorial, hoping he wasn't too late to join in the fun.

CHAPTER 43

Mara felt a burning in her chest as she walked toward her mom. She did her best to control the emotional reaction to seeing the woman she'd mourned for years standing in front of her, but it was a losing battle. Tears formed in her eyes, but they were as much anger as anything else.

For her part, Wendy looked unsteady at the sight of her daughter. She took a half step back. A show of weakness and hesitancy, but one that Mara registered as being a calculated movement. She knew she couldn't trust anything this woman did. The fact she was still breathing instead of being at the bottom of the Vltava river was proof of that.

"You did all of this?" she asked. "You had Joey taken?"

"He was never going to be hurt," she said.

"Bullshit," Hawthorn said. "Those weren't the orders you gave."

"Jesus, Wendy. Why?" Scott said. "Betray your country. Betray me. All right. But sacrifice your daughter? Your own grandson? For what?"

Wendy set her jaw, held her head higher, eyes signaling nothing but scorn. "The movement of history is greater than all of us. Just think for a second. What is a single family in a world of billions of people? What is a single life compared to the drive and thrust of all humanity?"

"There's a homeless guy in Lafayette Park who says crazy shit like that to all the tourists," Scott said. "Maybe you can hang out with him after your prison term."

"The difference is that guy in Lafayette Park is crazy. I'm just telling you the truth."

"The truth?" Mara spit out. "Nothing about you has been the truth. Not ever."

Wendy's features softened. "I never wanted children, but it was determined it was better for my cover. To anchor my relationship with your father. For what it's worth, I enjoyed it more than I ever imagined."

"For what it's worth?" Mara said, raising her gun to point it at her mom's head. "Nothing. That's what it's worth. Absolutely nothing."

"Mara, no," her dad said.

"Why not? We thought she was already dead. Why not make that a reality? What would change?"

It was Hawthorn who answered. "We need to know what she knows. We need her to get inside Omega."

"She won't talk," Mara said. "Look at her. She'll never talk."

"Everyone talks," Scott said. "Eventually."

Wendy pursed her lips as if in pity. "No, I'm afraid Mara is right. Besides, I'm not going anywhere."

The first two shots hit Hawthorn in the chest. The involuntary clench of his right hand discharged his gun, but it fired harmlessly up in the air.

Mara, gun still trained on her mom, saw the muzzle flash in the shadows behind the monument less than thirty yards away. Nine-mil fire. It was the woman who had first pretended to be Hawthorn's contact.

"Mara!" her dad yelled.

Her training told her what to do. Even if it meant more exposure to fire, secure the primary target. A wounding shot to disable her mom, a bullet in the shoulder or the leg. Then turn her attention to the threat in the shadows.

She moved the gun from her mom's head to her shoulder, going for the minimum amount of movement, knowing every split second counts. Her brain was running hundreds of options, weighing odds and probable outcomes. It all came out the same. Either her or her dad was going to take a bullet from the shooter. It just mattered which target the asshole chose first.

Her finger pressed on the trigger of the Sig Sauer. Slowly, as she'd been trained, even with the very real possibility that more than one bullet could already be in flight toward her.

She'd nearly reached the exact pounds of pressure to fire her gun when she froze.

It was her mom standing in front of her.

She couldn't do it.

In that split second, her mom knew it, too. And the look she gave Mara was one she would never forget.

Pure disdain.

A grunt of pain to her left and she knew her dad had taken the next bullet.

She lowered to a knee, double-handed her gun, and fired five shots at the muzzle flash in the shadows.

A woman's voice cried out, and Mara saw the outline of the woman as she stood, clutching her side.

There was no hesitation this time. Two more shots and the target went down hard.

Mara pivoted to her right to see her mom running. She trained in on her as she ran, her brain screaming at her to take the shot.

She did, aiming low at her legs, and was rewarded with a spark off of one of the metal statues of the memorial. Missed. Her mom continued to run, south toward the Lincoln Memorial.

"Jim!" her dad yelled to her left.

Her dad ran with his right arm hanging limp, a red stain spreading through his shoulder. He reached Hawthorn and turned him over.

Even from where she was, she heard him groan in pain. A good sign. Dead men didn't make a sound.

Her dad said something to Hawthorn she couldn't hear. "How bad?" she shouted.

"Crafty son of a bitch was wearing a vest," he said. "He'll be all right. Go. Don't let her get away."

Mara sprinted toward the last spot she'd seen her mom, cussing herself for choking on the shot to disable her. At least she wasn't armed. She at least had that advantage.

She ran past the soldier statues, cutting diagonally on the path that led to the Lincoln Memorial. There was a drop-off area right next to the Memorial and easy access to Independence Avenue. She worried her mom might have a driver waiting for her there. Or at least a car. She hoped that the woman with the 9mm and the man she'd left tied up were the only two operatives in the field. She thought that if there were more, they would have brought their firepower to bear already.

As the wooded path opened to the concrete plaza in front of the Lincoln Memorial, Mara's stomach dropped.

A man was curled up in a ball on the ground, his neck twisted unnaturally. A uniformed cop.

Mara knelt next to the body, gun raised toward the dozens of places her mom could have been waiting for her. She took a chance and reached out to check for a pulse. Nothing.

She didn't need to look, but she did anyway. Her suspicion was right. The man's gun was gone.

Her mom had just evened the playing field.

CHAPTER 44

Scott watched Mara run into the night, fighting the urge to follow her. The gunshot was the same shoulder that'd been hit when they escaped the prison. It felt like the slug was lodged in his flesh, burning its way through the muscle. But he'd been shot enough times to know that wasn't the case. It hurt like hell but getting shot always did.

He gathered his gun that he'd dropped when he was hit and then propped up Hawthorn, who groaned as his eyes fluttered open.

"You took a couple in the vest," he said. "Are you hit anywhere else?"

Hawthorn's eyes bolted wide open, as if just realizing where he was. He tried to sit up. "Where . . . you have to . . ." Then he groaned and slouched back to the ground.

"Easy," Scott said. "Let me take a look." He tore at Hawthorn's shirt, popping the buttons off. He inspected it for any sign of blood. Nothing.

"Can't breathe. Get this thing off me."

Scott pulled him up into a sitting position, peeling his suit jacket off first, then the dress shirt. The Kevlar vest had thin armored plates, an advanced body armor Scott had never seen before. Courtesy of the CIA tech masters. Fortunate given the firepower they'd gone up against. Scott wrangled it over Hawthorn's head using only his good hand.

Finally, he got it off and Hawthorn slumped against him, eyes clenched in pain. "I don't think I'm hit."

Hawthorn had worn a white T-shirt beneath the vest, which made an inspection quick and easy. "I don't see anything. You got damn lucky."

"Few broken ribs, I think. Hurts like hell, but I'm okay. Leave me here. I'll call in backup. Go help Mara."

Scott hitched his good hand under one of Hawthorn's arms and dragged him over to the Korean War Memorial wall so he had something to lean against. Hawthorn already had his phone out.

"Have them send a medic for you. I'm going after—"

The phone exploded in Hawthorn's hand, the unmistakable sound of a bullet ricocheting off the granite inches from his head.

Scott knew a second bullet would come, and he instinctively stepped in front of his friend.

A searing pain in his leg made his shoulder feel like a bee sting. He had the presence of mind to realize the shot would have been directed at Hawthorn's head. Whoever was shooting would aim at him next. And he wasn't likely to miss.

With a yell, he dove for the vest on the ground in front of him, hearing a bullet whiz past his head. He just hoped it hadn't found its mark with Hawthorn.

Adrenaline helped mask the pain as he grabbed the vest, held it up, and crouched behind it.

Two rounds hammered into it, twisting the vest violently in his hand. But the bullets didn't penetrate. The geniuses in the CIA lab had done their work well.

He fired three quick shots in the general direction of the on-slaught. Hoping to get lucky. Or to just slow his attacker down.

To his surprise, he heard a grunt of pain.

A quick look revealed his target. The operative from the farmhouse. Slouched to one side, injured from a lucky shot, but with his gun still in hand.

On instinct, Scott rushed forward, keeping low to the ground. Kevlar vest held in front of his chest and head, not sure if it would do a damn bit of good, he fired, hoping to keep his adversary pinned.

His legs churned as he closed the distance.

But then another round hit his already injured leg and he lost his balance.

His momentum carried him into the shooter, crashing into him with all of his bulk like a linebacker making a highlight film tackle.

Scott kept the vest up in front of him, covering the man with it as they fell to the ground together.

The pain that had somehow taken a backseat during his rush forward came flooding back. It hit him so hard that he thought he might black out. If he did, he was as good as dead.

The man beneath him recovered quickly. Scott's upper body was covered by the vest, so the man ducked down and landed a rapid series of punches on the bullet wounds in Scott's leg.

Scott yelled and dropped an elbow on the man's neck, a shaft of white-hot agony shooting up through his shoulder.

He connected and the man rolled away, crouching like an animal, favoring one side.

Neither of them had their guns. Scott had lost his when they collided. He didn't know if his adversary had lost his, too, or if he was out of ammo. The fact Scott was still alive now that they had separation between them meant it was one or the other.

The two men stood face-to-face with each other, gladiators in the ring, bleeding and ready for blood.

Sirens erupted nearby. First to their left. Then their right. The cavalry was on the way. Hawthorn's call must have gone through. Then again, the gunfire in the nation's capital was enough to spin up a dozen or more law enforcement agencies into action.

"In a minute or two, this place will be sealed off," Scott said, hoping to put off another attack. He swayed unsteadily on his feet, not sure he would last longer than one punch if the man charged him.

The observation surprisingly had an impact. Scott watched as the man raised a hand to his own neck and rested it there. As if taking his own pulse.

The sirens grew louder. The *thump-thump-thump* of a helo rose in the distance.

"You were injured before we met," the man said.

Scott put a hand up to his gunshot wound. "Shoulder."

The man stood upright, no longer in a fighting position. He had the look of a man who had reached a decision. "Next time, we'll start on even ground. I want your best."

"My best was twenty years ago," Scott said, stretching for time. "But if you come for me, you'll find what I have now can still kick your scrawny little ass."

The man smiled, as if he truly relished the insult. Then he turned and half-ran, half-staggered into the night, clutching his wounds.

Scott scrambled for his gun on the ground. It took him ten long seconds to find it. It might as well have been an hour. When he spun to where the man had run, there was nothing but shadows.

He remembered the shot that had gone past him. He feared the worst as he turned back to the wall. But Hawthorn was still there, raising his hand to signal he was okay.

Scott pulled his belt from his pants and wrapped it around his leg as a tourniquet, cinching it as tight as he could stand. The leg was turning numb, which wasn't a good sign, but he didn't have time to worry about that.

Grunting with each step, he hobbled in the direction he'd last seen Mara chasing her mother. He just hoped he wasn't too late.

CHAPTER 45

Mara heard the sirens as she ran around the left side of the Lincoln Memorial. Flashes of blue and red light reflected off the white marble walls told her they were close.

She spotted her mom running across the street, waving her gun at motorists, trying to get them to stop. DC residents, hardened by years of terrorist threats, weren't about to stop for someone with a gun. If anything, they sped up.

Mara dropped to a knee and lined up a shot. It was fifty yards and her hands were shaking. She waited until her mom was clear of traffic and then squeezed off a round.

By her reaction, the bullet hit the pavement just beside her. Where Mara had aimed. Just to get her attention.

She had it. Her mom spun toward her and unloaded several shots at her.

Mara pressed herself flat to the ground, hoping her mom wasn't a very good shot.

The shots faded and she risked a look up just in time to see her run toward Memorial Bridge.

Mara climbed to her feet and gave chase.

By the time she reached the bridge, passing by the gilded Arts of War statues that guarded the entrance, police cars sped toward her from all directions.

The far end of the bridge was already lit up with emergency lights and a blockade of police cars blocking the width of it.

The last civilian cars sped off the bridge as she ran onto it. Her gun was raised and she considered the risk that some fresh-faced police officer might mistakenly take a shot at her.

The safe bet was to surrender to the flood of cops rushing into position behind her. But she knew how that would go. They'd throw her on the ground, cuff her, then spend the next ten minutes trying to confirm her identity. That didn't work for her. So she rolled the dice and sprinted toward her mom.

"Stop," she yelled. "It's no use."

Her mom was in the middle of the bridge when she finally stopped. Mara didn't think it had anything to do with her command, but simply that she'd run out of options. That made her dangerous.

Mara held out her hands, the gun still in one, but now pointed away toward the dark Potomac River flowing beneath them. "It's over," she said, getting closer so she didn't have to shout. "There's no way out."

A helo approached from downriver, a powerful spotlight painting the area around them. Her mom grinned as she watched it approach, the harsh white light giving her eyes a crazed look. Mara saw the cop's gun she'd stolen was still in her hand. To her relief, she saw her mom was pulling the trigger over and over. Out of bullets.

"C'mon," she said. "Let me take you in."

Her mom looked around with a mix of disbelief and jagged amusement. "Hard to believe I ended up on another bridge."

"I don't think you'd get away with a jump over the edge this time."

She made a show of looking down at the black waters below. "You're probably right. No SCUBA divers waiting for me this time."

"I'd ask you why all this happened, but I don't think you'd give me an answer," she said. "Not a real one. Not one that would matter."

"How about the truth? Would the truth matter, Mara?"

She felt her throat tighten. The way she said her name made her feel like a teenager again. "Try me."

Her mom smirked, as if amused by the whole thing. She pointed back to the end of the bridge they'd come from. It was now cordoned off with rows of police vehicles. "Do you know what those statues are called? The ones on horseback?"

"No, I don't."

"Valor and sacrifice," her mom said. "Fitting, isn't it?"

"Valor is courage, especially in battle. I don't see how that's fitting at all."

"That's because you don't know the ways of the world. Not yet. Not really," her mom said. "There are forces at work greater than you can appreciate."

"Enlighten me."

"The world is already dead, Mara. It just doesn't know it yet. We can't escape population growth, global warming, nuclear proliferation in the hands of terrorists, the rise of automation that will create massive revolts from the working class. The coming unrest will tear down every structure of civilization we know. The future will destroy us all, unless someone is ready to take control."

"Omega."

"I have sacrificed everything for this fight, but it was necessary. And I've been proven right. Things have deteriorated worse than imagined. Everything hangs on a thread, you have to sense that. You always were the smart one, Mara."

She hated the swell of pride she felt at the compliment. She pushed past it, not wanting to give her mom the satisfaction of seeing it.

"Smart enough to know bullshit when I see it. What's this really about? Money? Power? Who do you really work for?"

Her mom looked disappointed. "You must see it. The evidence is everywhere. Even here in America, the police have been equipped with military vehicles. DHS last year stockpiled over two billion rounds of ammunition, for training purposes they say. They know it's coming just like we do. Only they won't be ready to do what's necessary."

"So this group, this Omega, they'll be ready? They'll be the ones to save us all?" Mara said, feeling sick to her stomach. She found herself wishing the reason for her mom's betrayal was more simple. Misplaced nationalistic fervor. Patriotism to Russia. Anything but this madness.

"Oh no," her mom said, looking at her like she was too slow to be believed. "Omega isn't going to save everyone. It's going to make certain most of the world dies. But the important people live. We are the Omega and the Alpha. The end and the beginning. The right people will live so that civilization can be reborn."

Mara didn't want to hear any more. "The right people? You mean the smart ones like you who got taken down by an old man and a washed-up CIA operative? A two-man operation against big bad Omega and they really stuck it to you. I got to say, if you guys are supposed to be the world's salvation, then maybe we really are screwed."

Her mom's smirk disappeared and Mara raised her gun. "While I can't stand to hear another goddamn thing you say, the people at Langley are going to have a great time talking to you."

Her mom walked toward her. "I'm not going in. I can't. I think you already know that."

"That's where you're wrong," Mara said. "There's no way out."

She took a deep breath and then slowly pulled a knife from a side pocket. "I'm sorry I didn't reach out to you, Mara. With enough time, I think I could have opened your eyes to the truth. What a force we could have been working together. I see that now."

Mara's eyes were locked on the knife. "You try to hurt yourself and I'll put a hole through your hand," she said.

"I'm not going to hurt myself," her mom said. "You don't think Omega has people at either end of this bridge? We're everywhere."

"They'll never get you out of here," she said.

"You could have learned so much from me." She glanced up at the helo, staring into the light for a few seconds before closing her eyes, swaying slightly in place.

"It doesn't need to end here," Mara said. "You can come in."

Her mom opened her eyes at the words. She gave the barest inclination of her head as her eyebrows raised, a gesture straight out of Mara's childhood. "Don't be silly, Mara. You know better."

Her mom lunged forward, knife raised.

"No!" Mara shouted, holding her hands out toward the police at the bridge.

But it was no use. Her mom's movement was precise, fast enough to sell it, but slow enough to give the SWAT teams a clean shot.

Multiple bullets entered her from both directions almost simultaneously. High-powered rounds that left puffs of red in the air, illuminated by the helo floodlights from above.

The violent twisting of her body was made worse because the bullets effectively propped her up as more rounds slammed into her. Finally, the shooting stopped and she fell to the pavement.

Mara stood in stunned disbelief as pools of blood spread from her mom's body. She staggered forward and then dumped to the ground so that her face was next to hers.

She was surprised when the tears came, then the wracking sobs as she pulled her mom to her. The feelings came from somewhere deep inside, the same place that had prevented her from taking the shot earlier. The same place that had so desperately wanted her to surrender. The same place that made it impossible to hate her own mother.

Police cars roared in from either side, and the air filled with men shouting for her to move away from the body. They sounded distant, nothing more than echoes.

But then another voice shouted over them all and it quieted down.

A hand touched her shoulder, but she didn't flinch. Somehow, she knew who it was.

"C'mon," her dad said. "Let her go."

Mara shook her head. She knew it made no sense, she knew she ought to hate this woman, but she couldn't make herself move.

"This isn't your mom," he whispered. "Your mom was the person we both loved years ago. Kind, genuine, brilliant. It doesn't matter what she said tonight, or what she became since you saw her last, that past life with her was real. You still have that. And so do I."

Mara let go of the woman's body and leaned into her dad, clinging to him. He wrapped an arm around her and they cried together, the police waiting respectfully around them. As Mara's head cleared, she glanced around at the group of them, thinking about what her mom had said, wondering which of the men here worked for Omega. There was no way to know, but she resolved to one day find out.

CHAPTER 46

Ryker read the message on his tablet device a second time; then he threw it at the nearest wall, shattering its glass screen. One of his men ran into the room, gun half-drawn from his shoulder holster. Ryker turned on him. "Leave me," he roared.

The man followed the orders without hesitation.

Ryker stood and paced the room. It was his favorite in the house. Floor-to-ceiling bookshelves, his prized collection of ancient scientific texts. Da Vinci, Copernicus, Newton, Edison. Rational men who had all dared to think outside the constraints of the accepted wisdom of their ages. They were creators. Visionaries. And he would one day join their ranks.

But not as soon as he wanted.

The Director was dead. The asset she'd deployed in the field had laid out the details in the message, but he'd skimmed over that. There would be time for that later. Time to analyze the series of events that had led to the failure. Time to grasp on to the lessons learned. Time to make adjustments.

But right now it was time for him to be angry.

He hadn't realized how much he'd invested himself in moving the timetable of his plan forward. Now, with the prospect of a year or more delay, it seemed an interminable wait.

And it was his fault. His poor judgment had insisted she go to

America for the meeting. A stupid decision, especially when the stakes were so high.

He slammed his hand on his desk, trying to purge his self-pity. It was a wasted emotion and he hated waste.

This was a setback, nothing more. The plan would continue. In fact, if he manipulated the Council to put the right person into the Director's chair, he would be able to use that person the way he'd planned to use Wendy Roberts. Perhaps he wouldn't have to wait the extra year or two after all.

He straightened and drew in a deep breath to steady himself. The plan wasn't ruined, he could see that now. In the long chain of history, this was no more than a blink of the eye. Even if Townsend released his book, or if Scott and Mara Roberts kept at their investigation into Omega, it wouldn't be in time. That was where the Council and the Director had both been wrong. Focus on such trivial matters was beneath him.

Because, if things worked out as planned, all of those people would be dead soon enough.

Feeling better, he decided to make a trip to his lab the next day. Deep in underground facilities in the mountains of Berchtesgaden, his scientists closing in on the final solution to the world's more intractable problem.

Man.

His scientists were the best in the world. They and their families had all been promised a spot in the new world he would create, so their loyalty was absolute. They were close, so close. Their fault so far was that their solution was too efficient, too perfect. Ryker didn't want to kill off the entire human race. He wasn't a madman.

The men whose books surrounded him had been geniuses of their age. Creators. Like them, he would also create a new civilization out of the ashes of the old. But for that to happen, he had first to set fire to the world.

And he took great pleasure at the thought of it.

CHAPTER 47

Mara stared at the door that led to the Oval Office, apprehensive about how she'd react when it opened. Her dad sat in a chair across from her, head leaned back against the wall, eyes closed. He didn't seem to share her anxiety, but that might have been because of the pain meds. He wore a full cast on one leg and a sling on his shoulder.

Joey ran into the waiting room followed close behind by a Secret Service agent, who looked like he was having just as much fun chasing his little protectee as the kid was having running from him. The agent caught himself once he entered the room, withering under the disapproving stare of President Patterson's executive secretary, a stern, ancient woman named Ms. Ferris. The agent stood up rigidly, assuming the don't-screw-with-me look all the Secret Service had down to perfection. Mara found it funny the old woman could have such an effect on the large man.

"Agent Hallsey says there's ice cream in the mess," Joey said, running up to Mara.

"The mess?" Scott said, opening his eyes barely enough to look at the agent. "Are you turning my grandson into a navy brat?"

The agent let a smirk turn up the corner of his mouth for all of two seconds. "No, sir, I'm an ex-Army Ranger. I'd advise the young man to stay far away from the navy."

"You're talking to an ex-Marine," Scott said.

"I'm sorry, sir," Agent Hallsey said. "But it's not my fault you chose the Marines."

Scott grinned, gave him a nod of approval, and closed his eyes again.

Joey tugged on Mara's sleeve. "He says they have all kinds of flavors down there."

"Is that right, Agent Hallsey?" Mara said.

"Yes, ma'am. Chocolate. Vanilla. And, sometimes, mint chocolate chip."

He delivered the list as if sharing state secrets, and Joey ate it up.

"Can I go? Hallsey said he'd take me."

"Can I go, too?" Scott said.

She pointed to her dad. "You're staying here." Then she turned to Joey. "And it's Agent Hallsey."

"I mean, Agent Hallsey. Pleeeease."

Mara laughed. She was amazed at Joey's resilience. Since being recovered from the safe house, he'd fallen back into his routine faster than any of them had. True to his word, Hawthorn had kept Joey comfortable the entire time. Even equipping his room with a PlayStation along with a box of games. Joey had actually asked when he could go back to the house for a visit.

By comparison, Mara's own state of mind was bordering on paranoia. Everywhere she turned she thought she saw evidence of Omega. Once she was reunited with Joey, she'd demanded he be put into protective custody.

But the agents assigned to her were junior people she didn't know, which only made her more paranoid that they could be working for the other side. It took three days before she'd let Joey leave her sight. Now, a week out, she was finally starting to feel like herself again.

"So, can I go?"

"Only on one condition," she said.

"What's that?"

"That you bring me back some ice cream."

"Yes," Joey said, his tiny hand clenched in a fist. He turned to the agent. "You hear that? We can go."

The agent gave his own fist pump and mimicked Joey's, "Yes!"

As Joey left, Mara said, "Thank you, Agent Hallsey. You're making his day."

"My pleasure, ma'am. He's a good kid." He looked like he was about to say something else, but he glanced over at Scott and seemed to think better of it. "We'll be down at the mess. If you want to join us after your meeting."

The agent left the room and Mara felt herself flush. She thought maybe she'd read into the man's tone, but when she turned, her dad was grinning at her.

"What?"

"Picking up dates in the White House? Now that takes game."

"Shut up."

Another Secret Service agent entered the room, his thick, barrel chest blocking the doorway. Once he passed through, Jordi appeared behind him, looking nervous and uncomfortable.

Unlike most White House visitors who dressed up to meet the dignity of the office, he wore Bermuda shorts and a tattered T-shirt that said, THERE'S NO PLACE LIKE 127.0.0.1. Mara had seen him wear the shirt before and knew the numbers referred to the IP address of a local host computer, essentially whatever computer the wearer happened to be in front of. Jordi definitely looked like he would have given anything to be home back in front of his computer instead of standing just outside the Oval.

Mara jumped to her feet and wrapped her arms around his wide girth. "I can't believe they got you to come."

"They didn't give me much of a choice," he whispered. Mara noticed there was almost no trace of his fake English accent. He was scared.

Scott extended his hand. "Good to finally meet you in person."

Jordi shook his hand. "If we go to prison, I'm counting on you having my back."

"Sorry," Scott said. "The president gave me a full pardon. I can give you some good pointers on prison yard etiquette, though."

Jordi wobbled on his feet and staggered over to a chair. It groaned as he plopped down in it, drawing a look from Ms. Ferris, the secretary.

"You're terrible," Mara said, taking a seat next to Jordi.

"No, I'm terrible," Jordi said. "All those top-secret systems I've broken into, tweaking their code so funny sayings pop up on people's screens. Poop emojis. I can't tell you how many senators and congressmen have poop emojis show up in their documents because of me. And Area 54. I was just curious. I didn't know what I was going to find there when I broke in. I'm a bad person. Maybe just because I can do something, doesn't mean I should. That's a saying, right? People say that?"

Scott and Mara exchanged a look. "I can't let you be this miserable," Mara said. "Listen close. The president is going to give you a blanket pardon, absolving you of any acts you committed while assisting us. And all acts prior to this. That's why you're here." She grabbed his hand, noting it was covered with cold sweat. "You're not going to prison. You're being handed a get out of jail free card."

Jordi took a few seconds for the words to register; then he lit up. "Not only for what I did to help the two of you? Are you saying . . . ?"

"Everything," Mara said. "In exchange for you keeping Townsend's document secret, like we discussed. But it doesn't cover anything on the go-forward. So I suggest you keep your nose clean from here on out."

He grinned. This time when he spoke, his accent was back in full force, as if channeling Dick Van Dyke's chimney sweep from Mary Poppins. "Would've thought they'd have given me a medal or something nice like that. A pardon? Still better than a finger in the eye, ain't it?"

Ms. Ferris picked up a phone, listened, and then hung up. "You and Mr. Roberts can go in now. Mr. Pines, if you would wait here," she said.

Mara swallowed hard as she prepared herself for the interview ahead. Her dad got to his feet next to her with the help of his crutches.

"In my experience," he whispered, "it's better not to hit the president in the face when he's talking to you."

"Thanks for the tip."

"Just trying to be helpful."

Mara turned the handle and entered the room.

Mara had seen the Oval Office so many times on TV and in movies that it felt unreal as she stepped inside. What made it even more surreal was there wasn't only one president of the United States waiting inside, but two.

Ex-president Townsend sat on a sofa, while President Patterson rose from the chair in front of the fireplace. If press accounts were to be believed, Mara thought she was witnessing the first time the two had been in the same room together since the campaign.

Patterson, then vice-president, had publically rebuked his old boss, trying to distance himself from the scandals. It'd made the way Gore sidelined Clinton in the 2000 election look like nothing. Entire books had been written about the bad blood between the two men, but there they were, sharing the same space together. Still, the body language between the two men told a story. And it wasn't one of forgiveness.

"Mara," Townsend called out as if they were the oldest of friends. "How's Jim Hawthorn doing?"

Mara shook his hand politely, her head spinning as to what his presence meant. "Jim's recovering at Walter Reed. A broken rib punctured a lung, but they expect a full recovery."

"My old man always said Jim Hawthorn was the toughest son of a bitch on God's green earth. He'll be up on his feet in no time," Townsend said.

Patterson waited for Townsend to quiet down, clearly used to his old boss trying to be the center of attention. Townsend seemed to remember himself and nodded to Patterson. "Have you met the president before?"

"Kyle Patterson," the president said, as if genuinely feeling the need to identify himself. He extended his hand and Mara shook it.

"Pleased to meet you, Mr. President. Thank you for ordering the protection for my nephew. I really appreciate it."

"It was the least we could do," the president said.

"And thank you for my father's pardon, although I'm not sure if he deserved it completely."

"I have done some pretty terrible things," Scott said. "Have you ever heard me sing? That's something that shouldn't be forgiven so easily."

Patterson held up his hands as if he was worried Scott might break into song to prove his point. He focused his attention on Mara. "The pleasure's mine, Agent Roberts. We owe you a debt of gratitude."

"Not agent," she said. "Just miss. Recently retired."

"I heard," he said, indicating to the couch facing Townsend for both she and Scott to sit. "I'd like to talk to you about that."

They all sat, Mara glancing over to Townsend, who regarded her without expression.

"Preston filled me in on the details of what really happened at the Tribune Tower in Chicago," he said. "I didn't think animal rights activists had the skill to pick apart the Secret Service that way."

Scott squirmed in his chair. "That pardon extended to everything, right?"

"Hell, Kyle probably wants to give you a commendation or something for punching my lights out," Townsend said. "I didn't come here to complain about you. I wanted him to know everything so he'd know why we can't afford to lose the two of you."

"Preston brought me an interesting idea," Patterson said. "We have a problem. Based on the debrief I read, you both agree that Omega remains a threat."

"Wendy may have risen to tactical control," Scott said, his voice strained at the use of her name. "But Omega existed before her and it certainly exists now. Their mission hasn't changed. I believe"—he glanced at Mara—"we believe that while their reach and influence may be overstated as a tactic to sow confusion and paranoia, they are dangerous."

"If you take their mission at face value, their goal is no less ambitious than the complete destruction of society, to rebuild it with themselves at the head," Mara said.

"Do they have the resources? Who is at its head?" Patterson asked. "If Wendy Roberts had tactical control, who was setting strategy? Whom did she report to?"

"And just how deep have these little buggers burrowed into our institutions?" Townsend added.

Mara remained silent. None of this was new. Her dad and her had been discussing this for the last week. If her mom was to be believed, Omega was everywhere. And their mission was to reduce the world to rubble so that a new society could grow. If that was true, then it was impossible to know who to trust.

"You want us to set up shop and go digging," Scott said slowly.

"You're half right," the president said. "Yes, I want you to set up shop. Your own people. Ones you trust. You'll report directly to me through Jim Hawthorn. But let's be clear, when it comes to Omega, I'm not asking you to go digging," the president said. "I'm asking you to go hunting."

Mara held Joey's hand as they waited for the elevator in Walter Reed Medical Center. She smiled when he reached up and took his grandpa's hand on the other side. Scott looked down and gave him a wink.

"Was that cool meeting the president?" Scott asked.

"Yeah, are you friends with him?"

Mara chuckled. "Kind of like friends. Grandpa works for him now."

"Do you work for him, too?" he asked her.

"I'm thinking about it. My most important job is to take care of you."

"But who's gonna take care of Grandpa? Isn't he always getting into trouble?"

"Hey, bub, I heard you like getting into trouble yourself," Scott said.

"Sometimes," he giggled.

The door opened and the questions stopped as Joey's world condensed down to who got to press the button inside the elevator. But she caught a questioning look from her dad.

She hadn't been ready to commit to the president's proposal the way he had, and he hadn't tried to talk her into it. When she'd brought up her concern about Joey, the answer had been that she could work in an analytical capacity. No fieldwork.

That was better. But after almost losing Joey once, and knowing their adversary would stoop to threatening kids to reach their goals, she couldn't stomach putting him at risk again.

Townsend's argument had been the strongest. His were the words that rattled in her head since leaving the Oval Office.

They rode up together to the fourth floor, where they passed through a security checkpoint before being given access to the hallway where Hawthorn's private room was located. The armed guard outside the door had been on a shift during an earlier visit, so he gave them a nod and waved them through.

When they entered the room, Hawthorn was gingerly pulling on his suit jacket, looking like a man who hurt everywhere.

"What the hell are you doing?" Scott said. "You're not supposed to be released until tomorrow."

Hawthorn adjusted his jacket and straightened his tie. "I got a phone call from the president. He told me he wanted me back to work when I was ready. I'm ready now."

"Is he going to fall over?" Joey asked.

"He might," Mara said. "If he does, you catch him."

Hawthorn sat on the edge of the bed, a bit out of breath. He looked at Mara. "So?"

She didn't have to ask what he meant by the question.

"Jim," her dad said, ready to tell him to give her space. But she put up her hand to stop him.

"Townsend asked me a question when we were in the Oval Office," she said. "And I can't stop thinking about it."

"What's that?" Hawthorn asked.

"What if I don't help and Omega succeeds? What then? Where would that leave us? Where would that leave Joey?"

Hawthorn glanced over to Scott, then back to Mara. "Maybe with all of our efforts, Omega still wins. But if they do, we'll have thrown everything we have at them to prevent that from happening. That's all we can do."

Mara picked Joey up off the ground and settled him on her hip. On reflex, he wrapped his arms around her and she hugged him tight. This was the reason to fight. This was the reason to go to war.

"I'm in," she said. "Let's go hunting."